# Wild Rain

**By Beverly Jenkins**

Wild Rain
Rebel
Tempest
Breathless
Forbidden
Destiny's Captive
Destiny's Surrender
Destiny's Embrace
Night Hawk
Midnight
Captured
Jewel
A Wild Sweet Love
Winds of the Storm
Something Like Love
Before the Dawn
Always and Forever
The Taming of Jessi Rose
Through the Storm
Topaz
Indigo
Vivid
Night Song

# Beverly Jenkins

# Wild Rain

Women Who Dare

AVONBOOKS

*An Imprint of* HarperCollins*Publishers*

This is a work of fiction. Names, characters, places, and incidents are products of the author's imagination or are used fictitiously and are not to be construed as real. Any resemblance to actual events, locales, organizations, or persons, living or dead, is entirely coincidental.



First Avon Books mass market printing: February 2021
First Avon Books hardcover printing: February 2021

Print Edition ISBN: 978-0-06-307515-3
Digital Edition ISBN: 978-0-06-286172-6



FIRST EDITION

21 22 23 24 25 LSC 10 9 8 7 6 5 4 3 2 1

*To the women who love horses, and those who refuse to change their minds.*

# Wild Rain

# Chapter One

Spring Lee held tightly onto the reins of her wagon and cursed the blinding blizzard she was driving through. With her hat pulled low, muffler wound up to her eyes, and wearing the thick oversize buffalo coat given to her by her cantankerous grandfather Ben, she was dressed for the brutal weather. It was early afternoon and having spent the past fifteen hours helping a friend with a difficult foaling, she was exhausted and wanted nothing more than to get home, take a hot bath, and sleep. Instead, she and her mare, Lady, were as snow covered as the surroundings and could barely see the road. It was mid-April. By all rights winter should be on the wane, but the seasons in Wyoming Territory moved by a calendar all their own. Buffeted by the howling wind, she chanted inwardly: *Another half mile. Another half mile.* And she and Lady would be home.

Up ahead on the deserted road, a horse appeared out of the storm. She thought she'd imagined it, but a break in the gusts showed the animal walking slowly, head lowered, its mane and body crusted with the elements. As she came abreast of it and stopped, she took in the bags attached to the saddle and the thick bedroll riding the rump. *Where's the rider?* She scanned the area. Not seeing anyone, she got down and waded through the calf-high drifts. Urging the animal forward, she trailered its reins to the wagon's bed, climbed back up to the seat, and resumed the drive.

She was familiar with the mounts of her neighbors, but she'd never seen this horse before. Had the rider been thrown and was hurt somewhere up ahead? Weariness and the freezing cold might have made another person leave the mystery for someone else to worry about, but she'd been raised better, so she kept an eye out for the rider as best she could.

It didn't take long.

She rounded a bend and saw a hatless, snow-covered man slowly limping his way up the road. He turned to look back, revealing a brown-skinned, ice-crusted face. Upon spotting her, he waved frantically.

When she reached him, she pulled her muffler down and yelled over the wind, "Climb on!"

He didn't hesitate, but his injury made the ascent slow. "Thank you!" he said, once settled.

"There's a couple of blankets under the tarp behind you! Wrap up!"

While he complied, she got them underway. A glance over her shoulder showed he'd placed one blanket over his head and wrapped the other around his brown wool coat. She had no idea who he was, but his story would have to wait. Getting them home came first.

A short while later, the sight of her cabin filled her with a weary joy. She alerted her passenger, "We're here! Go on inside and start a fire. I'll take care of the horses."

Draped under the blankets, he climbed down and haltingly made his way to her door while she drove to the barn.

By the time she got Lady and the man's gelding bedded down and a big fire built in the grate to keep her other three horses warm, she was weary enough to lie down where she stood. Hating having to face the weather again, she rewound her muffler, pulled on her gloves, and stepped out into the frigid wind.

Inside her cabin, there was no fire. The stranger, still wrapped in the blankets, was stretched out on her fancy new sofa, head back, snoring loudly. She set his bedroll and bags on the floor.

The younger, wilder Spring Lee would've given his foot a swift kick to wake him up, but the more mature version of herself settled for grumbling while tossing logs into the fireplace. As the flames rose, she viewed him. He was handsome, she supposed, but a pretty face often masked an ugliness inside, so she wasn't impressed by the strong jaw or the pleasant features it anchored. "Hey! Wake up!" she called crossly. The wet blankets would ruin the sofa her sister-in-law Regan recently convinced her to buy, and Spring was the only person allowed to damage it.

As he snored on, she shook his shoulder. "Mister. Wake up."

His eyes opened.

"I have a spare room. You can sleep there."

He looked confused.

"Ruin my couch and I'll feed you to a bear."

He startled.

"Can you stand?"

His eyes swept her face. The confusion gave way to wariness. Finally, he whispered, "Yes. Sorry for falling asleep."

She noted his shivering, but she was too bone tired to fire up the boiler to heat water for the hot baths they both needed. "This way."

He rose, took a step, and cringed.

"Is it your leg?" she asked.

"My knee. Hurt it when the horse threw me."

She raised an eyebrow and he responded with, "The horse reared when a big cat ran into the road chasing a deer."

"They tend to do that. Lean on me," she offered.

"I'm too heavy for you, ma'am."

"I'm stronger than I look, so let's try. Otherwise, you'll have to sleep here on the floor."

"I'd do fine in front of the fire. I have a bedroll."

She gritted out, "Just come on, please. You can be a gentleman after I've had some sleep."

He seemed amused by that. "Yes, ma'am."

With her supporting him, they slowly made their way to her spare room. Inside, he dropped onto the bed and offered his thanks.

"You're welcome." She opened a nearby trunk and withdrew blankets and quilts. Still wearing her buffalo coat, she made a fire in the grate. "Should warm up eventually. There's a washroom through that door. Tub, too, but I've been gone a couple of days, so there's no hot water for now. What's your name?"

"Garrett McCray."

"I'm Spring Lee."

"Related to Dr. Colton Lee?" he asked.

"Why?"

"I'm a reporter. Here to do an article about him for my father's newspaper."

Her brother had mentioned a reporter was on the way. "Colt's married to my sister-in-law."

As if confused by her response, he studied her for a moment, before asking, "Dr. Lee is your brother?"

"Smart and a gentleman. Rare as the white buffalo. I'll bring your bags and bedroll. You should get out of those wet clothes."

She exited.

GARRETT STARED AT the empty space she left behind. Did she live here alone? Did her brother and his wife reside nearby? Had her confusing responses been deliberate? His numerous questions about her would have to wait. Her advice about his wet clothes was sound. The last thing he needed was to be laid low by illness, so doing his best to keep his weight off his injured knee, he shed the blankets and his coat. Seeing no place to hang them, he laid them in front of the fire, then hobbled to the room's lone chair to remove his boots. Raising his leg hurt. It only took a few more attempts to realize that between the pain and the boots' tight fit, removal was impossible. The boots were new and so tight and uncomfortable that during the ride to Paradise he'd wanted to snatch them off and toss them into the nearest stream. Now his feet were probably so blistered and swollen, he'd need a surgeon to cut them free.

She returned. After placing his belongings beside the chair, she asked, "How's the knee?"

"It's been better. Can't seem to remove my boots." He hated admitting that.

"Can you raise your leg?"

He nodded.

She took off her big coat and let it drop to the floor. Back home women didn't wear men's shirts, denims, or gun belts, so he forced himself not to stare.

"Show me."

He hadn't any idea why she'd asked, but she didn't appear to be in the mood for a discussion, so he raised his leg as requested.

"Hold on to the chair."

He grasped the arms, she turned her back to him, and took his booted foot in hand. He forced himself not to stare again. This time at her behind.

"Yell, if you have to."

And before he could ask what that meant, she pulled with a strength that was surprising, and the boot came free. The pain put a catch in his breath, but he didn't yell. Not in front of her.

"Now the other one."

She repeated the process with the same expertise and once it was done, he melted with relief. "Thank you."

"Boots new?" she asked.

"Yes. Bought them a few days ago. Storekeeper said they'd be tight."

"Where are you from?"

"Washington."

"Territory?"

"No. District of Columbia."

Her thoughts on that information were kept unspoken. "I've water boiling on the stove for bark tea. It should help with the pain. Once it stops snowing and Odell clears the road, we'll ride over to my brother's place and see if he's back."

"He's not here?"

"I'm not sure. He left a few days ago to help with a measles outbreak over in Rock Springs."

"When will the road be cleared?" He wondered who Odell might be and hoped the doctor had returned.

She shrugged. "Depends on how long it takes the storm to blow through. I'll be back with the tea."

She picked up his wet coat and hers. His eyes followed her strong stride until she closed the door and disappeared.

She was gone long enough for him to change into a dry union suit. He longed for a hot bath to take the chill off his bones, but he'd have to wait. With the door closed, heat was finally warming the space, but it was still cold enough to bring on shivers. Outside, the wind continued to wail. Knowing gentlemen didn't allow themselves to be seen in their underclothing by a lady, he climbed into the bed. He'd just settled under the quilts and blankets when a knock sounded on the closed door. "Come in."

She entered carrying a large drinking cup. "It's hot," she cautioned, handing it to him.

It was and tasted awful. "What's in this?"

"Bark."

"From a tree?"

"No, a dog. Yes, it's from a tree—a willow. It's a Native remedy. Tried and true."

He kept his skepticism hidden but wasn't sure he wanted more.

"Drink it or not," she stated as if having read his mind. "Your pain. Your knee."

Was she always so direct? Another question to add to his list. Still skeptical, he drank the rest and handed the cup back.

"It'll help you sleep, too." She crossed to the fireplace and put in more wood. "Do you need anything else?"

"No. Thank you for everything."

"You're welcome."

She departed. He cocooned himself beneath the small mountain of blankets and quilts. Thoughts of his enigmatic hostess and the sounds of the roaring storm faded away as he sank into sleep.

SPRING AWAKENED IN bed, pleased that the room was finally warm and she was home. The mare she'd been helping with had delivered a stillborn foal, which left her sad, but she knew nature wasn't always kind. She wondered how the man down the hall was faring. Although McCray's arrival had been anticipated, she hadn't been involved with his travel arrangements, and certainly hadn't expected to make his acquaintance in the middle of a snowstorm. She admittedly didn't like houseguests. She'd lived alone for over a decade and preferred her own company. If visitors needed a place to stay, the Paradise boardinghouse owned by her sister-in-law, Regan, offered rooms to rent. However, the reporter hadn't asked to be caught out in the weather, so Spring supposed she'd have to be pleasant and put up with him until Colt took him off her hands.

She left the bed and walked to the window. She didn't hear the wind, but that didn't mean the storm had passed. She looked out. Snow covered most of the pane, making it impossible to see anything other than that it was dark. The small clock on her nightstand showed the time to be a bit past five, so she'd been asleep almost four hours. She could use a lot more, but her stomach wanted food, and she needed to check on her animals. The man was probably hungry, as well, so she dressed.

The moment she opened the bedroom door, the scent of what smelled like stew made her pause. Curious, she continued the short journey to the kitchen and found her guest stirring a pot on the stove.

"What are you doing?" she asked suspiciously.

"Found stew in your cold box. Didn't want to wake you, but

I'm as hungry as the bear you threatened to feed me to." He offered a ghost of a smile to her confused face before returning to his task.

Spring was prickly by nature and a part of her wanted to rail at him for sneaking around her place while she was asleep, but her hunger took the lead. Without a word, she opened a cupboard, grabbed two bowls, and set them on the counter.

"Thanks," he told her.

She didn't reply. Instead, she retrieved two forks and set them beside the bowls. He filled both bowls with the steaming mixture of vegetables and beef. Seeing that he was struggling to keep his weight off his injured leg, she picked up both bowls and carried them the short distance to her small dining table. Limping, he joined her and eased himself into one of the chairs.

To show him she did have manners, she said, "Thanks for heating up the stew."

"You're welcome."

For a few moments they ate in silence until he said, "This is very good."

"My sister-in-law, Regan, makes it for me."

"It's spicier than I'm accustomed to."

"She's from Arizona Territory. Her cooking is mostly Spanish. She uses peppers and chilis."

He nodded his understanding. "How long have she and your brother been married?"

Spring debated answering. He was a stranger after all but reminded herself Colt would undoubtedly expect her to be nice. "A bit over a year."

"Children?"

"Two."

"And you?"

She met his eyes. "Me, what?"

"Do you have a husband?"

She shook her head.

"An intended?"

"Are you always this nosy?"

He chuckled softly. "Asking questions is part of the job."

"No husband, and I don't intend to have one."

"Why not?"

"Why should I? I have land and horses. I'm content."

He eyed her as if he had more questions, but he kept them to himself. "I see."

She asked, "Are you married?"

He shook his head. "No."

"An intended?"

"My father says yes. I say no."

It was her turn to chuckle.

"What?"

"That was quite the answer."

"Meaning?"

"Either you have an intended or you don't. Why do some men find it difficult to answer a simple question?"

He opened his mouth as if to respond, then closed it.

Smiling inwardly, she resumed eating.

But he wasn't done. "Are you one of those women who thinks poorly of all men?"

"No. I know some who're good as gold and others I'd not turn my back on. Not intending to marry either kind."

"Society thinks a woman should marry."

"Good thing I don't live by what society thinks. Otherwise, I'd've married the lecherous old snake my grandfather tried to shackle me to when I was eighteen. Probably be out of the penitentiary by now though."

He stared. She returned to her stew. Although he kept further questions to himself, there were unasked ones all over his brown-skinned face.

They finished their stew at about the same time. "Do you want more?" she asked.

He nodded and made a move to rise. She stopped him. "You're still favoring that leg. I'll get it."

She brought their second helpings back to the table, acknowledged his thanks with a short nod, and asked him, "Did the tea help?"

"It did."

"There's more if you want it."

"I do. Maybe after I finish this."

"Still going to taste awful."

"Understood. Is that one of the remedies your brother uses?"

"Along with everyone else out here. My brother trained at Howard's Medical School. Don't write something wrongheaded and insulting about him using so-called savage concoctions."

"And have you feed me to a bear? Don't worry."

She knew he was making a joke, but his face was so serious, she was thrown off her stride for a moment. "What do you do back in Washington besides ask a lot of questions?"

"I read for the law at one point, but the newspaper is a sundown paper, so I make my living as a carpenter."

"What's a sundown paper?"

"The editor works on it in the evenings after his day job. My father owns the paper and I help when I can. He couldn't take the time off work to interview your brother. I volunteered to make the trip instead."

"So you work as a carpenter and not a lawyer?"

"Yes. I prefer working with my hands."

Her eyes settled on them. They looked strong and capable like most men she knew, except for maybe banker Arnold Cale. His hands were as pink and pampered as a lady-in-waiting to Queen Victoria.

He'd apparently viewed her hands, too. "What happened to your finger?"

The top of her right index finger still bore the ugly black bruise from a hammering mishap. "Hit it with a hammer instead of the head of a nail."

"Ouch."

"Yes. I cussed a lot, but it's healing." She flexed the battered finger. "Not the first time. Probably won't be the last, either." Lady ranchers didn't have pink and pampered hands.

"I've never met a woman rancher."

"I've never met a newspaper reporter carpenter. Makes us even." Spring didn't mind the conversation, but she didn't want him to think her being friendly was an invitation to something else. He was a stranger after all, and she was a woman alone. "Do you have a sister?"

"Yes. Her name's Melody."

"What would you tell her if she took in a strange man and they had to be alone together for a few days?"

He stilled and searched her face. She waited.

"I'd—I'd tell her to be watchful and careful, and to be ready to protect herself if need be."

Spring nodded. "Good advice."

Silence settled over the room for a few moments, before he said quietly, "You're a very unique woman, Miss Lee."

"I also sleep with a Colt Peacemaker."

"Noted."

She stood and gathered up their empty bowls. "I'll get the water boiling for your tea and then go check on the horses."

While the water boiled, Spring went to her room to dress for venturing out. With the windows snowed over there was no way of telling what she'd be facing outside, but the wind had stopped, a good sign.

He was still seated at the table when she returned. His curious eyes scanned the buffalo coat as she set it on a chair, but he didn't ask about it. In the kitchen the water was ready. After putting the bark in and letting it steep, she carried a mug out to him and set it down. Under his gaze she put on the coat, did up her muffler, and donned her battered, wide-brimmed, gray hat.

He asked, "Do all the women here dress like you?"

"All the ones with sense. I'll be back shortly. Providing I can get out. If the windows are snowed over, the doors probably are, too." Her hope was that the temperatures hadn't dropped low enough to freeze the snow.

Leaving him with the tea, it took a few shoves with her shoulder to get the back door open. Holding the lantern she'd lit, she stepped out into the knee-high snow covering the back porch. It was cold, the moon was just rising, and the snowfall had transitioned to flurries. Her land was covered by a beautiful glistening sea of white as far as she could see. According to her grandfather Ben, the tribes had different words for various types of snow, from heavy and wet, to light and fluffy, and everything in between. He'd never taught her the words though. With a gloved hand, she scooped some up, tossed it, and it floated light as goose down. A blessing, at least for the moment. Were it heavy with moisture, making her way to the barn would be a lengthy, tiring struggle. Due to the snow's sheer depth though, it would still take time, but its fluffiness would make the trek easier. Unable to see the porch's stairs, she descended carefully. The last thing she needed was to fall and break something. As she reached what she guessed to be the bottom, the depth rose to midthigh. With the lantern held high, she waded slowly. The barn was a good distance from the house. With any luck, she'd make it before summer.

# Chapter Two

Garrett sipped the terrible-tasting tea and mused on his journey so far. Having left Washington, he'd journeyed by train to Chicago, changed trains in Denver, and boarded another for Cheyenne. From there, he'd been surprised to learn it was the train's last stop and he'd have to travel via stagecoach or horseback to his destination, Paradise. A few questions put to the conductor informed him that the stagecoach only ran twice a week, and wasn't due in for another three days. Not wanting to wait, he chose horseback. The conductor sent him to the livery, where after negotiating a price for the mount and a saddle, he was advised by the owner that his thin-soled back-East shoes should be replaced by boots to protect his ankles from snakebite. Uncertain as to whether the man was pulling his leg or not, he'd counted out the coin owed and spent the night at a local boardinghouse. He set out at first light and spent the next two days atop the stiff, uncomfortable saddle and wearing the tight, ill-fitting new boots. He was then waylaid by a blizzard, thrown from the horse, and forced to walk. Between his wrenched knee and saddle-sore rump, a less determined man might be ready to return home at first light. Instead, he was seated with his belly full of the best stew he'd ever tasted in the cabin of the most unconventional woman he'd ever met.

Spring Lee was seemingly as untamed as the Wyoming mountains, and frankly, just as impressive. Unlike some of the women he knew at home, there was no artifice or pretentiousness. She was candid and frank. The question she'd asked about his sister had been unexpected yet sent the message she wanted to convey: if he got out of line she'd shoot him. He planned to mind his manners and be on his best behavior.

This was his first trip west of Chicago. Having learned of Dr. Colton Lee from a family friend, Garrett and his father thought their paper's subscribers would be intrigued by a Colored doctor practicing medicine in a place not usually associated with members of the race. Spring mentioned a grandfather. Garrett wondered just how long the family had lived in the Territory and why'd they'd settled there. Their story would be a feather in the cap of his father's struggling newspaper, the *Crier.* As far as Garrett knew, the *Washington Wasp,* the leading Colored paper in the District, had never run anything like the story the *Crier* planned to publish, and that would no doubt anger its owner, Emmanuel Beal. Beal prided himself on having the most influential and most subscribed-to newspaper around and took great joy in poking fun at those lacking his funding and readership. If the *Crier* could show Beal up just once, Garrett's being subjected to the stiff saddle and the agony of his new boots would be well worth it.

He'd exchanged a few wires with Dr. Lee to set up the interview, and hoped the man was still open to being questioned. He didn't relish having come all this way only to return home empty-handed. If that occurred, he'd at least have the memories of Wyoming's mountainous beauty and meeting the remarkable Spring Lee.

After downing the last of the tea, he set the cup aside and wondered how his hostess was faring outdoors. Hearing a scraping sound, he glanced around the room to determine the source. When he heard it a second time, he turned to the window beside him and saw a square piece of wood drag the snow down the pane. His hostess was clearing the windows. Aided by the light of the moon and bundled up in the hat, muffler, and burly brown coat, she resembled an eerie apparition. The gentleman in him felt guilty watching her work alone, then reasoned, she'd still have to accomplish the task were he not there, but it didn't make him feel any better. Men worked. Women rested. At least where he was from. After a few more passes the window was cleared, and she moved on.

Although his nap had restored him somewhat after his long unnerving day, he needed more sleep. Much more. The weariness coupled with the effects of the bark tea and his full stomach had him on the verge of nodding off when he heard her return.

"I heated the boiler," she said, freeing herself from her outerwear. "Water should be hot enough for a bath in a few hours if you're willing to wait, or have one in the morning."

That her cabin had indoor plumbing also raised questions, but he kept his curiosity for another time. "How long has your family been in Wyoming?"

"Since the twenties. My grandfather Ben was a trapper. He and his friend Odell opened a trading post that eventually became the town of Paradise."

Her response gave rise to more questions. He watched as she removed her boots and set them by the fire.

"Where was your grandfather born?"

"Canada."

"Was he enslaved?"

She shook her head. "His parents were indentured servants to a French fur trader in Quebec. After they cleared their debt, they founded a small trading outfit of their own. My grandfather became a trapper and a guide for the French and English wanting furs."

"And your grandmother?"

"What about her?"

The tight tone of her voice matched the frank, dark eyes. He almost told her to ignore the question, but his curiosity propelled him forward. "Who was she?"

"A Shoshone woman who left him soon after my father was born because Ben has always been a terrible person. Anything else?"

Her abruptness gave him pause. Having interviewed many people, Garrett had learned to delve beneath the surface of their answers to gain a truer sense of the response, and what he saw and heard under her tough, no-nonsense exterior was bitterness and pain. "No. Nothing else."

"Good. I'm exhausted and going back to bed. If you'll be up for a while, make sure you douse the lamps and throw more wood on the fire. It gets cold in here at night."

"I will. And thanks again for the rescue."

She responded with a terse nod and left him alone.

As he sat there, the crackling of the fire played softly against the silence. There were so many things he wanted to know about Spring Lee. What kind of life had she led? How had she been shaped by it? She'd mentioned her grandfather twice now, giving Garrett the impression that they were at odds. Was the acrimony tied to more than her refusal to marry the man she'd described as an old snake? He had no answers. He was intrigued though. Yes, she was beautiful with her ebony skin, jet-black eyes, and the thick braid down her back, but what drew him more was the fierce granite-like strength. Deciding to head to bed, he remembered her request and added more wood to the fire before dousing the lamp.

THE NEXT MORNING, after a good, long soak in the tub filled with hot water, Garrett's knee was less stiff, his bones no longer frozen, and he almost felt human again. Spring had been correct about the cabin being cold. Overnight the fire in the grate had burned down to embers and he was surprised there weren't icicles hanging from his nose. He quickly dressed, layering on as much as he needed to stay warm, and added more wood to the fire. Pulling his thin, back-East work boots out of his carpetbag, he put them on. Moving on the less painful knee he went in search of breakfast. The cabin was quiet. He didn't see her or hear her moving about, so he guessed she was either outside checking on the animals or still asleep. Not seeing her big coat hanging from the peg on the door made him assume the former. The view through the window showed a blue sky and sunshine sparkling on a world covered in white. Wispy eddies of snowflakes danced in the breeze and off in the distance—the mountains.

In the small kitchen he found eggs, bread, and bacon. Being unmarried, Garrett was accustomed to taking care of his own needs. If he didn't cook, he didn't eat. Hoping he wouldn't be shot for helping himself to her eggs, he cracked a few into a bowl and lit the stove. He was stirring a bit of cream into the eggs when he heard someone knocking on the front door. Unsure if he should answer, he waited a few moments to see if Spring would appear. When she didn't, and the knocking came again, louder this time, he left the bowl and made his way there.

He opened it to find an old man with a long white beard and a coat similar to Spring's on the other side. Hair the color of the snow streamed from beneath his hat made of furs. "Who the hell are you?" the visitor asked pointedly.

"Garrett McCray."

"Where's Spring?"

"I believe she's out checking on her animals."

The confusion on his face might have been amusing if the sky-blue eyes weren't glaring with such hostility.

"And you are?" Garrett asked.

"Odell Waters."

Recognizing the name from last night's talk, Garrett was tempted to let him in, but again, he didn't want to be shot by the lady of the house for being presumptuous. He also wanted to let the old man inside because it was too cold to be conversing in the open doorway.

"Let him in, McCray."

He turned to see Spring removing her coat and hat. Her weary tone matched the weariness in her face. It was plain she needed more sleep. Garrett stepped aside.

Still exuding suspicion, Odell took a moment to take off his snowshoes before entering. Garrett closed the door.

Removing his coat and hat, Odell asked Spring, "What's he doing here? Who is he?"

"Name's McCray. Back-East newspaper reporter here to interview the good doctor. Found him walking in the storm yesterday. Got thrown by his horse."

He sized Garrett up again. "He giving you any trouble?" Odell hung the coat and his hat on one of the pegs nailed to the door.

"No."

Garrett wanted to announce that he could speak on his own behalf, but the old man seemed intent upon ignoring him. Grumbling inwardly, Garrett spoke to Spring. "I hope you don't mind me eating your eggs, but I'm cooking breakfast. Do you want a plate?"

She paused and did some sizing up of her own before replying, "Sure. Two eggs."

"Bacon? Toast?"

"Both."

Odell finally addressed him, "If there's more eggs, I'll take two. Bacon and toast for me, too. Any coffee? Cold out there."

Garrett wondered how wanting to repay Spring for her hospitality by offering her breakfast had turned him into a diner cook. "Where's your coffee, Miss Lee?"

"Come. I'll show you. Odell, have a seat."

Odell asked, "You sure you're okay with having him here?"

"If I wasn't, he'd be out in the snow waiting to be turned over to Beck."

Confused, Garrett asked, "Who's Beck?"

"Town undertaker."

"Oh." He had no further questions.

As they ate, his hostess and their visitor talked while he listened. Odell had spent the morning checking on his snowbound neighbors. Garrett had no idea how large an area that entailed, but the idea of a man his age venturing out on such a mission was impressive.

"Everyone okay?" she asked.

Forking up some of the scrambled eggs on his plate, Odell nodded. "Seems so."

"How's the road?"

"Impassable still, but temperature's rising. Another day or two and it should melt enough for folks to get out." He glanced Garrett's way. "How long are you staying?"

"Just long enough to get what I need from Dr. Lee for my story."

Odell studied him. "Good."

Garrett tried not to take offense, but it was difficult.

"Quit poking at him, Odell."

"Just don't want him getting any ideas." He gave Garrett another hard stare. "I'm a man. I know how they think. Woman alone."

She shook her head in response but didn't say more.

Holding on to his temper, Garrett asked, "Mr. Waters, would you mind being interviewed for my story?"

"Thought you were here to talk to Colt."

"I am, but Ms. Lee said you and her grandfather founded Paradise. My readers might be interested in hearing a bit about that, as well."

Odell grumbled for a moment before responding, "Ain't saying yes. Ain't saying no. Let's see how you get along with folks first."

Garrett's eyes met Spring's. Hers revealed nothing. "Okay, sir. I'll ask again at another time."

Odell turned to Spring. "How'd Ed's foaling go?"

She replied softly, "Not well. Foal was stillborn."

Odell's blue eyes showed sympathy. "How's the mare?"

"He may lose her, too."

"Sad news. Was Colt there to help?"

"No. He was up at Rock Springs. Not sure if he's back yet or not."

Garrett had hoped to conduct his interview and promptly return home. He hadn't considered medical emergencies, a blizzard, or snow-clogged roads. Also not considered was a woman he wanted to know more about, and an insulting old curmudgeon Garrett wished would put on his snowshoes and depart.

Odell asked Garrett, "Where's home?"

Garrett told him.

"You ever been West before?"

"No."

"Figured that. You losing your seat and all."

Garrett shot him a look.

"Odell," Spring cautioned.

"Good thing he won't be staying," the undaunted Odell continued. "Man can't handle his horse should stick to those fancy back-East streetcars."

"Are you always this rude?" Garrett asked, glaring.

"Depends." But Odell was smiling. "Just wanted to see how long you'd let me poke at you, newspaper fella. Good to see it wasn't long."

Garrett wasn't sure how to respond but was glad he'd passed the test.

Odell pushed back his chair and rose to his feet. "Thanks for breakfast."

Garrett nodded. A glance Spring's way showed a small smile above her raised coffee cup.

Spring walked Odell to the door. After returning and seeing the displeasure Garrett didn't bother masking, she said, "Don't mind Odell. He's my godfather and likes to needle. The day my sister-in-law arrived from Arizona, she shot my brother. Odell teased her mercilessly."

Shocked, Garrett echoed, "She shot your brother?"

"Yes. Mistook him for an outlaw."

"Do you think she'd let me add that to my story?"

"Only Regan speaks for Regan."

He was now anxious to meet the doctor and his wife. "That's quite a tale."

"My brother will never live it down."

"Was he seriously injured?"

She shook her head. "She plugged him in the shoulder. He was fine."

Garrett wanted to know more but knew not to pepper his hostess with the dozens of questions the story had given rise to. He'd learn all, eventually. He hoped.

She began clearing the table. "Thanks for breakfast. How's your knee?"

"Better." Where he came from it was considered ill-mannered to discuss bathing in front of women, so he said simply, "Thanks for lighting the boiler."

"You're welcome."

"I can help you clean up in the kitchen. My knee's strong enough, as long as I don't stand too long."

She eyed him dubiously.

"I know how to wash and dry dishes. I live alone and since I can't afford a housekeeper I do all the cooking and chores myself."

"Am I going to have to put up with a load of nosy questions?"

He smiled wryly. "Yes, if you don't mind."

She didn't appear pleased. "Come on, then."

SPRING'S KITCHEN WAS perfect for one person. For two, it was crowded. Especially with a man as tall and broad as McCray. She washed. He dried. Their shoulders bumped as he placed the dried dishes in the cupboard beside her. Their hands grazed as she handed him dishes to dry. As promised, he asked a wagonload of questions, which she preferred to deal with rather than why their accidental touches kept sending unnerving little sparks up her arms. His questions began with wanting to know the name of the mountain range, then to how long she'd lived in her cabin. "About twelve years now. Place used to belong to Odell. He and his family lived here when Colt and I were growing up."

She saw him survey the walls and ceiling and she wondered if he was evaluating them with a carpenter's eye.

"Did he build this himself?"

"Yes, with help from friends like my grandfather. All of the old trappers built their own places."

"Is your grandfather still living?"

"Yes." She handed him a wet plate to dry. And if meanness defined the length of a person's life, Ben would be around until the mountains turned to gravel. "And your grandparents?"

"I don't know. They've probably passed on by now. Never knew them. We were captives."

That brought her up short. She searched his face. "Really?"

"Yes. In Virginia. Some people are ashamed of their time before the war. I'm not. I ran when I was fourteen and joined the Union Navy."

"At fourteen? That's young, isn't it?"

He gave her a smile. "Yes, but there were some boys even younger."

When Spring worked for the Ketchums after Ben put her out, she'd felt like a captive, too, but knew her experience and his were worlds apart. "Did you escape with your parents?"

"No. My uncle Quincy ran when I was just a babe. He returned in sixty-three hoping to help my father escape, but Hiram, my father, wouldn't leave without my mother, Fannie, so my father sent me with Quincy instead."

She wondered why his mother couldn't leave. Then reminded herself that his time in Paradise was limited, and that when he left for home she'd never see him again, so asking a bunch of nosy questions served no purpose.

"Did the war affect you here?" he asked.

"In some ways. The cattlemen got rich shipping beef to the Union troops. The army sent most of the soldiers back East to fight and left local militias to defend the Territory. They started their own war."

"What do you mean?"

"Some militia members massacred the Cheyenne at Sand Creek in Colorado and the Cheyenne rightfully wanted revenge. There were raids and battles. The tribes eventually lost and were forced onto reservations."

"You sound as if you have sympathy for the Indians."

"Don't you?"

"Back East, they're portrayed as bloodthirsty killers."

"The bloodthirsty killers were the men who gunned down the Cheyenne children and women, then returned to mutilate the bodies and set the village on fire. Chief Black Kettle and his people had already signed for peace."

"The newspapers at home never tell that side of the story."

"Maybe they should."

"I didn't mean to upset you."

She handed him the skillet he'd used to fry the bacon. "Those were upsetting times. In many ways nothing's changed." She poured the dishwater down the drain. "We're done here. Thanks for your help."

"You're welcome," he replied quietly. "May I ask a final question?"

She nodded tersely.

"Do all the people here feel as you do about the Indians?"

"Some do, but the big cattle ranchers don't. They own the land now and it's made them rich. They don't care if the tribes are fenced in, starving, and destitute, as long as they can ship their beef. Anything else?"

"No."

"I'm going to go out and shovel a path to the barn."

"I'd like to help."

She glanced down at his knee.

"I can wrap it. There's a lot of snow out there."

"True, but wrapped or not, I'm the one who'll have to listen to my brother fuss when you do more damage. Thanks for offering your gentlemanly assistance, but it won't be the first or last time I've done this alone."

She saw him open his mouth to protest. "You should go write a story or something. Better yet, make a list of a hundred more questions you want to ask."

He lowered his head and amusement filled his eyes. "Okay. If you insist."

"I do." For a moment, she acknowledged how easy it was to be around him and his handsome face. Appalled, she shook it off and glanced around the kitchen to make sure she hadn't overlooked a stray dish or spoon. Satisfied, she left the kitchen, bundled up again, and left him inside.

While shoveling, she tried to make sense of her uncharacteristic physical reaction to the newspaper man. There was no good reason for her to have felt sparks and tingles or linger on his looks. As she'd noted yesterday upon finding him asleep on her new couch, a pretty face could hide all manner of inner ugliness, something she knew well. Had the sparks been a simple reminder of how long it had been since she'd had a man in her bed?—not that any of the previous experiences ever set her barn on fire. Especially not the way her brother and sister-in-law Regan acted with each other. Colton and Regan's arranged marriage had evolved into a love match, and they were forever stealing kisses when they thought no one was looking. Spring knew nothing about that kind of bond and wasn't sure she wanted to, but as she'd reminded herself, McCray wouldn't be staying around, so it made no sense to have this conversation with herself. Once he was gone, she'd return to what she enjoyed and did best. Being a woman alone.

# Chapter Three

Garrett took her advice and brought out his journal and made short notes on what he'd experienced so far. Not everything would be incorporated into his story on Dr. Lee, but he was certain his readers might find further stories interesting, like the plight of the Indians. Being a Colored man, he was sympathetic to their plight. Their beliefs and way of life, trampled by the nation's movement west, had been no more valued than those held by the people of Africa forced into slavery. Unfortunately, his only knowledge about them came via the garish and often sensationalized stories put out by the press, both Colored and White, portraying them as soulless, murdering demons. He'd not seen anything in the newspapers on the Colorado militia murdering and mutilating Cheyenne women and children. Spring mentioned the massacre had taken place during the war. Even though the nation's eyes had been focused on the conflict, it was no excuse for the incident not to have been more widely reported. Her description of the events left him feeling both ignorant and ashamed. He wondered how many people in the East were aware of what had transpired. Had they been appalled by the murders? Spring couldn't have been very old at the time, but apparently, the story remained a bitter memory.

He had his own share of bitter memories. At the age of eight, he and his family were put on the block to pay down their master's debts. Garrett and his father, Hiram, were purchased by a carpenter in Richmond, while his mother, Fannie, was sold to a wealthy female plantation owner. And for the first time in his life, he learned what being a slave truly meant. Seeing his mother's anguished tears as she was driven away, and knowing he might not ever see her again, had been one of the most horrific, heartbreaking days of his life. As his father explained later that evening, "The masters own us. To them we're no more than pigs or mules. If they want to sell us, they can, and we have no recourse."

By his twelfth winter, his mother had been sold twice more, each time farther away. How his father kept track of her whereabouts Garrett never knew, but when Richmond fell and the war ended, his father knew exactly where to find her and her infant daughter. A few weeks later, when Garrett left the navy and returned to Virginia, they became a family again and he was delighted to have gained a little sister, but for many of the enslaved there were no such reunions. Even now, twenty years later, the nation's Colored newspapers continued to publish pleas from those searching for sold-away kin.

According to Spring's account, her grandfather had been free. Garrett assumed her father had been, too, but what about her mother? Spring hadn't shared much of anything about her parents. Were they still living? He didn't know why learning all he could about his hostess seemed so important. Due to his short stay in Paradise, most of his questions would remain unanswered and more than likely they'd never meet again. Why that fact left him unsettled, he didn't know, either, but it did. What made her smile? What put the light of joy in her eyes? Had any man ever loved her for all that she was? Although having only known her two days, Garrett didn't see her masking her true nature to secure a man's affection as society often forced women to do. Reminding himself again about the briefness of his stay and the unanswered questions he'd leave behind, he sighed wistfully, and returned to his journal.

When she entered the house a short while later, he had his list of questions written out for the doctor. More would surface during their talk, but for the moment he was content.

"You have your questions ready?" she asked after removing her coat and boots.

"Yes. Is that coat a real buffalo hide?"

"Yes, and much warmer than wool."

"May I try it on?"

"Sure. It's very heavy though."

He slipped his arms into the sleeves and the weight buckled his knees. It was like having an anvil on his shoulders.

"As I said—heavy."

He scanned the shaggy garment. Although its size and length didn't dwarf him as it did her, he couldn't imagine having to wear it for an extended period. "Do you wear this all winter?"

She shook her head. "Just when the weather is like it's been for the past few days."

He shrugged out of it and, glad to be free of the weight, handed it back. "Thanks for indulging my curiosity."

"I'm stuck with you and your curiosity," she quipped. "So I haven't much choice."

Although the words were pointed, her eyes held a hint of playfulness that added to his growing interest in her. "Is there a place in town where I can rent a room?"

"Yes. Regan owns a boardinghouse run by the town seamstress, Dovie Denby. Paradise doesn't get a lot of visitors, so the place is never full."

"Good to know." He expected her to leave him after that, but she sat instead and that pleased him. "Have you ever lived anywhere else?"

"No. I've been here my whole life. Farthest I've been from Paradise is Laramie and Cheyenne."

"Never been back East?"

She shook her head.

"Are you curious about what it might be like?"

"Not really. When Colt returned after his medical studies at Howard, he said it was full of people, streetcars, and the noise of both."

Garrett thought about that. "I suppose he's right, and it can be overwhelming."

"I've no need for overwhelming. I like the quiet and the peace of waking up every day to the sun rising over the mountains."

He'd yet to witness that but remembering the beauty of the sunrise over the water during his stint in the navy, he understood. There'd been breathtaking sunsets, as well.

"Besides," she continued, "from what my brother said, none of the women wear denims or gun belts, and aren't allowed in the saloons."

Although parts of him were afraid to ask her to explain that last part, his curiosity refused to be denied. "Why would you want to go into a saloon?"

"For a drink."

He stared again.

"I take it the women you keep company with don't drink whiskey?"

"Not even a little bit." She'd caught him so off guard, he wasn't sure what to ask next. "Does your sister-in-law imbibe, too?"

"She'll have an occasional shot of tequila, but not now. She's nursing."

"And her husband approves?"

"Why would she need his approval? Oh, I forgot. You're from back East. Your menfolk get a say in those kinds of things there."

"Here they don't?"

"Some men do, or at least they try. My brother was that way until he married Regan. Now he minds his own business."

"I see." He didn't really, but pretended to. "So you just waltz right into the saloon and order a shot of whiskey?"

"Maybe not waltz, but yes, McCray."

"Is there a separate room for ladies?"

"I've never seen one." She eyed him with a hint of a smile. "Why do you look as if I've grown another head?"

"I'm just surprised." Still outdone, he asked, "And no one cares that you're in the saloon?"

"The gossips do, of course."

"Ah." There was now challenge in her eyes, as if she was waiting for something. Judgment from him, maybe. That made him wonder if she continued to be the subject of gossip. If so, he couldn't imagine her backing down. *Lord, this woman was interesting.*

She asked, "Anything else?"

"Maybe. I'm just not sure what."

"While you figure that out, I'll get some meat thawing for supper. Steaks or trout?"

He thought that over. "Steaks."

"Good choice."

LATER, SPRING PULLED the skillet of cornbread out of the oven and left the kitchen to alert her houseguest. He was in his room, so she knocked on the closed door. "Dinner, McCray."

"Be right there."

She didn't know how he'd been occupying his time all afternoon, but he hadn't bothered her while she sorted seeds for her garden, so whatever he'd been doing was fine with her.

She'd just taken the plates down from the cupboard when he appeared in the kitchen.

"Anything I can do to help?" he asked.

"Grab that pot holder and put the cornbread on the table."

She followed with the plates and tableware, then went back to retrieve the platter of steaks and the bowl of root vegetables.

"Steaks smell good," he said, standing behind his chair.

She forked a steak from the platter and set it on her plate. Noticing him still standing, she asked, "You plan to eat standing?"

"Waiting for you to sit."

"Why?"

"Being a gentleman again."

She waved him off. "Not necessary."

"It is for me."

His soft tone did something to her insides. "Just sit, McCray."

"I will, after you do."

Spring growled quietly.

"It's a show of respect, Spring."

She blew out a breath. "Christ and three fishes. Fine." She sat.

He followed.

"Happy?" she asked.

He simply smiled.

"I drink whiskey, remember. I'm not a lady."

"Doesn't make you less deserving of my respect. You took me in, fed me, doctored me."

Not comfortable with the conversation, she grumbled, "Eat before the food gets cold."

"Yes, ma'am."

She hazarded a look his way to gauge whether he was toying with her, but the seriously set eyes holding her own touched her in a way that made her break the contact in favor of something less discomforting, like putting vegetables on her plate.

They ate in silence for a few moments. "My apologies if I made you uncomfortable," he said. "It's how I was raised."

"My brother does that with Regan. He tries with me, but I just ignore him. I don't need that kind of respect."

"What kind do you need?"

She paused. He had a way of asking questions she had no ready answers for. "None really. Not being respected hasn't made me lose sleep."

"But respect is a way of acknowledging how valued you are, or how much you mean to a person."

She shrugged. "I suppose, but I value myself. I don't need it from anyone else just because it's the gentlemanly thing to do."

"But what if it's genuine, and not because of what society dictates?"

Spring had spent the past fifteen years focused on what she didn't need: a man, respect, to be coddled. She wasn't sure how to respond to his attempts to make her consider what else she might need besides the support and friendship of Ed Prescott, Odell, her brother, and Regan. "How's your steak?"

"Steak's fine."

That he didn't push her to answer earned him a measure of her respect. "So do you stand at the table and wait until the woman who may or may not be your intended sits down?"

He glanced over. "I do."

"Does she have a name?"

"Yes. Emily. Emily Stanton."

"Not known to frequent saloons?"

"No."

"Does she mind all your questions?"

"No, just that I prefer carpentry to law. My father isn't happy about it, either."

"Then why are you entertaining the idea of maybe marrying her?"

"My father and hers are convinced we'd be a good match."

"What do you think?"

"She and I are certain they're wrong."

"Problem solved, then."

"If only our parents would agree."

Spring was confused. If he and this Emily were of like minds, why was a match still being discussed? It sounded fairly simple to her. She reminded herself that the answer didn't matter because he'd be returning home eventually and the outcome wouldn't affect her life one way or the other, but she was admittedly curious.

"Emily is a crusader. She doesn't believe marriage holds much benefit for women," he explained.

Spring raised her cup in silent tribute.

He smiled. "I sensed you'd agree with her."

"So you don't want to marry her because she doesn't want to marry you?"

"In part, but the other part is if I do marry, I want it to be to someone who fills my heart the way my mother fills my father's heart. He adores her."

Something rippled through her that was both faint yet powerful. For a moment she felt entranced, unable to do anything but look into his eyes and let him do the same to her. She broke the invisible thread and concentrated on cutting her steak. Realizing her hand was shaking, she cursed inwardly and drew in a breath to calm herself. "So you believe in love." It was more statement than question.

"I don't know if that's what it's called, but for the sake of conversation, yes. My mother is the light of my father's world. You see it in his face whenever she walks into a room. I'd like to feel that way about the person I pledge my life to."

"And it doesn't happen with Emily," she stated quietly.

He shook his head. "But she's incredibly smart, funny, and a good friend."

Spring thought him way more complicated than she'd initially assumed. His description of his father and mother fit how Colt and Regan felt about each other.

He added, "Of course, I may never find that person, but I'd like to hold out and see."

Once again she was caught by the spell in his gaze. Tearing herself away, she said, "Good luck." What she didn't say aloud was: *What in the hell is wrong with me?*

"Thanks." He offered up a toast. "Have you ever been in love?"

She glared.

"My apologies. Even I know that was too nosy to ask."

"Just eat."

After the meal, they did the dishes. This time he washed, and she dried. They worked silently, which suited her just fine.

Because of her mood, she wanted to ignore him but found that difficult. Like before, there were inadvertent touches, and though she tried not to, she found herself studying his strong hands, along with the cut of his jaw and the slope of his shoulders in the blue shirt he wore. That her eyes kept straying to his was frustrating. She uncharacteristically wondered if her glare had hurt his feelings, but there was nothing in his face or manner that said she had. Oddly enough, when their eyes brushed, he seemed quietly amused, as if he held the answer to a private riddle. She wanted to ask what it meant because it further fed her inner grumbling. Instead, she took the wet dishes he handed her, dried them, and put them away.

When they finished the task, he asked, "Is there anything else I can help you with? You've taken me in and fed me. I'd like to feel as if I'm at least earning my keep."

"No, but thank you for asking."

"Then I've some reading I want to catch up on. Have a good rest of your evening and thanks for dinner. I'll see you in the morning."

And he walked out and left her alone in the kitchen. She told herself good riddance because she'd had enough of his company and nosy questions for one night, even as a voice inside called the lie.

The following morning, after feeding the horses, Spring looked around the landscape surrounding her place and decided the snow had melted enough to make the trip to her brother's place.

McCray had breakfast started when she entered the house. "Morning," she said. The air was fragrant with the scent of bacon.

"Morning."

He paused scrambling the eggs to take her in while she did the same, and for a moment that was all either seemed capable of doing. Whatever was happening seemed to be growing but she was determined it not become any stronger. Pulling herself free, she said, "The snow's melted enough that we can ride over to my brother's today. It'll be muddy, but I don't think it'll be too bad on our mounts. Is your knee healed enough to ride?"

He nodded.

"If my brother's back, he can take you into town to get your room."

"And if he isn't?"

"Then I guess I'll have to do it."

"I don't want to impose upon you any more than I have already."

"If I don't take you, who will? I can ask Odell if you prefer."

"No. I'll take your company over his any day."

"He's not so bad once you get to know him."

"If you say so. Once I get my gear packed, I'll be ready to leave. How far away does your brother live?"

"On horseback about twenty minutes. It'll probably take us a bit longer today with it being so muddy."

"Does he live on a ranch, too?"

"No, but he has a fair amount of land."

After breakfast they saddled their mounts.

"That's a fine-looking stallion," he said to her as they rode slowly out to the road.

"This is Cheyenne. Have had him now about eight years. He was a sickly foal when I found him. I don't know if he lost his mother or got separated from his herd, but he was near death, so I brought him home. We've been together ever since."

"I've never seen such a magnificent animal."

"There are hundreds of wild horses here. Wranglers bring them in, break them, and sell them. Where do your horses come from back East?"

"Usually from the owners of horse farms, but I've no idea where their stock comes from. Many breed them, I suppose."

"You should always know where your mounts originate. Some sellers aren't always honest. If you don't know what to look for they can take advantage and stick you with a sick or deformed animal."

"I'll remember that."

As they kept the horses to a slow walk down the road, Spring wouldn't admit to having enjoyed McCray's company, only that he'd been a houseguest she hadn't immediately wanted to be rid of. It made her wonder if that meant she'd been lonely over the course of the long winter months. Having her breakfast prepared for her had been novel, and holding conversation with someone other than her horses had been, as well. Usually when she wanted talk or company, she rode over to Regan's or Odell's. Rarely were conversations held at her table.

She glanced his way and wondered what he thought of her. Not that it mattered. She made no apologies for who she was, but knew she probably wasn't like his female acquaintances at home. Would he go home and make jokes to his friends about her buffalo coat, buckskins, and unconventional ways? Not that that mattered, either, or at least she told herself it didn't. Being a hothouse flower needing care and watering by a man wasn't anything she desired to be. Like many unmarried women in the West, she saddled her own horse, chopped her own wood, and shoveled her own snow. Society dictates or not, she didn't want children—never had, which would undoubtedly shock any man loco enough to come calling; not that there'd been any nor would be, for that matter. And that meant she wouldn't have to worry about being challenged to change her mind.

"What's it like around here in the summer?" he asked.

"Beautiful. Green. Lots of wildflowers. Big blue sky."

He studied the still snow-covered landscape and mountains off in the distance. "I'll bet it's something."

"It is. No streetcars though."

He shot her a smile. "Do folks climb the mountains?"

"Sometimes, but I've never known anyone to go all the way to the top. Odell said the Natives worshipped them. They believed their gods lived on the summits."

"So they have stories?"

"Yes, just like most groups of people do, I suppose."

"My father said when he was young, the old slaves told stories of the African gods. Sadly, most of the tales died with them."

She wondered what those tales had been like. Were there tricksters and magical beings? Were some gods evil and others good? Her mother, Isabelle, had been enslaved then freed as an adolescent. She'd never talked about her experiences though. McCray said he wasn't ashamed of his past. Had her mother felt differently? Was that the reason she never discussed those years, or did she simply want to forget because life had been too painful? Spring wondered what her mother would think about what her daughter had been forced to do to survive after her untimely death. Not wanting to open old wounds, she turned her thoughts away from those heartbreaking times and concentrated on the warmth in the air and the brilliant blue sky above.

Like the road, the gravel path leading to her brother's house was thick with mud from the melting snow. "We're here."

They dismounted and he eyed the surroundings. Seeing the unfinished structure behind the house, he asked, "Are they putting on an addition?"

"No, it's going to be the town's first hospital. Colt has an office in town, but he'd like to treat people away from town, too. He's also adding a room where patients can stay overnight if need be."

She led McCray up the steps to the porch and knocked on the front door. It was opened by her seven-year-old niece, Anna.

"Aunt Spring!" the girl cried joyfully and launched her small frame into Spring's embrace.

Grinning, Spring picked her up and hugged her close. "Hello, Anna. How are you? How's your pony Shadow?"

"I'm fine. Shadow, too. I have to wait until the snow melts some more before I can go riding. It's so good to see you.

Colton Fontaine spit up all over Mama. She's in her room cleaning up."

Spring saw Anna eyeing her companion, and so made the introductions. "Anna Lee, this is Mr. McCray. He's a newspaper man and is going to do a story about your father. McCray, this is my niece, Anna."

"Hello, Miss Anna. It's my pleasure to meet you."

"Hello," she replied shyly. "Pleased to meet you, too."

Spring put her back on her feet, and they entered the house. She was just closing the door when Regan appeared with her son in her arms. Spring noted the bags of exhaustion below her eyes.

"Hello, Spring," Regan said. "Is this the newspaper reporter Odell told me about when he stopped by yesterday?"

"Yes. Name's Garrett McCray." Spring turned to him. "McCray, this is my sister-in-law, Regan Carmichael Lee."

He nodded. "Pleased to meet you, Mrs. Lee."

"Same here. My husband's been expecting you. I'm sorry he isn't here. This small bundle of sometimes joy is our son, Colton Fontaine Lee."

McCray stepped closer and peered down at the blanket-swathed infant in her arms. "Hello there, little fella. How are you?" He then asked Regan, "How old is he?"

"He'll be six weeks old tomorrow."

"Congratulations."

"Thank you."

Anna said, "He cries so loud sometimes."

McCray said to Anna, "Crying is what babies do. They grow out of it, though."

Anna replied, "Libby has a baby sister. She cried a lot when they first got her, too. Now she crawls around on the floor."

Regan explained. "Libby is Anna's best friend."

"Ah."

Regan said, "My husband has been looking forward to your arrival but unfortunately, there's a measles epidemic up at Rock

Springs. Hopefully, now that the weather has broken, he'll be home soon. Odell said Spring rescued you from the storm. Good thing she found you."

Spring cracked, "As long as we have Odell, we'll never need a newspaper." The old trapper had ties to nearly everyone in the Territory, and if there was news to be told, he could be counted on to spread the word. "I'm going to take him into Paradise so he can rent a room from Dovie."

"Okay," Regan replied. "Welcome to Paradise, Mr. McCray. As soon as my husband returns, I'll let him know you've arrived."

"I'd appreciate that. I'll let you get back to your day. Was nice meeting you."

"Same here."

Spring placed a kiss on the cheeks of Regan, Anna, and Colton Fontaine, then led McCray back out into the sunshine.

"Sorry for having to take up more of your time, Spring."

"I'm fine. Just mount up." She couldn't recall a man quite so apologetic, and she wondered who he really was beneath the gentlemanly facade. Could he simply be who he'd shown himself to be so far? A well-raised, nice man?

They resumed their ride and at one point he asked, "What are the politics like in Paradise? Might need it for background for the story."

"Things are more progressive now that there's a new mayor. His name is Randolph Nelson. That was his beef we had for supper last night."

"Ah. He's Republican?"

"Yes. Head of the local party. The old mayor, Arnold Cale, was Republican, too, but he and his cronies were voted out mainly for refusing to pay for a schoolteacher."

"Why would anyone be against that?"

"Just cheap and not being very educated themselves."

"Is your brother active in the political arena?"

"No. Colt's more focused on his doctoring."

"I see. Is it true women vote out here?"

"Yes. Since sixty-nine."

"Some folks back East are against women voting."

"Just the men, right?"

His amusement showed. "Mostly, yes."

"The Territory hoped giving us the vote would draw women from back East and help grow the population."

"Has it worked?"

"A bit, but women aren't arriving in the droves hoped for."

"Do you vote?"

"Of course."

"Colored people aren't challenged?"

"Not yet, but I'm guessing it's on the way. Last year Regan was on a stagecoach outlaws tried to rob, but she wasn't allowed to testify against them at the trial because of her race. How is it back East?"

"Getting worse by the day, seemingly."

"Another reason to stay out West."

"Might not be a bad idea. Just seeing all these trees and imagining what they look like in warm weather, and what I could build with the wood, makes me want to stay and find out. I've met some interesting people here, too."

"Yes, Odell is interesting."

He laughed. "I meant a certain woman who wears buckskins and a buffalo coat. She's somewhat prickly but that seems to be part of her charm."

Spring turned to him. "I thought you were talking about me until you added that charm part."

"I find you very charming."

She stopped her horse and searched the sky.

"What are you doing?"

"Looking for the lightning that's coming to strike you dead for lying."

"You don't think you're charming?"

"*Charming* is used to describe dainty women wearing pretty dresses who drink tea from little china cups."

"Not to me," he said quietly. "Charming can be strength, intelligence—an unconventional way of looking at life."

She found herself entranced again but fighting free because she had no business being attracted to a nosy newspaper man. She said, "Let's go so you can get settled in town, and I can ride home."

"Lead the way."

# Chapter Four

Garrett's first thought upon arriving in Paradise was how small it was. As he rode beside Spring down the main street, he took in the businesses and shops: Miller's Grocer, the medical office of Dr. Lee, the sheriff's office, and Beck's Undertaking. A few men on the walks in front of the grocer's called hello to Spring, and asked, "That the newspaper fella?"

"It is."

"Heard he was being chased by a bear when you found him."

Garrett's jaw dropped. *A bear?*

She smiled. "There was no bear."

Someone yelled, "He going to let other people be in his newspaper story?"

"I don't know. You'll have to ask him."

Garrett was amazed that they already knew about him. He supposed small-town folks had nothing better to do than share gossip—true or not.

"Is there a telegraph office?" he asked Spring. "I want to let my family know I arrived safely."

"Yes. Odell runs it. It's across the street from the boardinghouse."

Garrett still wasn't sure how he felt about being tested by the old man, but having passed it, he supposed he shouldn't hold a grudge.

She stopped at the far end of the street in front of a simple house whose green paint looked new. "This is the boarding-house. Regan owns it but Dovie Denby runs it. She also has her seamstress shop inside."

They stepped up onto the porch and before she could reach for the latch to open the door, he reached for it first.

"What're you doing?" she asked.

"Getting the door."

"Being a gentleman again?"

"Yes."

"I can open the door for myself, McCray."

"I know that."

"Then step aside."

"Remember the talk we had about respect?"

"Remember what I said in response?"

A female voice interrupted them. "For heaven's sake, Spring. Let the man open the door. Nobody else around here has balls enough to try and treat you like a lady."

Garrett turned to see a red-haired woman dressed in an elegant green day gown. She was standing at the base of the steps with a small group of curious onlookers that included Odell.

Spring groused, "Go away, Glenda, and take Odell and his checkers partners with you."

Garrett had no idea who the woman was, but that was quickly remedied. Ignoring Spring, she walked up and stuck out a hand encased in a green glove that matched her dress. "I'm Glenda Cale. My husband, Arnold, owns the bank and is the former mayor."

"Garrett McCray."

"If you're thinking about courting our Spring, know that she's going to ride you hard and put you up wet, but she's worth every argument the two of you are going to have. Welcome to Paradise."

"Glenda," Spring snarled warningly. She then turned on the men. "Odell, don't you have someplace else to be?"

Garrett stood fascinated and confused. Where did the notion

that he might be courting Spring come from? He looked out at Odell, who smiled and nodded a greeting.

Glenda then asked where he was from, and the name of his newspaper. After his replies she said, "Nice meeting you, Mr. McCray. Have Regan and Dr. Lee bring you over for dinner while you're in town."

"Yes, ma'am."

"And Spring. Be nice. Any man willing to fight you for a door may be worth keeping."

That said, she strode away.

Outdone, he turned to Spring who growled, "Open the damn door, McCray."

He did, and Odell and his friends applauded.

Inside, the house was quiet, clean, and well-furnished. A tall large-boned blonde woman came from a room off the parlor.

"Hey, Spring."

"Dovie."

"You look angry. What's wrong?"

"Nothing."

Dovie didn't appear convinced and Garrett had no plans to add to Spring's ire by offering an explanation. He was still trying to process the encounter outside.

"Is this the newspaper man you rescued?"

"Yes. Garrett McCray. Dovie Denby."

"Nice to meet you, Miss or is it Mrs. Denby?"

"Legally, it's Mrs., but the mister is off living with another woman. Left me high and dry."

Her frankness caught him off guard.

She explained, "More than likely you'll hear the story from somebody else. I just wanted to get ahead of it before you did."

He wasn't sure how to respond. "Um. I appreciate that. Thank you. It's nice to meet you."

"Same here. So you need a room?"

"Yes."

"There aren't any other boarders at the moment, so since

you're doing a story on the doc I'll put you up in the Rhine room, and you can have it for the price of one of the smaller ones."

He didn't know what the Rhine room was, but she gave him the impression that it was a bit fancier than the others. "Are you sure?"

"Positive. Come on with me."

He picked up his carpetbag and valise.

Spring said, "I'll get the bedroll—or am I supposed to leave that for a gentleman to handle?"

Not bothering to hide his smile, he added the bedroll to the other items he was carrying, and he and Spring followed Dovie up the stairs.

The Rhine room was spacious and well appointed. Dovie explained that it was named in honor of Regan Lee's uncle, Rhine Fontaine. There was a big four-poster bed atop a wide expensive-looking Oriental carpet, an attached washroom with a tub, and a small desk with a chair. A large wardrobe made of a beautiful oak stood against one wall.

Dovie asked, "Will this do you?"

"Yes. How much is it, may I ask?"

She quoted him a very reasonable price.

As he placed the bedroll on the large rug near the foot of the bed, Spring said, "I'm going to head home."

Even though he knew they'd be parting, he was still disappointed. He wanted to discuss his supposed courtship to assure her that wasn't his intent, but the terseness on her face showed now was not the time. "Thanks for everything."

"Telegraph office is across the street. The livery will take care of your horse. Have Dovie or Odell show you where it is. If you get the chance, walk down and introduce yourself to the sheriff, Whit Lambert. He and my brother are good friends."

"Okay. I hope to see you again before it's time for me to go back to Washington."

She didn't respond, but turned and left, and he was fine with that. If she didn't wish to see him again, she'd've had no problem saying so.

"She likes you," Dovie said.

Amused, he replied, "I'm not so sure about that."

"I am. If she didn't, she'd've sent you off with Odell after the storm. In the ten years I've known Spring, I don't remember her ever taking a man in, blizzard or no blizzard. Makes you special."

Garrett didn't know what to say to that, so he set it aside to ponder later.

Dovie moved to the doorway. "I'll let you get settled. Come find me if you need anything."

"Thank you. Will do."

As he unpacked, he thought about Dovie's words and the fascinating run-in with Glenda Cale. Why did she think he was courting Spring? Was it a rumor started by Odell? He admittedly found Spring intriguing, but courting her? He couldn't imagine how difficult such a challenge would be. Granted, pursuing her wouldn't be boring, but would he survive? She didn't suffer fools nor offer quarter. He'd stood a better chance of walking back to Washington wearing a blindfold. But there was an attraction between them. He was fairly certain she felt it, too, even if she'd probably go to her grave denying it. She impressed him as keeping a tight rein on her emotions and took pride in the control, but he wondered how she'd respond if the reins were loosened. What was she like with a lover? Did she embrace passion as fiercely as she embraced life? Last night at supper, when he asked if she'd ever been in love, her glare would've turned him to stone had it the power. Later, in the kitchen, she seemed set upon ignoring him yet couldn't stop meeting his eyes. He for sure couldn't stop looking her way. He'd found the episode somewhat amusing only because she seemed angry about her inability to control what her eyes were doing. Dovie called him special. He didn't know how truthful that was, but the more time spent with Dr. Colton Lee's iron-willed sister, the more captivating and intriguing he found her to be.

The telegraph office was in a small log building. A barely legible weather-beaten sign above the door read PARADISE TRADING POST. He entered and found Odell and some of the men who'd been with the old trapper earlier gathered around a checkerboard that appeared to be as old as the sign. There was sawdust on the hard-packed dirt floor. On the walls were the heads of an elk, a bear, and a big cat with one eye. The three men looked up at his entrance and Odell said, "Can I help you, McCray?"

"I'd like to send a telegraph back East, if I may."

"Sure." He stood and told the elderly Colored man on the other side of the checkerboard, "Keep your hands off my men, you old cheat."

His opponent, his right leg in a cast and propped on a listing cane chair, shot back, "I can beat you in the middle of the night wearing a blindfold. I don't need to cheat." He then addressed Garrett. "Name's Porter James. Welcome to Paradise."

"I'm Garrett McCray. Pleased to meet you, sir." James's hair was white as snow, but his face, the color of dark maple, was unlined. Garrett certainly hadn't expected to meet another Colored man. He'd have to remember to ask Dr. Lee just how many other members of the race lived in the area.

The other man seated by the checkerboard introduced himself as Moss Denby. He was short, plump, and had graying mutton chops gracing his cheeks. "I drive the stagecoach. Dovie is my daughter-in-law and mother of my grandson, Wallace."

"She's been very helpful." Garrett wondered what Moss thought about his son living with another woman and leaving Dovie high and dry, as she'd claimed.

Odell handed Garrett paper and pencil. "Write what you want to say and where you want it sent. Storm's now east of us, so it may take your message a few days to get where it has to go."

"That's fine." When he finished writing, he handed the paper back to Odell.

"I'll send it right out."

"Thank you."

Moss asked, "Is working for a newspaper the only thing you do?"

"No. I'm a carpenter by trade."

Porter James turned and looked him up and down. "How long?"

"Most of my life."

"You any good?"

"I think I am. Why do you ask?"

"I'm a carpenter, too. Only one within miles. I also own the mill. If you need work while you're here, me and this busted leg could sure use some help."

"I'm not planning on staying after I speak with Dr. Lee, but thanks for letting me know I'd have work if I did."

Garrett spent a few more minutes being quizzed about where he was from and what other places the newspaper business had taken him to.

Odell asked, "So you and Spring getting along?"

Garrett paused and wondered where this might be going. "I'm very grateful that she took me in. I'm concerned about folks thinking I'm courting her. Farthest thing from my mind."

"Why?" Porter asked.

Garrett studied him. "I doubt Miss Lee is interested in being courted by a man who will be leaving soon."

Moss asked, "If you weren't leaving, would you be interested?"

More accustomed to being the nosy questioner, he kept his voice calm. "I think that would be between me and Miss Lee, don't you?"

Moss smiled. James did, too. Odell said, "See? He'll do fine, won't he?"

Garrett was afraid to ask, but did anyway. "Fine as what?"

"As the man Spring needs to court her," Odell replied as if it was obvious.

Exasperated, Garrett said, "But you don't know anything about me. Suppose I'm already married or engaged?"

"Are you?"

"No."

"Then, there you go," Odell said.

He wondered if the people in Paradise were prone to insanity. As he contemplated that, a tall auburn-haired man entered. There was a brass star pinned to the front of his brown wool coat.

"Name's Whitman Lambert," he said, sticking out his hand. "I'm the sheriff. Call me Whit."

Thankful to be rescued, Garrett shook the man's hand. "Garrett McCray. Pleased to meet you."

Whit explained, "Dovie asked me to show you around."

"I'd like that." Anything to get away from Odell and his matchmaking friends.

Garrett turned to them. "Nice meeting you gentlemen."

Odell said, "Whit, give this to Heath. It came in with this morning's mail." He handed the sheriff a small package wrapped in brown paper. "And take real good care of our guest there."

The sheriff appeared confused by that, but replied, "Sure, Odell."

Outside, Lambert asked, "What was that all about?"

Garrett said, "You don't want to know. Where to first?"

"Let's go take this to Heath Leary over at the saloon."

BEFORE GOING HOME, Spring rode over to the Irish Rose, the town's local saloon. She'd asked the owner, Irishman Heath Leary, to order a bottle of scotch from a Denver importer, and she wanted to see if it had arrived. Unlike the wild Spring of old, she rarely set foot in saloons anymore. If she wanted to sip, she preferred to do it in the evenings, at home—alone. As she entered the establishment, she scanned the near-empty interior, noting a few men seated here and there. A small group sat together at a table in the far corner. Baxter, the aged piano player, was dressed in his usual threadbare black suit. He was also slumped against the piano, asleep. She walked over to the bar where Leary was stacking glasses. Dark hair and eyes, he was easily one of the most handsome men in the Territory. He was also hopelessly in love with Dovie Denby, who refused to give him the time of day.

"How are you, Spring?"

"I'm okay. Has my scotch come in?"

"Not yet. Any day now though, I'm sure."

A man called out from across the room. "If it isn't the most well-used mouth in the Territory. How you doing, Spring?"

She froze. She hadn't heard Matt Ketchum's smug voice in years, but her hate rose fresh and raw.

Leary's dark eyes moved to the speaker and back to her tight face. She saw his concern. Ignoring Ketchum, she said to Leary, "I'll check back in a couple of days."

Ketchum stormed, "Don't try and ignore me, you little whore."

He'd drawn everyone's attention. The scrape of his chair as he got to his feet was loud in the silence.

She turned to face him because she wasn't afraid. Not anymore. "No one can ignore your stench, Matt. They probably smell you in Laramie."

The men seated with him turned around to get a good look at her.

Her sidelong glance showed Whit Lambert entering the saloon with McCray. *Great.*

Matt boasted in a loud voice, "Boys, she didn't complain about my stench when she was on her knees, sucking my dick."

"Yeah, I did," she countered coldly. "I've sucked ryegrass straws with more girth than you've got."

A few guffaws were heard.

Face beet-red, he charged her. The sight of her drawn Colt aimed his way froze him midstride. She heard Whit say warningly, "Spring."

She didn't take her eyes off the furious Ketchum. "Need to settle this, Whit."

Ketchum sneered. "Shoot me in front of all these witnesses and you'll hang for sure."

"And I'll do it gladly because you'll no longer be walking this earth. The girl you enjoyed beating up has wanted you dead a long time."

She waited.

The hate in his glare flared. Her raised gun was an equalizer; even a man known as a bullying coward was smart enough to figure that out. He didn't advance. She'd bested him. They both knew it.

"This ain't over," he promised.

"Then have Beck measure you for a pine box." Wasting no more time on him, she holstered the Colt and told Heath, "Let me know about my scotch."

On her way to the door, her eyes briefly brushed McCray's concerned face. He was probably appalled, but she kept walking. Outside, she mounted Cheyenne and they raced home ahead of the demons rising from her past.

She put Cheyenne in his stall and was walking back to her cabin when her grandfather rode up. She wondered if her day could get any worse. "What can I do for you, Ben?" She went inside; he followed.

"Odell said you had some fella here for a couple of days."

"Yes, and he probably also told you the man is here to do a story on Colt and got caught in the storm." She knew what he'd really come to find out. "And if you're wondering how we entertained ourselves, we cavorted like rabbits the entire time."

His jaw tightened beneath his slate-gray beard. "Show some respect."

She asked challengingly, "To whom? You? That is what you wanted to know, isn't it?"

"Odell says he's a nice fella."

"He is, but I'm sure you'll find a way to be rude. Just like you are with Regan." Her brother had forbidden Ben to have any contact with his family until Ben could be civil to his wife.

"Your brother should've never married her."

Spring felt a headache forming. "Go home, Ben. I'm not in the mood to argue with you today."

"Just came to make sure you're okay."

It was a lie and they both knew it.

He gave her a terse nod and departed.

Spring put on a pot of coffee, and while it brewed, sat on the sofa to try and shake off the day. The memory of her run-in with Matt Ketchum still angered her. After Ben threw her out of their family's home for refusing to marry his aged choice of a husband, she'd gone to Matt's father, Mitch, to ask for a job. He bred and sold horses, and since she'd loved horses all her life and had done odd jobs for him while growing up, she was willing to take whatever employment he had to offer so she could eat and have a place to stay. His price. Her innocence. She was eighteen, homeless, and desperate. Her parents had passed away and Colt was back East studying at Howard's Medical School. Seeing no other choice, she followed him to his bedroom and started working for him the next day. She rode with his ranch hands, and he rode her whenever he had a mind to. He let Matt ride her, too, and didn't care that Matt used his fists on her as punishment for sins real and imagined whenever he'd had too much to drink, which was often.

She scrubbed her hands down her face and went to the kitchen. The coffee was ready, so she poured some and took a sip. The sharp bitterness mirrored how she felt inside. Her Ketchum years had been hell and she'd masked her horror, and yes, shame, by fighting, gambling, and strutting drunkenly through town as if she owned the place. When Colt finished his studies and returned to town, her wild behavior gave him nightmares and the local gossips fuel that still burned today. But she saved her money, and when she accumulated enough to pay for the land she now called her own, she quit working for the Ketchums and never spoke to them again. A month or so later Matt left town. Rumor had it he'd used his fists on the daughter of a state legislator and fled the Territory to escape the man's wrath and jail, but Spring didn't know how much of that was true. His father, Mitch, died in a rockslide a few years ago. She didn't mourn.

And now Matt Ketchum had returned. She hoped he was just passing through, but her gut said no. Regardless of the why, he'd want revenge for having his manhood ridiculed, so she'd have to keep an eye out. He was a coward and wasn't above ambushing her and shooting her in the back.

Coffee cup in hand, she stood before the window in her small dining room and looked out. It was still sunny and bright. Usually when she needed to clear her head, she'd pack some gear, saddle Cheyenne, load a pack horse, and camp out in the foothills for a few days because the change in scenery it offered always seemed to be the balm her frayed mind needed, but there was still too much snow. She wondered what McCray thought of the encounter. She assumed the show she'd put on wasn't common where he was from. Parts of her wished he hadn't witnessed it, but other parts shrugged. He now knew more about the true Spring and her past. What he did with that was his own business. She would miss him cooking her breakfast come morning though.

She knocked around her cabin for the next hour and realized she was becoming more and more antsy, so she packed an overnight bag, saddled Cheyenne again, and rode back to her brother's place. Maybe if she stayed until Colt returned, Regan could sleep when the baby did and thereby get some well-needed rest. As it stood now, that was next to impossible because Anna needed looking after, too. Spring refused to admit how empty her house felt and why. Regan needed her help, so she focused on that.

"Did Mr. McCray get settled in at Dovie's?" Regan asked as she led Spring into the parlor. Colt Fontaine was sleeping.

"Yes."

"Are you heading home?"

"No. Heading here."

Regan appeared confused.

"I saw how tired you're looking, so I thought I'd come over, keep Anna company, do some chores, and maybe cook some meals so you can rest."

Regan met her eyes and began to cry. "Thank you."

Spring moved to the sofa, draped an arm over her sister-in-law's shoulders and eased her close. "If I'd known you were going to start crying, I'd've stayed home."

Regan wiped her eyes and laughed before saying seriously, "I didn't know this baby business was going to be so difficult. I feel like I haven't slept in a hundred years, and poor Anna has been so good, but I'm spending all my time with her brother and neglecting her—I—Lord, this is hard, Spring."

"That's why I'm here. Once you're rested you can go back to ruling the world. So what do you need done first?"

"I haven't been able to make bread all week. Anna usually helps me. Can you do that and let her assist?"

"Sure can. That will give us some time together."

"Good, and after I'm back on my feet, you can tell me why you've really come."

Spring stared.

"I don't doubt you came to help me, but something else is on your mind, too."

Spring smiled. "You know me well."

"I do, so whatever is bothering you, I expect you to spill all."

"Yes, ma'am. Now, go to bed while your son is asleep and leave the rest to me and Anna."

Regan kissed her cheek and left. Watching her go, Spring realized just how much she loved having Regan Carmichael Lee as a sister. She was more of a blessing than either Spring or her illustrious doctor brother deserved.

As she and Anna began the bread, a knock sounded on the front door. Spring turned to her niece. "Let me see who it is. I'll be right back."

Opening it, she found a tall man whose blue eyes appeared startled by her appearance. He was wearing a bowler hat and an expensive coat that seemed to say *back East*. His pale middle-aged face was craggy. His hair and beard sandy. "May I help you?" she asked. She wondered if his surprise was tied to her color. There weren't many members of the race in the Territory.

He gathered himself. "I, um, hope so. My companions and I seem to be lost."

Out on the road was a large fancy buggy. The lowered canopy hood showed a man, dressed similarly to the one on the porch, holding the reins. Behind him sat a young woman wearing a pert navy blue hat. Her coat, a matching blue, was edged with black fur.

"Where are you traveling to?"

"Paradise."

"You're on the right road. You'll come to a fork in another mile or so. Take the one on the left. It'll lead you straight into town."

"Thank you." He looked her up and down. The speculative gleam in his eye gave the impression that he liked what he'd seen. "May I ask you a question?" he asked.

"Yes?"

"Are there many of your kind here?"

"My kind, meaning women?"

He chuckled. "No, I—I mean Coloreds?"

"Will the answer alter why you're going to Paradise?"

Her serious tone seemed to give him pause. "Well, no. I just . . . You're a very striking woman and I'm wondering if you ever entertain—"

"Remember to take the left fork."

His thin lips tightened, and the gleam was replaced by what may have been anger or embarrassment. "Thank you, miss."

He left the porch. She closed the door and returned to the kitchen.

# Chapter Five

Touring Paradise with the sheriff didn't take long but proved helpful in meeting some of the other townspeople. After the saloon the first stop had been Miller's grocer. Garrett was surprised by the establishment's large interior, and how well-stocked it was. He spied everything from farm implements and children's clothing, to back-East newspapers and a few Singer sewing machines. The Millers were middle-aged. The gray-haired wife, Lacy, had a twinkle in her blue eyes when Lambert introduced Garrett. Her husband, Chauncey, with his black-framed spectacles, was standoffish, and eyed him suspiciously. Next, he and the sheriff walked to the town's lone bank, owned by Glenda Cale's husband, Arnold, who appeared years older than his wife. Cale boasted about the bank's large deposits on hand, and told Garrett, "Too bad you won't be staying. I'd have some sure-fire investments for you to consider."

Their final stop—the undertaker's, where he shook the cold hand of owner, Lyman Beck. And throughout it all, his thoughts were dominated by the encounter witnessed at the saloon.

"So who was the man Spring was arguing with?" he asked the sheriff as they finished up their lunch in Dovie's small dining room.

"Name's Matt Ketchum. Spring worked for his father, Mitch, when she was younger."

"In the house as a cook or a maid?"

"No, as a ranch hand and the only woman on the place."

Garrett paused over his coffee and studied him. "Really?"

"Yes. She was pretty wild back then. Arrested her regularly for disturbing the peace, public intoxication, shoplifting. Colt and I were afraid we'd find her dead somewhere."

Garrett's lips tightened in response to Lambert's description and concerned tone.

"But as soon as she got her own place, she settled down," the sheriff continued, "or as settled down as Spring can be."

"Do you think Ketchum will harm her?"

"He may try, but he'll have a helluva time doing so, and he knows it. He doesn't have his father to make things smooth for him anymore. Man's basically a coward. Always has been."

That made Garrett feel somewhat better. He was still trying to reconcile the Spring he'd met a few days ago with the one Whit had regularly arrested. Granted, she'd admitted patronizing saloons. It never occurred to him that she'd also run afoul of the law.

"Some people still judge her for her past, others don't, but just about everyone points at Ben Lee for sending her life off the rails. Ben, and Mitch Ketchum. Both deserved to be horsewhipped for the parts they played."

Garrett wanted to know the full story but didn't see himself asking Spring about what had to have been a difficult time in her life. He couldn't claim to respect her one minute, then turn around and casually ask, "Oh by the way, I heard you called a whore and were arrested for public drunkenness. Can you share the details with me—a stranger?" If she shot him with her Colt, he'd deserve it.

Whit drained the last of his coffee and stood. "I have to get back to my office. If you need anything, you know where to find me."

"Thank you. I appreciate you taking the time to show me around."

"You're welcome."

The tall lawman departed and Garrett's thoughts slid back to Spring. His entering the saloon just in time to hear Ketchum brag about Spring being on her knees had been shocking. Her withering retort referencing something he'd never heard another woman say in his life still had him reeling. Rather than judge her as some might, Garrett considered the life she'd led. It had to have been challenging being the only woman on the place. She'd undoubtedly had to forego what society saw as proper female behavior in order to measure up and hold on to her position. She would've needed to be physically strong, have a thick skin, and an even quicker wit to pull her weight.

She said her grandfather kicked her out at age eighteen. Had working for Ketchum been her only option? She must have seen it as such, and he could only imagine how difficult making that choice must have been. When Matt Ketchum came charging at her for comparing him to less than a ryegrass straw, Garrett's first instinct had been to jump between them to protect her. He sensed the sheriff was of a like mind, but Spring had drawn the Colt with such deadly calm, neither of them got the chance to intervene. She didn't need protecting. Watching her face Ketchum down so fearlessly made him want to cheer. He'd never seen a woman radiate such ice-cold purpose and doubted he ever would again. That Ketchum had used his fists on her made him furious. Had she been forced to service him? Was that the reason she wanted him dead? It was a disturbing question, one he had no answer for and with his return home on the horizon, probably never would.

LATER THAT EVENING, after Anna went to bed and Regan put the baby down for the night, Spring sat with her sister-in-law in the parlor. The temperature outside had dropped so they built a good-size fire in the grate.

"Thanks again for coming to my rescue today," the still-weary Regan voiced softly.

"You're welcome."

"So other than being a good sister to me, what was the other reason?"

Spring thought back on the altercation at the saloon. "Had a run-in with Ketchum earlier today."

Confused, Regan sat up straight. "The Ketchum you told me about last year? The one you once worked for? I thought you said he died in a landslide?"

"Mitch Ketchum did. This is his son, Matt."

"What happened?"

Spring relayed the incident.

"That's what he said to you?" Regan asked angrily. "And you didn't shoot his bastard arse?"

A small smile curved Spring's lips. She loved her fiery sister-in-law. The fuming Regan switched to Spanish as she always did when her emotions ran high. In the year they'd been family, Spring had learned to pick out a few of the curse words but little else. "He's still alive. For now."

More angry Spanish was spoken before Regan calmed enough to ask, "Did any of the men there come to your aid?"

Spring shook her head. "My Colt did that. But . . ."

"But what?"

"Whit came in, along with McCray."

"And?"

Spring shrugged. "I sort of wish McCray hadn't witnessed and heard everything. That's all."

She met Regan's eyes.

Regan studied Spring for a long, silent moment before asking in a wondrous voice, "Do you have feelings for this man, Spring Rain Lee?"

"Doesn't matter. He'll be going back East soon."

"You didn't answer the question."

"I don't know. This is all new for me, Regan." She then admitted, "Maybe it's simply lust."

"Nothing wrong with lust—ask your brother."

Spring held up a hand. "Stop. I don't want to think about my brother in a sentence tied to lust."

"Neither did he, at first."

Regan laughed, and unable to hold back, Spring joined in. "Poor Colt's up in Rock Springs wondering why his ears are suddenly burning."

"Probably."

After the laughter Spring said honestly, "The last thing I want in my life is a man cluttering up things."

"As you said, he won't be here long enough to do that."

"But there's something about him that makes me want to know more about him."

"Then use the time he's here to do that, and if you end up with him in your bed, whose business is it besides his and yours? Just make sure you don't get caught. I know you don't want children."

"I'll protect myself, that's a given."

Regan reached out and took Spring's hands. "I'm aware you aren't seeking my approval, but I'm all for any woman snatching happiness wherever she finds it—especially if the woman is my sister. And if it's lust—so what?"

"Please don't bring up my brother again."

And they laughed once more.

"I won't promise. McCray is quite handsome."

"So is Matt Ketchum, but something's drawing me to McCray besides his looks, and I can't put my finger on what it is. He can be annoying. Asks far too many questions and won't sit at the table until I'm seated. I don't need a man to treat me that way. Sit down."

"If he wants to—let him. No skin off your nose."

"He wants to open doors for me. I break horses. I can open my own doors."

"Has nothing to do with strength, Spring."

"That's what he said."

"Dare I mention your brother again? He treats me like a hothouse flower at times and it can rile me no end. I talked to my aunt Eddy about it when she visited, and she asked if Colt made me happy. I said yes. She said then let him do those things that make him happy—unless he begins acting as if I'm not smart enough to cross the road alone."

"So I should let him open doors for me?"

"I know better than to try and tell you what to do because we're very much alike in that way. Just offering things to consider."

"Okay. That's fair, I suppose." Yet, she remained opposed to his shows of chivalry because at the end of the day who cared as long as the damn door was opened.

That night, lying in bed in Colt and Regan's spare bedroom, Spring thought back on having admitted her attraction to McCray. She didn't like having feelings she didn't understand. Avoiding him until he left town might be a way to solve the problem, but what if that only left her pining? Another way might be to invite him into her bed and let nature take its course. In her mind, one quick romp was all she'd need. If he were anything like the other men she'd danced between the sheets with in the past, quick was what it would be. None had ever taken more than three, four pumps before doing up their trousers and going on their way. She'd never minded the briefness when she needed an itch scratched. Coupling was for relieving lust or creating children; it wasn't supposed to take all day. McCray was a self-professed gentleman, however. Would he be appalled by her invitation? She'd yet to meet a man who'd willingly turn down such an offer, especially one with no strings attached, so he probably wouldn't, either—gentleman or not. Deciding to make the invitation in hopes it would rid her of the troubling attraction once and for all, she turned over and went to sleep.

THE NEXT MORNING Garrett was eating breakfast in the dining room when Odell came in and approached him with a smile.

"Morning, McCray."

"Morning, Odell. Any replies to my wire yet?"

"Not yet. Want to ask you something."

"Sure. Have a seat."

"Thanks. Are you busy this morning?"

Garrett wondered where this might be leading but responded honestly, "I was going to work on my notes but nothing more. Is there something I can assist you with?"

"Yes. Porter could use some help. You know anything about sawmills?"

"Other than picking up lumber my uncle and I ordered, no. What kind of help does he need?"

"Getting the mill up and running because he can't do much on his busted leg."

"What about his employees?"

"They always leave when he shuts down for the winter. They're due to return in a week or two. I have a small group of volunteers lined up, and thought with you being a carpenter and all, maybe you knew something about how mills run or could help with some of the repairs."

Garrett thought it over. He did want to interview Mr. James, and this might be a way to accomplish that. "I don't know if I'd be a help or a hindrance, but I'd be willing to give it a try."

With Dr. Lee still away and Spring keeping to herself, his time was his own. "When does he want me to start? Is he at the telegraph office?"

"He is, so come over when you're done with your breakfast. I'll round up the rest of the volunteers and we'll meet you at the mill. Thanks," he said, rising to his feet.

"You're welcome."

When his breakfast was done, Garrett walked over to the telegraph office. When he entered, Porter James nodded a greeting. "Appreciate your help. You ready?"

"I am."

Aided by a cane, James rose and made his way outside to where a wagon waited. Garrett started to ask if he needed help but waited and watched as the old man slowly but smoothly maneuvered his way up to the seat and picked up the reins. Impressed, Garrett climbed aboard, and they got underway.

They headed north and were soon following a river. He'd not seen the area before, but like the rest of the surroundings, the land was filled with towering pines, birdsong, and stands of brightly colored wildflowers. Off in the distance the snow-capped mountains rose majestically. The countryside seemed to grow more beautiful with each passing day. "How long have you lived here, Mr. James?" he asked.

"Long time," he replied. "Was young when I first got here though. Maybe fifteen, sixteen years old. I was a slave owned by a Methodist minister from Georgia. He and his wife came west to save the souls of the savages."

Garrett heard sarcasm in his tone.

"By the end of the first winter though, the minister was dead from fever. His wife buried him, freed me, and took the train back to her family."

"And you've been here since?"

"Yes. Worked traps for a while, learned to build cabins from a friend of Odell and Ben Lee, then got into the business of lumber because it was needed."

"Family?"

The question made him smile fondly. "Sent away for a mail-order bride. A sweet little brown-skinned beauty named Molly responded. Loved her like summer sunshine. We were married five years before she died birthing our twins, a boy and a girl."

"My condolences."

"Thanks. Sent away for another bride. She was pretty, just like my Molly, but inside she was ugly as the devil. I came home from the mill one evening and found a bruise on my son's face the size of my fist. She said she'd punished him for not eating his supper."

Garrett was appalled. "How old was he?"

"Three. She didn't like my twins. Wanted me to send them away so we could raise children that were hers. The next day I drove her to the train station, bought her a ticket, and left her there. Don't know where she went. Didn't much care."

"Sorry to hear that."

"Wasn't sorry to see her go, and neither were my twins."

On the far bank Garrett spotted deer drinking from the river, but the animals looked stronger and more robust than the ones at home.

"They're elk," Mr. James explained. "In the fall, their antlers can grow three, four feet across. They use them to fight over who gets the ladies. You can hear them bashing each other for miles."

Garrett found that fascinating. "This is a truly beautiful place."

"I agree. It's one of the reasons I stayed. Winters aren't much fun, but once spring comes you forget all about how cold you've been."

"What's it been like living here as a man of the race?"

"Haven't had too much trouble. You run into prejudice every now and then just like any other place else, but folks here are generally too busy surviving to worry about what color you are."

"Does your family live nearby?"

"Daughter is in Denver. She's married and has three boys. We lost her brother ten years ago. He was laying track for the railroad and got crushed beneath a load of steel that fell."

"My condolences on losing your son."

"Thanks."

They arrived at the mill a short time later. The barnlike building made of wood weathered gray by the elements and time was set on the riverbank. Like many old mills it was powered by water. Waiting nearby were a few men on wagons and horseback.

They were put to work cleaning the conveyors, checking for breaks in the heavy steel chains, and repairing the many internal joists and platforms. Garrett spent his time hammering in new wooden supports for some of the blades and adding new two-by-fours to the dock where the cut trees entered the building. Ten men had been recruited, all strangers to him except for Odell, Moss Denby, and saloon owner Heath Leary. The men he didn't know were a bit standoffish at first, but by the time they broke for lunch to eat the sandwiches sent to the mill by Dovie, he was included in the laughter, joking, and assistance they extended to each other.

After lunch a large man wearing a buffalo coat arrived. As he left his wagon and approached, Garrett sensed the atmosphere change from loose and easygoing to a guarded wariness.

Moss Denby, who was working beside Garrett on the dock, glanced the man's way and said, "That's Ben Lee."

A surprised Garrett studied Spring's grandfather, noting his height, girth, shaggy gray hair and beard, and that his presence was commanding. What little Garrett knew about the man could fit on the head of a pin and he wanted to know more, not only for the newspaper article but also for the reasons behind the estrangement with his granddaughter. The urge to go over and introduce himself was strong. He paused, however, choosing to wait and watch instead.

Odell solved the issue by bringing Ben Lee over to meet Garrett. After the introductions were done, Garrett said, "Pleased to meet you, sir."

Eyes sharp with disapproval, the imposing Lee studied him silently.

Garrett continued, "I'd like to interview you for my article, if I might."

"Got nothing to say." And he walked off.

Odell observed the retreat with a shake of his head. "Sorry."

"You've nothing to apologize for."

"He can be rude as a bear just out of hibernation."

"I understand."

Odell sighed and left Garrett to his work.

At the end of the day an exhausted Garrett rode back to town with Odell. He was pleased to have contributed to the effort, and glad to have met a few more people. Ben Lee was still on his mind, however.

"Is Mr. Lee always so cheery?"

Odell chuckled. "You'd think he was raised by wolverines the way he acts. Sorry again for his rudeness."

"Is the rudeness why Spring speaks so poorly of him?"

"Partially. Has she told you what happened between them?"

"Just that she refused to marry his choice of a husband."

"Can't blame her. Ben wanted to give her away because he was tired of looking after her."

"What do you mean?"

"Spring's father, Lewis, died during the war and his wife, Isabelle, joined him in death a few years after the Surrender. Ben was the only family the children had left. After Colt went off to Howard, Ben had had enough of child raising and decided to marry Spring off so he could head back to the mountain, but Spring wanted no parts of the plan."

"Did you know the man?"

"Yes. Cyrus Russell. He was old as Ben and I back then, and frankly, was just looking for a young woman to warm his bed."

Garrett thought about his sister Melody. Even though they had different fathers, his father, Hiram, loved her and even though he'd been trying to arrange a marriage for her for years, he'd never palm her off to a terrible man. "Ben didn't see Spring's side?"

"No. He had his mind made up. He refused to let her live in the house alone. Told her it wasn't proper. She asked to go East to be with Colt. He said there was no money. Which was a lie, of course. In the end he demanded she marry Russell or leave, and so she did."

Garrett couldn't imagine how hurt she must have been.

Odell continued, "She stayed with me for a while. I offered her a home for as long as she wanted but the girl has a lot of pride. I didn't know she'd signed on with Ketchum until the day after he gave her the job. I was furious with Ben. He and I fell out for months after that. And he had the nerve to be mad when she started running wild."

"And Spring is still angry."

"And hurt. She left the home she'd been born in with nothing but the clothes on her back. I loved Ben like a brother. Still do. But I'll never forgive him for what he did to my godchild. Never."

Garrett now had more pieces to Spring's puzzle and thought he understood her a bit better. He admittedly didn't like Ben Lee. He was the root cause of her being publicly called a whore by wastrels like Matt Ketchum.

When they reached town, Odell stopped the wagon in front of the boardinghouse. "Thanks for your help," Odell said to him.

"You're welcome." Garrett had already agreed to rejoin the crew the next day. "See you in the morning."

"If there's a wire waiting for you from your folks, I'll bring it over."

Garrett gave him a nod and went inside.

The next day, Garrett once again volunteered his help with Porter James's mill. Ben Lee didn't make an appearance and Garrett didn't mind. Thanks to the story Odell shared, Garrett didn't care if their paths ever crossed again. At the end of the workday Mr. James thanked everyone and announced plans to travel to Denver for the christening of his new grandson. The remaining work on the mill would resume when he returned.

That evening, Garrett received a wire from his father saying the family was happy he'd arrived safely, and all was well at home. Smiling, he went to bed and slept well.

# Chapter Six

After lunch the following day, Dovie came to Garrett's room to let him know Dr. Lee was waiting for him in the parlor. Ecstatic, Garrett picked up his journal and pen and hurried down to meet the man he'd traveled halfway across the country to see. Dressed in a worn black suit, Colton Lee was much taller than his sister, but they favored each other in skin tone, leanness, and features.

"I'm Garrett McCray," he said, extending his hand.

"Colton Lee. My apologies for not being here when you arrived."

"No need. Seeing to your patients was more important. Shall we sit here, or would you be more comfortable in your office?"

"I'd prefer my office—just in case I'm needed."

Garrett understood. "Let me get my coat."

Thanks to rise in temperatures over the past forty-eight hours, the bulk of the blizzard's snow was just a memory. The sun was shining, the air warm. Garrett was no expert on the Territory's weather, but it appeared that spring had arrived.

As they entered the office, Garrett looked around, taking in the desk and chair, and a door that he thought maybe led to an examination room.

"Have a seat," Lee invited. "I hear you were rescued from the storm by my sister."

"Yes, and she took me in."

"She said you injured your knee? Do you need me to look at it?"

"No, it's still a bit sore but that's all. She encouraged me to stay off it, and I took her advice."

"She has a way of making you listen to her."

Garrett nodded. "Yes, she does." He hadn't seen her since the incident at the saloon and wondered how she was faring. He doubted she missed his presence but he liked to think she did.

He and the doctor spent the next hour talking about everything from Colton growing up in the Territory, to his training at Howard Medical School under Dr. Alexander T. Augusta, the famous Colored Civil War surgeon.

Looking up from his notes, Garrett asked, "Why not practice medicine back East?"

"It would probably be more lucrative, but there are only a few doctors here and I'm needed. Plus, I'd miss the mountains."

"They are rather inspiring." The pull of them and the towering timber seemed to be growing in him with each sunrise.

"And being here brought me Regan after the death of my first wife. Life for my daughter Anna and I would be infinitely poorer without her."

"Congratulations on your son."

"Thank you."

Garrett wanted to ask if he knew about Ketchum's threats against Spring but thought that wasn't his place. Lee and the sheriff were reportedly good friends. Lambert would tell him about the confrontation if he hadn't already.

The office door opened and in walked banker Arnold Cale. Short and round as a turnip, he exuded the air of being the biggest fish in the Paradise pond, even though it was no more than a puddle by back-East standards.

"Afternoon, Arnold," Lee said. "What can I do for you?"

"The wife's having a dinner party and wants to invite McCray along with you, Regan, and Spring."

"When?"

"Tomorrow evening, if possible." He looked at Garrett. "You available, Mr. McCray?"

"Yes, and thank her for me, please." It was short notice, but he had nothing else planned. That he might see Spring again also fueled his ready acceptance.

"What about you, Dr. Lee?"

"I'll have to see how Regan feels. Tell Glenda I'll let her know as soon as I'm able."

"The wife says she can bring the baby and Anna if she needs to."

"I don't think an adult dinner is a place for our children, but her offer is very kind, and I'll pass it along. Thanks for the invitation."

Garrett expected Cale to depart after that, but he didn't.

Lee asked curiously, "Is there something else I can help you with, Arnold?"

He drew himself up importantly. "The town council wants to know if Mr. McCray plans to interview us for the newspaper story, too. Miller and I think your readers might like to learn more about our town and some of the other people who reside here."

Garrett sensed Cale was really referencing himself. "I'd be very interested in talking to the council. Newspapers have limited space, so I can't promise all we discuss will be in the final draft, but let me know when's a good time to speak to everyone."

He beamed. "Can we meet this evening at Dovie's? Say around seven?"

"Sure. I don't see why not."

"Good. We'll be there. I'll let you two get back to your business."

Once he was gone, Lee said, "Let's hope he and Miller don't end up fighting over who gets to talk the most."

"Are they competitive?"

"Yes, and spend a lot of time attempting to top each other."

"How so?"

"Last year on the Fourth of July, they tried to outdo each other with the size of the American flags they displayed on their businesses."

"Who won?"

"Arnold. They both had flags big as the Territory, but the bank sported two. Miller was furious for weeks."

As the conversation continued, Lee had questions of his own for Garrett, such as what he did for a living, how life back East was faring for members of the race, and the future plans for the newspaper.

"I'm a carpenter by trade and frankly, my father's paper is not very successful. He's determined to keep at it, but sundown papers can be difficult to keep afloat." He saw Lee's confusion and explained as he had to Spring. "Sundowns are newspapers worked on after the editor gets home from his day job."

Lee nodded his understanding. "What's your father's occupation?"

"He's the doorman at one of the white hotels. He couldn't take the time off to travel here, so he sent me instead."

"Those are prestigious positions for men like us."

"True. He was a coachman during slavery, so he knows how to conduct himself, even if the guests sometimes forget we're free now." His father was often infuriated by the more bigoted encounters such as those who slurred him for not opening the door fast enough, or accused him of ogling their wives. But as Lee pointed out, it was a prestigious position and the pay provided his parents a comfortable life when compared to those forced to live hand to mouth by picking rags, or shoveling horse manure from the streets.

Lee said, "When I was in Washington, the most coveted jobs were low-level patronage positions at places like the post office."

"That's still true, but most people lack the necessary political connections with the Republican party to secure one."

They talked for a short while longer and when they were done, Garrett was pleased. "I think I have all I need for now," he said, closing his journal. "Would it be possible to accompany you on some of your doctor visits? I'd respect your patients' privacy and not get in your way."

"I'm sorry, no, but I can let you attend the visits I make with animal patients."

"Animal patients?"

"Yes. We don't have a local veterinarian, so I do what I can to help with ailing stock and pets."

Garrett found that intriguing. "My father's readers might be very interested in that side of your practice." He certainly was.

"Then if you're still in town when I go out, you're welcome to come along."

Garrett stood and the men shook hands. "Thanks, Dr. Lee."

"Thank you for coming all this way. Makes a man feel important."

On his walk back to Dovie's, Garrett thought back to his interview with Colton Lee. The doctor was impressive not only for his accomplishments, but also for not looking down his nose at him for having been enslaved. Some freeborn people did, and back East it often influenced how you were perceived for things like employment and your social circle.

As a former slave and a lowly carpenter, he'd never been invited to the homes of many of the people holding the coveted government jobs he and Lee briefly discussed. Although not everyone wrapped themselves in the born-free snobbery, there were those who did. His father was a bit of a social climber. Being a coachman had given him a status lacked by those who labored in the fields. In his mind, being a doorman offered the same elevated rank, but his past enslavement often barred him from the higher social circles he wanted to be a part of.

It was one of the reasons he was pushing for Garrett to marry Emily Stanton. Her father, Henry, a celebrated chef at the same hotel, was a descendant of people free since the Revolutionary War, and so was accepted in the rarefied places his father was not. The two men were longtime friends, and the Stantons occasionally invited Garrett's parents to dinner. Mr. Stanton looked upon Garrett as someone he wouldn't mind his daughter marrying if she could be convinced to do so, and if Garrett returned to the practice of law.

Garrett loved his father, but he refused to be a pawn to further his social ambitions. Creating furniture and working with his uncle Quincy to build homes held all the satisfaction he needed in life. The feel of the tools, the scent of the wood, and turning that wood into something functional and often pleasing to the eye, was a joy difficult to convey. His uncle understood; his father did not. Garrett respected his father's desire for a son who championed the law; the race needed such men, but it wasn't his calling. Being enslaved, who he wanted to be had been beyond his grasp. Now free, his life, ambitions, and dreams were his own. He'd not turn the reins over to anyone else.

PER THE ARRANGEMENT, Arnold Cale and Chauncey Miller arrived promptly at seven, and joined Garrett at a table in the back of the boardinghouse's dining room.

As they took their seats, Garrett asked, "Are the other council members on the way?"

"No," Cale replied. "Mayor Nelson is in Laramie on business, Heath Leary's doing inventory at the saloon, and Beck's handling a funeral, so it'll just be the two of us for your story."

Garrett had hoped to speak with the entire group. "Shall we postpone the interview until they're available?"

Cale shook his head. "I think Chauncey and I can provide you with all you need to know."

The dour Miller studied Garrett through the thick lenses of his spectacles and asked, "Do lots of people read your newspaper?"

"A fair amount. There are a number of newspapers to choose

from in Washington, so many people subscribe to more than one."

Cale appeared pleased by that.

"How about President Cleveland? You think he'll read about us in your paper?"

Garrett smiled. "I'm not sure. I don't know if he reads Colored newspapers."

Both men appeared perplexed, and Miller asked, "What do you mean by Colored newspapers?"

"Newspapers for the Colored population."

They drew back as if he was contagious. "Coloreds have newspapers?" Cale asked.

The astonishment on his face forced Garrett to swallow an urge to laugh out loud. "Yes. There are quite a few, to be honest. In fact, the first one, *Freedom's Journal*, was published way back in 1827."

Miller's eyes were wide, as well. "And that's where your story about us will be? In a Colored paper?"

"Yes." He opened his journal. "So tell me how long you've both been on the council."

Cale began to stammer. "I—I just remembered Glenda needed me to do something for her this evening. So sorry. She always teases me about how forgetful I am." He stood up so hastily he knocked his chair to the floor.

Miller rose, too. "I have a shipment coming in I need to see to. I don't think I'll have free time to talk to you again before you leave town."

"I understand," Garrett replied. "Have a nice evening, gentlemen."

They practically ran to the exit.

Garrett sighed with irritation. Although their reactions were common, he still found them disappointing.

Dovie walked over. "Are you ready to eat? What happened to Arnold and Chauncey?"

"When they found out I write for a Colored newspaper they suddenly remembered they had someplace else to be."

She shook her head. “I'm sorry they were so rude. We have spittoons with better manners.”

“No apologies needed. And yes, I'm ready to eat. I'll have the pork chops and rice, please.”

“Coming right up. If you decide to write about a tall blonde woman making her way alone while raising her son, I'm available.”

“Good to know.”

# Chapter Seven

Although Spring got along well with Glenda Cale, the idea of having to attend a dinner party at her home was not something she would've agreed to on her own, so while Regan did up her hair, she simmered silently.

"There," Regan said, placing the curling iron in the brazier for the last time. "I'm done."

Spring looked at herself in the mirror and scowled. Regan ignored the displeasure on her face and said, "Get dressed. You don't want to be late."

A short while later, stomping through the house in the fancy, off-shoulder burgundy gown and thin-soled slippers she didn't want to wear, Spring snatched up her shawl and went to seek out her sister-in-law.

"You look lovely," Regan said. "But please don't glare at Glenda's guests that way."

Spring glared at Regan instead. "Tell me again why I'm going to this party?"

"Because I have to stay with the children, and Colt is away handling an emergency, so you, my dear angry sister, have to represent the family. Mr. McCray is our guest after all."

"Not mine."

"Yours, too. Didn't you rescue him from the blizzard?"

"Yes, I did. I also fed him, helped him out of his boots, and gave him bark tea. My obligations are done." So maybe she was curious about how he might be faring, but it wasn't necessary for her to get all gussied up to find out.

"You'll have fun."

"Lightning is going to strike you dead."

"Didn't you say you wanted to know more about him?"

"I lied."

Regan laughed softly. "Colt hitched up my buggy for you before he left."

Spring blew out a breath. "I'll bring it back in the morning."

"Thank you, Spring."

Waving dismissively, she left the house.

STEPPING UP ONTO the Cales' porch, Spring wondered sarcastically if she should wait for a man to open the door. Inside, the Chinese maid greeted her with a smile and took her shawl. Spring thanked her, drew in a calming breath, and followed the voices to the parlor. Once there she paused for a moment to survey the people in the well-furnished room with its dark emerald drapes and large portrait of Glenda in an off-shoulder, emerald gown hanging above the fireplace. The Millers were in attendance as were most of the area's prominent ranchers, along with their wives. Upon seeing Spring, some of the women deliberately turned their backs.

"Spring," Glenda said fondly. "Welcome. You look lovely."

"Thanks. Regan and Colt couldn't come, so I'm here to represent the family."

"Are you still angry with me?"

"No, but I did manage to open the door without male assistance."

Glenda smiled. "You're going to pay me back for that sometime soon, aren't you?"

"Probably." Spring scanned the small crowd again. McCray, clad in a brown suit, was in a conversation with rancher Randolph Nelson and Heath Leary. As he glanced up, their eyes met, and she did her best to ignore the rush in her blood. He sent her a smile and a slight nod of greeting. She returned the gesture and thought about the invitation she wanted to extend. His suit wasn't as fancy as the ones worn by Arnold and some of the others in the room, but it fit his lean frame and broad shoulders well and gave his appearance a level of sophistication she found appealing.

"Help yourself to the buffet," Glenda said.

Before she could do so, her attention settled on someone else. Forcing down her anger, she asked in as casual a voice as could be managed, "What's Matt Ketchum doing here?" By the glassy sheen in his glare he was already drunk.

Glenda sighed. "Arnold invited him. I'm sorry. I heard about the incident at the Irish Rose. Arnold hopes Ketchum and the people visiting him from New York will invest in the bank."

Standing with Ketchum was the man who'd needed directions to Paradise. "Is he one of the friends?"

Glenda turned to see who she was referencing. "Yes. His daughter Hazel arrived with him, but she chose to stay in her room at Dovie's. The younger man with him is a business associate. His name escapes me."

Spring planned to avoid the lot of them. By then, McCray had excused himself from Nelson and was making his way to where she stood.

Glenda said, "I'm going to see to my guests. Thanks for coming, Spring."

"You're welcome." But the entire time she was focused on the advancing McCray.

When he reached her side, he said, "Evening, Spring."

"McCray."

"How are you?"

"Fine. You?"

"Fine, too. You look very nice."

"Thanks."

The man who'd asked her for directions to Paradise turned her way. He appeared surprised by her presence and nodded a greeting. She responded tightly in kind before returning her attention to McCray, who'd glanced over to see who she'd greeted.

"Do you know him?" he asked.

"No. I was at Regan's home when he stopped to ask for directions to town." Refocusing on McCray, she asked, "Did you get enough information from my brother for your story?"

"I did. He was very forthcoming. I thought he'd be here tonight."

"He'd planned to but was called away earlier this afternoon. A rancher was kicked in the head by one of his horses."

"How on earth did that happen?"

"Had something to do with a horseshoe and a dog nipping the horse . . ." She shrugged. "I don't know the exact details, but the man was kicked. His son rode over to get Colt."

"Your brother stays busy."

"He does."

A male voice interrupted them. "Thank you for those directions."

Spring sighed and looked up into the cold blue eyes of the speaker. "Glad you arrived safely."

"Name's Avery Jarvis."

"Spring Lee."

Jarvis eyed McCray. "And you?"

"Garrett McCray."

"This your little lady, McCray?"

"I'm no one's little lady," she responded icily, adding, "If you gentlemen will excuse me, I'd like to sample the buffet."

At the buffet table, she picked up a plate. Randolph Nelson was there adding food to the plate in his hand. "You're looking right lovely, Spring."

"Thanks," she replied, viewing the variety of dishes on display.

"I want to get with you about acquiring a few new mustangs."

"I'm sure that can be arranged. Stop by when you can, and we'll talk."

"Will do."

Leary stepped up next to let her know her whiskey had yet to arrive, then moved on. While wondering who else needed a word with her, Lacy Miller approached. "Spring, my cat just had another litter. Can you take a couple of the kittens off my hands?"

Spring placed some slices of beef, potatoes and carrots on her plate. "Sure, always in need of mousers."

"Thanks. I'll drop them by in a day or two."

Across the room, Matt Ketchum's drunk voice rose above the quiet conversations. "Hey, Spring. Tell my friend Jarvis here how you used to spread those legs you're hiding beneath that fine dress."

Spring froze.

"Better yet," he continued loudly, "how about the time you—"

There was a loud crash and she turned to see a furious-looking McCray holding the much shorter Ketchum against a wall at eye level with a hand around his neck. Her jaw dropped.

McCray barked, "Apologize!"

Apparently too drunk to perceive the danger he was in, Ketchum laughed, "Boy, if you don't get your hands off me, they'll find you hanging—"

McCray slammed him bodily against the wall and growled, "Don't ever mention her that way within my hearing again. Do you understand?"

"She's a fucking whore. Get your hands off me, nigger!" And spat in McCray's face.

He retaliated with a fist that drew a sharp-pitched cry from Ketchum, who grabbed his bleeding, busted nose, and a smug smile of satisfaction from Spring.

Face filled with thunder, McCray tossed him away. Ketchum tried to rise, but his drunken legs refused to cooperate. Dragging a handkerchief from his pocket, Garrett cleaned his cheek.

Nelson gave his plate to the stunned Heath Leary, and called out tightly, "Chauncey, how about we take Matt home?"

As Nelson moved past Spring he said to her in a low voice, "You got a fine man there."

Spring agreed and wondered if any of the other men in the room would've come to her defense had he not been there. She knew the answer. While Nelson and Miller dragged Ketchum to his feet and out of the parlor, Jarvis studied her for a long moment before he and his business partner, accompanied by Arnold Cale, hastened to follow. She didn't know nor care what he might've been thinking.

Still radiating outrage, McCray said to Glenda, "My apologies for the ruckus. I'll understand if I'm never invited to your home again, especially after breaking whatever fell. Let me know the replacement costs, and I'll wire the money when I reach home."

Spring saw broken pieces of glass scattered on the floor.

Glenda waved him off. "That cretin Ketchum will be the one never invited back, and as for the broken figurines, they belonged to Arnold's mother. I never cared for them anyway, so no payment is required."

"That's very gracious of you," McCray replied humbly. "And thank you for your hospitality, but I'll be leaving. I've had enough excitement for the evening, and I'm sure your guests have, as well. My apologies to everyone." On his way out, he gave Spring a brief glance but didn't stop.

Ignoring the whispers and the condemning glares sent her way by some of the wives, Spring asked the maid for her shawl and went after him.

Outside, the moon was high and the April night was both warm and chilly. Seeing McCray walking towards Dovie's, she pulled the shawl closer and quickened her pace. "McCray. Wait."

He stopped and turned. When she reached him, she said, "You throw a pretty good punch for a newspaper man."

Remnants of anger remained in his voice. "Thank the Union Navy. When you're on the bottom rung, learning to defend yourself against the older sailors is one of the first things you learn. That and if sailing makes you sick."

"Did it?"

"No."

Spring viewed his strong features in the moonlight. "I just wanted to say thank you. Never had anyone stand up for me that way."

"I figured if I didn't shut his mouth, you would, and I didn't want you messing up your pretty dress."

Touched, she smiled and replied, "Always the gentleman."

"Always." He flexed his hand.

"Sore?"

"Yes. Been a while since I've done something like that. It'll be worse in the morning if I don't get some ice. Hope Dovie has some." He paused for a moment as if weighing what he wanted to say, all the while viewing her with a soft intensity. "Listen, I know you don't need protecting, but I couldn't help myself. If I stepped in where I didn't belong, my apologies."

"You did fine," she softly replied. "And you're right, I can take care of myself, but sometimes a girl gets tired of fighting alone."

Silence rose between them. She didn't know why he set off the feelings he did, but the longer she held his gaze, the higher the draw rose.

He reached out and a whisper-light fingertip trailed down her cheek. "Anytime you need a partner, let me know."

Her reactions to him were slipping past the reins of her legendary control. She covered his hand with hers and gently pressed her lips against the knuckles. "A kiss to make it feel better."

He smiled. "If I kiss you in return, will you feed me to a bear?"

"If it's a bad kiss, I might."

"I'll have to make it a good one, then, I guess."

"Yes, you do."

"I'm out of practice."

"Are you going to kiss me or talk me to death?"

He leaned in, brushed his lips against hers, and murmured, "I love a woman who says what she wants." The potency of the kiss that followed awakened her senses and kindled the embers of her lust. He was no novice at this, and before his seductive magic reduced her mind to jam, she took a step back. "Come home with me. I've ice and whatever else you may want."

"Are you sure? I've a long list of what I want to do with you."

Her knees went weak. "Do I impress you as being unsure?"

"A gentleman always asks."

"I want you in my bed, McCray. That plain enough for you?"

"Yes, ma'am. It is."

A male voice interrupted them. "Quite a display you put on back there, McCray."

They turned to see Avery Jarvis standing there. Where he'd come from or how much he'd seen or heard, she didn't know.

He continued, "Man like you could draw a lot of unwanted attention putting your hands on a man like Ketchum. You might want to be careful."

"A man like me draws unwanted attention from men like Ketchum just for waking up every morning, but thanks for your concern. Good night." He offered Spring his arm. She responded, and together they set out towards the livery to retrieve the buggy for the drive to her cabin. Neither looked back.

Led by the light of the full moon, Spring guided the buggy slowly. McCray hadn't said anything since they'd left the livery. There wasn't enough light to see his features clearly, but she sensed distance. "If you've changed your mind, McCray, that's fine."

"I haven't. Jarvis has me angry at Ketchum all over again."

She understood. She'd been angry at Ketchum for years. "Should I distract you?"

He chuckled against the night. "Your invitation is distracting enough, honestly. I'll be better shortly."

"Good, because when we get home, I'll need your full attention."

"And you shall have it."

Garrett knew he'd placed himself in jeopardy defending her. He'd embarrassed and humiliated Ketchum. Scores of Colored men had been beaten and killed for less. Should he have chosen caution and waited for one of the other men in the room to shut Ketchum's vile mouth? And if none had, then what? Was he supposed to ignore it and pretend the verbal taunting was deserved? Spring admitted to being gossiped about; even the sheriff said she'd been no angel back then. However, that didn't give Ketchum the right to speak to her so disrespectfully. Garrett expected Ketchum to seek revenge but when the time came, he'd not go down without a fight.

Now, though, Spring had invited him home. Since their time together during the blizzard he'd sensed a mutual attraction. He hadn't expected such a bold offer though. He glanced over at her in the moonlight and wondered if she'd be as fiery in bed as she was in life. The brief kiss they'd shared gave him a taste of the passionate woman hidden beneath her tough exterior, and he was anxious to explore her fully and without interruption.

Once they arrived at her property, he watched while she swapped her fancy slippers for a pair of serviceable boots she retrieved from the buggy's backseat. "I have to unhitch the mare from the buggy and with the ground being so soft, I don't want these shoes ruined. You can go inside and start a fire. I'll join you as soon as I'm done."

He countered, "How about I be the partner we spoke of and help with the buggy?"

"What about your hand?"

"It's sore but not so much that I can't assist you."

He sensed she wanted to argue but seemed to think better of it and surrendered. "Okay."

Once the mare was bedded down and the other horses seen to, they let the moonlight guide them to the house.

The interior was as cold as it was outside. While he started a fire, she pulled her shawl closer and lit a few lamps. "I'll get the ice."

She returned with a small metal bucket. Seated on her sofa, he stuck his hand into it and hissed as the cold settled into his skin. After a few moments he lifted the hand free. He repeated the process a few more times before flexing the hand and wincing a bit.

"How's it feel?" she asked.

"It's so cold it's hard to tell, but I'm sure this is helping. I'll know better in the morning."

"I can make you some bark tea if you'd like."

"Maybe later."

An awkward silence rose. It was as if neither of them knew how or where to begin their night together, so he opted for small talk, hoping that might help. "Do you get your ice from an icehouse?"

"No. I have some stored underground inside one of my outbuildings."

She must've seen his confusion. "Once the rivers freeze, we harvest it, so to speak, by chopping out big pieces and hauling them home. They're put underground in a large hole and covered with straw. In a good winter we can store enough to last until mid-June, depending on how fast the temperatures rise in the spring."

"That's fascinating."

"It's pretty common here."

He withdrew his hand from the ice one last time and dried it with the towel she'd given him earlier. He flexed his fingers again. "I think that's enough for now."

She took the bucket. "I'm going to set this outside. Depending on how cold it gets it might be still usable in the morning if you need it."

When she returned the parlor was a bit warmer, thanks to the fire. She took him in, then looked away, saying, "I should get a fire started in my room. Come join me?"

He studied her silently in the wavering light of the flames. "You can still change your mind, Spring."

"I know," she said quietly, "but I won't."

"Okay, then." He rose to his feet and followed her.

SPRING LIT THE small lamp on the nightstand by her bed and turned it low. Shivering from the chill, she made a fire and watched while the flames grew. Across the room Garrett stood silently, framed by the doorway and the shadows. She drew in a deep breath to calm her uncharacteristic jitters. "Are you coming in or planning on standing over there all night?" she asked, attempting a light tone.

He closed the door, crossed the distance between them, and stopped behind her. Gently caging her with his arms, he nuzzled the edge of her hair. Her eyes closed as sensation flared. "Come sit with me while the room warms up," he invited.

He placed one of her upholstered chairs close to the blazing fire then sat. Spring could count on two, maybe three fingers the number of times she'd sat on a man's lap.

As she hesitated, he lightly took her hand and asked, "No?"

"Just unexpected."

He asked softly, "Meaning?"

"Usually, this starts with me on my knees, then after a few pumps inside, it's done and the man leaves."

She thought he smiled, but because of the shadows couldn't be sure.

"Let's try something different."

Although still hesitant, she sat. "Why can't I just take off my clothes, you take off yours, and we move to the bed?"

He outlined her lips with an adoring feather-light finger, then kissed her. "This way is more fun . . ."

And truthfully, as the kiss deepened, she decided he was right. His slowly roaming hands coupled with his heated mouth and the whispered promises of the many wicked ways he planned to have her stoked the embers of her desire back to breathless life. Leaning up, she returned the kisses with the same languid intensity, savoring the taste of him and the potent slide of his tongue against her own. The shawl slipped free, exposing the bare crowns of her shoulders to fervent brushes of lips that then descended and lingered against the hollow of her throat. She moaned with pleasure.

He drew the tip of his finger over the exposed tops of her breasts above her heart-shaped bodice. "I've wanted you since our first breakfast together."

Holding her eyes, his finger caressed the soft skin beneath her proud chin before moving down to lightly graze her already taut nipples. Her eyes slid closed. He kissed her and continued the slow, sweet teasing of her breasts until they pleaded silently. As if hearing the plea, he leaned in, freed a nipple, and sucked it wickedly. Heat flowed from his mouth to her core. His tongue circled lazily around the tightened peak. A gentled bite made her moan pleasurably, helplessly, for more.

He raised his head and recaptured her lips. "Is the other one as sweet?" His fingers kept the one he'd just treated hard and pleased. "Show me so I can taste it."

Propelled by the husky request, Spring boldly unveiled herself and was splendidly rewarded. The shadowy room spun deliciously as he feasted. She was unaccustomed to a man intent upon pleasuring her so skillfully, or at all. By now, those in her past were already done and on the way out the door. It was scary in a way. Her body was enjoying the hot slide of his lips across the hollow of her throat, and the sureness of his hand slowly mapping her silk-covered spine. Sex was supposed to be emotionless and quick, not this prolonged, languid descent into a heated realm she couldn't control. She backed away, closed her eyes, and fought to calm the wild lust he'd unleashed in her blood.

"What's wrong?" he asked softly, continuing to pay smoldering attention to her bared breasts. "Are you unhappy with the way I'm pleasuring you?"

Fighting to form words, she replied, "I like the pleasure, but I don't like how long this is taking, or not being able to remember my damn name."

He leaned down and drew her nipple into his mouth. When she gasped in shuddering response, he chuckled.

"I can still feed you to a bear, you know."

Rising up, he whispered hotly against her ear, "My apologies for being a man who knows his way around a woman's body and not a ham-handed rube who pumps inside you a few times and leaves you unsatisfied. Loving a woman properly is an art, my sweet Spring."

"I don't want art."

"You should. You're passionate and beautiful. You shouldn't be afraid of pleasure."

"I'm not." Her core was wet and pulsating even though he'd yet to touch her there. She was sure she'd burst into flames when he did.

"If you've changed your mind, and prefer I spend the rest of the night in your spare room, I'll understand."

"No." She didn't know how she'd lost the upper hand in the conversation, but apparently, she had. Even worse, she now had to prove she wasn't afraid of pleasure.

"Are you sure?"

She nodded.

"Then shall we get this gown off of you?" he asked, brushing his lips over the column of her throat and moving a thumb over a damp pebble-hard nipple. Leaning up to kiss him, she replied, "Yes." In spite of her slight show of pique, she was enjoying being kissed, and truthfully, couldn't seem to get enough of his mouth or the sensual dance of their tongues. All the quick couplings she'd had in the past had never involved her removing anything but her denims. Her shirt may have been opened to allow a fast grab at her breasts, but the men were mainly focused on what she had between her legs. There'd been no art.

"Turn a moment, please."

She complied and he deftly undid the small jet buttons that ran down her spine. Once he was done, she left his lap and stood, then slowly stepped out of the gown. Clad in her lace-edged ivory shift, garters, stockings, and drawers, she laid the silk gown on a nearby chair. Chin raised and savoring the heat in his eyes, she stood before the undulating light of the fire in anticipation of what would come next. He skimmed both hands possessively up and down the edges of her thighs and hips—circling her skin slowly, masterfully, until her head dropped back and her legs trembled.

In a voice as dark as the shadows he said, "Take your drawers off for me, Spring."

Her eyes blazed into his as she complied.

His hand moved between her thighs and she widened them in sultry invitation.

"You're very hot and wet . . ."

He impaled her with a finger and she responded with a crooning she'd never given any man before. A second finger joined the first, and as she rode the blissful strokes, all sense of time and place fled, leaving behind—lust. He soundlessly urged her to come closer and took a nipple into his wickedly splendid mouth while his free hand wandered over her spine. He bit her, pushed his fingers higher, and she shattered with a raw, smoky scream. The echoes pulsed for an eternity as he continued the strokes, sucks, and licks. She was still enthralled when he picked her up and whispered, "Now we move to the bed."

The rest of the night passed with such heat neither cared that the fire had burned low. She pleasured him on her knees, slowly savoring his girth, size, and sharp hisses of lusty response. When he could breathe again, her reward was an oral tribute so erotic, she grabbed fistfuls of the sheet, cried out, and broke into soaring pieces again.

Now he knelt above her and she was so dazzled and overwhelmed by Garrett McCray, she wondered if she should change her name because she was having difficulty remembering who she was. Reaching up, she lightly cupped his jaw before leveraging up to give him a searing kiss. And they began again. Kisses, touches, whispers, sighs. She stroked him with a firm hand. He teased the wet flesh of her core. Breathing hard, she backed away and reached into the drawer of her nightstand and withdrew a sponge.

He asked, "May I?"

She handed it over, and he inserted it with such finesse, her hips rose greedily in invitation. Moments later, their night entered a new realm. He was thick and gloriously hard, and had she the power, he'd stay right where he was for the rest of her days. The pace he set was slow at first, but as the desire rose and their bodies were spurred by desire's call, the rhythm increased. He gave, she took, until the bed shook and their verbal cries and calls became a lovers' passionate symphony. Spring couldn't believe such pleasure was possible, but another orgasm gathered like clouds of a storm, and when the lightning struck and the thunder ripped her apart, she screamed his name.

Roaring, he shattered, too, hips moving like pistons until he had nothing left to give. Slumping forward, he gathered her in and pulled her atop him so as not to crush her. They held each other until their breathing slowed and the world returned.

Later, watching him sleep, Spring admitted that for a woman intent upon walking through life alone, having him in her bed may have been a mistake. He'd left her feeling treasured, desired, something she'd never experienced before. It awakened a long-buried part of herself to the possibility of what could be, and that scared her.

# Chapter Eight

Spring slipped out of bed as quietly as possible. There were horses to feed and because she'd never had a man spend the night before, she had no idea how to navigate the morning after. With those things in mind, she tiptoed around the cold bedroom, gathering her clothes and everything else she needed to start the day, and left him sleeping.

When her chores were completed, she entered the kitchen and found McCray at the stove cooking breakfast. Still unsure how she was supposed to proceed, she said, "Morning, McCray." Removing her coat and hat, she hung them on the peg.

"Morning, Spring." He seemed to sense her mood. "Something wrong?"

She considered lying but chose to go with the truth. "I've never had anyone stay overnight and . . ."

"Is this awkward for you?"

"Yes."

"Do you regret last night?"

She shook her head.

"Had a good time?"

She gave him her first smile of the day.

"Good. Then let's just let the morning unfold and not worry about what to do. Unless you'd rather I go back to town."

"No."

His uncomplicated solution to the situation drained much

of her unease and she wondered if that, too, was part of his art. She noticed his slight limp as he moved around. "Your leg bothering you still?"

"It's a bit stiff after being put through my paces last night."

Embarrassment heated her cheeks. "Should I apologize?"

"Not on your life. I had a good time, too."

Memories of last night rose, bringing back the feel of his hands and the power of his kisses. She remembered how it felt when he filled her and the many ways his mouth made her moan. His claim of knowing his way around a woman's body hadn't been an idle boast.

"You keep looking at me that way and we'll be having each other for breakfast instead of bacon and these eggs."

Caught, she smiled and looked away. "I think breakfast is best for now."

"Pity."

His ability to spark desire with just a phrase or a glance was also new for her. She had no idea there were men with such skills walking around in the world. How many other women were going through life thinking sex was something to be endured or dealt with hurriedly because of ham-handed rubes? Last night's glorious feast of passion and pleasure had been prepared by a brown-skinned wizard who'd left her mesmerized and spellbound. And yes, she'd enjoy another night with him, but that would only amplify her mistake. Although he was someone she was on the cusp of developing feelings for, he'd be going home soon and she refused to be the wailing woman at the train station, clinging to his legs, begging he stay.

They were just sitting down to eat when a knock at the door made Spring sigh and get up to see who was there.

"Do you know where your newspaper fella is?" Odell asked as soon as she opened the door. "Dovie said he didn't come back to his room last night after Glenda's party, and she's worried something may have happened to him."

Spring released another sigh.

"Is that bacon I smell?"

Without waiting for a reply, he followed his nose. Seeing McCray seated at the table, he stopped in surprise and turned to Spring, who stood arms crossed, silent. Odell eyed McCray again. "Oh."

"Yes, oh," she replied.

"Well, that solves the mystery."

McCray asked, "What mystery?"

"Of where you were last night."

It was McCray's turn to sigh.

"Guess I'll get my bacon elsewhere. Good seeing you, McCray."

"You, too, Odell."

"Goodbye, Odell," Spring said tartly.

Grinning, he departed.

Shaking her head, she sat down again. "Pass me the eggs, please."

"Do I assume that by noon half the Territory will know I spent the night here?"

She placed some of the scrambled eggs on her plate. "Maybe. Maybe not. He can be discreet when he wants to be. Doesn't matter really. I'm not ashamed of you being here. Are you?"

"No."

"Good." Even if Odell kept the news to himself, more than likely he wasn't the only person Dovie had questioned about McCray's whereabouts. Once Spring drove him back to town and word got around, people would put two and two together. Again, she didn't care. Someone had to give the gossips something to do. "When are you going back to Washington?"

"My ticket is for four days from now. Your brother agreed to let me ride along on some of his visits, so I want to take him up on that first. I'd also like to speak with Mrs. Lee about her thoughts on living here. I'm hoping she'll share some of the details on how she and your brother met."

Spring wondered how he'd react were she to tell him Regan was an heiress, but that would be Regan's story to share or not, so Spring kept silent. Refusing to remain silent were her own thoughts of wanting him to stay longer. She had an uncharacteristic desire to show him more of her life: her favorite places to hunt and fish, her makeshift mountain cabin, the thundering herds of wild mustangs that always left her in awe. No man before had ever inspired her in that way, but he'd be leaving, so she pushed the thoughts aside. "Is there anyone else you want to speak with before you go home?"

"Yes. Mr. James. I heard some of his story when I helped with the mill, but I'd like to find out if there's more. I didn't expect to find another Colored man here. Do you know if there are more of us in the area?"

"My family and Porter James are it, as far as I know. Ben might know more."

"Your grandfather?"

"Yes."

"I met him while at the mill."

"How'd it go?"

"Let's just say he wasn't very forthcoming."

"I don't doubt it. He's not much for conversation."

"Does he live nearby?"

"He has a place not too far from here. If you want to try again, take my brother with you. If I take you, he and I will argue, I'll leave in a huff, and you won't get anything for your story."

Seeing the concern in his eyes, she added, "Just offering you the truth. We haven't gotten along in over a decade and I don't expect a thaw anytime soon."

"Okay."

And it was the truth. Both she and Ben were stubborn. They'd probably carry their rift to the grave. Deep in her heart, a years-old pain flared though. Growing up she'd loved him, in spite of his contrary ways, and he'd loved her.

Another knock at the door drew her to her feet again. She

opened it and found her brother Colt on the porch. "Morning," he said.

She backed up so he could enter. "Morning."

"I came to get the buggy. I'll need it today." Seeing McCray seated at the table, he paused.

"It's out back," she told him but didn't reply to the questions in his eyes.

He sighed softly and walked to the table. "Morning, McCray."

"Dr. Lee."

Colt studied him. McCray waited silently. Colt finally spoke. "Do you want to join me on my rounds today?"

McCray swung his attention to Spring. She responded with a tiny shrug. His day was his own. She had no claims on his comings and goings.

"Yes. I'd like that," he replied.

"I need to go into town first."

"Good, I want to stop by my room."

Spring assumed he wanted to change clothes. He was still wearing the suit from Glenda's party last night.

"Okay. Finish your breakfast and meet me outside when you're done."

On his way back to the door, Colt gave Spring a tight-jawed look. It wasn't the first time she'd been on the receiving end of his disapproval and probably wouldn't be the last, so she refused to let it rile her. She and McCray were adults. Their being together was none of Colt's business.

After his exit, McCray said, "Your brother doesn't approve of me being here."

She returned to the table. "The good doctor doesn't approve of a lot of things. Don't let it bother you. He thinks he's being protective. I appreciate his concern but it's unnecessary."

"Do you really not care what people think of you, Spring?"

His voice was so soft and serious. "If I did, I would've left town years ago, but running away would have meant they were right, so I stay."

"I'm glad you did, otherwise, we wouldn't have met."

She wondered if not meeting him would have mattered in her life one way or the other. After last night, the answer was yes. "How's your hand?"

He flexed it. "Still a bit sore, but I'll survive."

They viewed each other silently and she was again taken back to last night and all things they'd done and the ways he'd made her feel. He said finally, "I shouldn't keep your brother waiting."

"I know."

But he seemed as reluctant to leave as she was for him to go.

"Can we have dinner together this evening?" he asked.

"I'd like that. Shall we eat here?"

"If you don't mind."

"Then let's. Bring your overnight gear."

He nodded, rose from the table, and walked to where she stood. Looking up into his eyes made last night's lingering embers flare. He traced a light finger over her mouth and gave her a long bone-melting kiss that left her in a puddle on the floor.

"I'll see you later," he whispered and departed to join Colt.

Dr. Lee's stony face didn't invite conversation when Garrett climbed into the buggy, so as they got underway, he contented himself with the pleasurable echoes of his parting kiss, and taking in the beauty of the countryside. The trees were showing off their spring buds and awing him again with the variety: stands of pine, maple, birch. The carpenter in him noted how enjoyable working for Mr. James had been along with the feel of the wood and tools in his hands. Lee drove past flowering shrubs and eye-catching scatterings of colorful wildflowers. Off in the distance the snow-crowned mountains loomed against the blue sky.

As the buggy reached the fork in the road that led to town, Lee still hadn't spoken. Garrett tried not to be irritated by the man's chilly demeanor, but it was difficult. He let Spring's brother brood for another half mile, then said, "Dr. Lee, if you have something we need to discuss, let's do so."

Lee viewed him for a moment before replying, "I don't enjoy my sister being taken advantage of."

"You know Spring better than I. Does she seem weak-minded to you?"

Garrett held his gaze.

Lee paused then looked away. "She's not, but once you're back East you probably won't give her a second thought."

"And that's where you're wrong. If I could stay I would, because I'd like to be in her life for a very long time."

Lee showed surprise.

"I'm being truthful. She might not have me, but it wouldn't be because I didn't try. Spring's one of the most fascinating women I've ever met, and it will be a long time before I forget her—if ever."

Lee scanned his face. "You're serious, aren't you?"

"Very much so. She's not someone I'm using as a convenient amusement. Do you know about the altercation I had with Matt Ketchum at the Cales' house last night?"

"No. What happened?"

Garrett shared the details and Lee's face tightened. "Nasty bastard."

Garrett agreed.

"Thanks for standing up for her."

"You're welcome. As I told her, I didn't want her to mess up her fancy dress."

Lee showed a small smile. "If she'd've been of a mind to retaliate that gown would've been the last thing on her mind. Whit said she drew her Colt on Ketchum while I was up at Rock Springs."

"She did."

Lee looked up from the road. "You were there?"

"I was. My first thought was to help, but she didn't need it. Her Colt stopped Ketchum cold."

"And yet, you're still smitten with her?"

"I hear your wife shot you the first time you met. Yet, you married her."

Lee chuckled, "Touché." Lee studied him for a silent moment more as if reevaluating his former assessment of Garrett. "I'm glad we talked."

"So am I."

"I can say with authority that pursuing my sister is going to be akin to wrestling the wind."

"I sense that."

"So you'll be returning?"

"More than likely. I have some things to tie up at home first." He'd answered without thought but it felt right.

"If you decide being here is not for you and decide to return home, she'll never leave the Territory to live back East."

"I wouldn't ask her to. I don't want to cage her—just to be with her on whatever terms she chooses." And it could be two weeks, two months, or two years. Of course, she'd probably feed him to a bear were he to confess this to her. When they met initially, he'd wanted to know all about her and that hadn't changed. There were parts of herself hidden beneath her toughness he was certain she'd never shared, and he wanted to earn the opportunity to be trusted with them.

"I wish you luck, then."

"Much appreciated. I'll probably need it." And he would.

COLT DROPPED GARRETT off at the boardinghouse. He'd had a bath earlier at Spring's, so after exchanging his suit for a clean shirt and trousers, he threw an extra fresh shirt and his shaving kit into his saddle bag and left the room. He saw Dovie in the hall.

"Oh, there you are. When you didn't come back after the party, I was worried something had happened to you."

"My apologies. Didn't mean to cause concern."

"Have you had breakfast?"

"I have. I won't be back this evening."

Dovie eyed him. "Okay. Thanks for letting me know."

"You're welcome."

Descending the stairs, he passed Jarvis on the way up. Their eyes met. Garrett nodded a greeting, but the cold-faced businessman offered nothing in return.

Outside, Garrett set out for the short walk to Dr. Lee's office. Unlike Jarvis, the few people on the walk acknowledged him as he passed. He wondered how many of them knew about him and Spring, but refused to dwell on the question. Their opinions didn't matter.

Entering the office, he found Lee placing equipment and small vials into a worn black medical bag.

"Are you ready?" he asked Garrett.

"Yes. Can we stop by the livery? I want to retrieve my gelding."

"Sure. You can either ride or trailer him to the buggy."

"I'll ride for now."

Lee gave him a nod and they left to begin the rounds.

As he rode, Garrett thought back on his talk with Lee concerning Spring. Confessing his feelings about her had not been his intentions. He was usually more guarded with his intentions, another holdover from being enslaved, but the words seemed to have sprouted on their own. Yet, he'd spoken truthfully. He did want to be in Spring's life, and although he hadn't really considered returning to Paradise, the decision made sense.

Thanks to Porter James's offer, he'd have a job. The town's pace was slow and peaceful, unlike the frenetic pace of Washington. He'd saved up a bit of money with the hopes of one day moving out of his rented room, but what if he used it instead to buy a small piece of land and build a place of his own?

That possibility was exciting, and although there weren't many people of the race around, the Lees hadn't shared any tales of overt racial animosity or being targeted for the color of their skin. In the Territory, he might be relatively free to be himself and not constantly reminded of having to stay in his place. Jim Crow was infecting the country like a disease, and more than likely would eventually show its ugly face in places like Wyoming Territory, too, especially by men like Ketchum. Presently, however, it didn't seem to be as virulent or as ingrained as it was back East, and for him that was also a plus. The true plus though was Spring Lee. If in the end, she decided she wanted no parts of him, he'd accept that verdict because he'd still be free to work and live life on his own terms. Growing up enslaved, it was more than he ever thought he'd have the option to do.

The first stop on Dr. Lee's rounds was at the home of the Taylors to check on a bull terrier named Lucky. Walking to the porch, Lee explained the reason for the visit. "Lucky picked a fight with a porcupine and lost. He had so many quills in him I didn't think he'd survive, but he's a tough little fellow. I came to make sure I removed all the quills, and that none of the punctures are infected."

They were greeted at the door by Mrs. Taylor, who was short, thin, and had red hair. Her threadbare calico dress and apron indicated a woman with little wealth. Lee made the introductions.

"Nice meeting you, Mrs. Taylor," Garrett said.

"Same here. Come on in. Silas and Lucky are in the parlor."

Lee, carrying his medical bag, asked, "How's Lucky doing?"

"Limping a bit, but healing. I swear that dog is really a cat. He has nine lives just like one."

Garrett guessed the red-haired freckled-faced Silas to be about ten years old, and upon seeing Dr. Lee the boy smiled widely. "Hello, Dr. Lee."

"How are you, Silas?"

"I'm fine."

"How's Lucky?"

The black-and-white terrier was lying in a large basket atop a pile of blankets. At Lee's approach he shrank back and whimpered. Silas stroked the dog's back. "It's okay, Luck. Doc Lee just wants to make sure you're healing up right."

Lee hunkered down by the basket. "Removing those quills caused him a lot of pain. I understand why he's a little wary of me."

While Garrett and Mrs. Taylor looked on, Lee gently examined the dog's wounds. Garrett saw the small reddish patches that covered Lucky from nose to tail.

Lee said, "Looks like you've been taking real good care of him, Silas."

"I've been putting the salve on him like you showed me. He's still having trouble eating because of the quills that were stuck in his mouth."

Garrett was surprised by that. Mrs. Taylor told him, "You should've seen him, Mr. McCray. We couldn't tell where the quills ended, and Lucky began. It was terrible."

Colt added, "But once again, he lived up to his name."

Silas smiled. "I didn't think anything could be worse than him taking on One Eye."

Colt replied, "Me, either." He stood. "Okay. He's healing up well. Lucky, no more cougars and definitely no more porcupines."

Lucky whimpered as if agreeing.

"Silas, keep putting the salve on him, and give him soft things to eat."

"Yes, sir."

"Is he having any other problems?"

"No, sir."

Colt looked to Mrs. Taylor for verification, and she agreed with her son. "Nothing else that I can see."

"Good. I'll be back to check on him next week."

Mrs. Taylor escorted them to the door. "Thanks, Doc. Nice meeting you, Mr. McCray."

Walking back to the buggy and the gelding, Garrett asked, "Lucky tangled with a cougar?"

"Yes, last year, and saved Silas's life. One Eye's claws ripped open Lucky's rib cage, but he lived up to his name. He's a very lucky dog."

Garrett thought the tale would be a great addition to his story on the doctor. He mounted up. "Where to next?"

"Ed Prescott. Life-long friend, and Spring's business partner. He's also an engineer. We all grew up together. A mare of his lost a foal while I was in Rock Springs. Ed does a good job of doctoring his animals but wants me to check the mare, too, just as a precaution."

Garrett was anxious to meet the man. He assumed Spring held him in high esteem if they were partners. Of course, being a male, Garrett fleetingly wondered if the two had ever been lovers, but put that out of his mind because it was really none of his business. He did envy the fact that Prescott obviously knew more about Spring than Garrett ever would.

As Garrett rode beside the buggy through the gates of the Prescotts' Sweet Heart Ranch, he was impressed by the dozens of horses of all sizes and coat colors filling the vast pens. Some galloped while others milled about. The tall brown-skinned man who waved and walked to meet them as they arrived had long raven-black hair braided down his back.

Colt made the introductions. "Ed Prescott, this is Garrett McCray. He's a newspaper reporter from back East. McCray, my good friend, Ed Prescott."

Garrett shook his hand. "Pleased to meet you."

"Same here."

It was Garrett's first encounter with what the back-East papers called an Indian, and nothing about him fit what he'd read; not his speech, manner, or college training. Given how slanderous and insulting the press often portrayed the Colored race, he was again humbled that he'd even considered their reporting to be truthful.

As he followed the two men to the barn to see the mare, Prescott's home came into view and its grand beauty took his breath away. Built with timber, boulders, and more glass than Garrett had ever seen employed on a residence before, he wanted to immediately quiz Prescott about its construction and design. However, his curiosity wasn't the point of the visit and he didn't know the man well enough to pump him with questions. Maybe sometime in the future he would.

"She's still grieving," Ed said as he and Garrett watched Lee examine the black-maned chestnut mare named Maribelle. Ed added, "She wouldn't let me remove the foal's body until last night, and she won't leave the stall."

Garrett had never known horses grieved.

Lee asked about Maribelle's bodily functions and appetite since the stillbirth, and Prescott supplied the answers. After a few more questions and further examination, Lee stepped back and put his instruments away. "Physically, I'd say she's okay. You know to keep her away from the stallions for the time being. See if you can get her out into the fresh air. Might help with the grieving."

"Will do." Prescott walked over, gave the mare a long hug, spoke softly to her, and they all left the barn.

Prescott asked Garrett, "How long are you going to be with us?"

"Just a few more days."

"Nice meeting you."

"Same here."

Lee climbed into the buggy and Garrett mounted his gelding. "Where to now?"

"Hog farmer Sol Boyer's place. One of his sow's impacted."

Garrett was confused. "How do you treat that?"

"Usually with an enema."

Garrett's eyes widened. He'd never heard of such a thing. "Is this something I want to see?"

Lee chuckled. "Probably not," he said, and set the buggy in motion.

He was right. The sight and stench tied to the pig's relief

played such havoc with Garrett's own insides, he quickly sought cover behind a nearby tree and lost his breakfast.

Later, after the visit ended, he and Lee walked to the waiting buggy and gelding. "Are you okay?" Lee asked.

Still woozy, Garrett replied, "Honestly? No."

Garrett smiled and lightly clapped him on the back. "You'll be fine. Welcome to the world of the country doctor."

"Where to next?" Garrett asked.

"Back to town. We're done for the day."

Filled with relief, Garrett mounted up.

# Chapter Nine

Spring spent the morning mucking out the stable. Her horses were out in the grassy pasture enjoying the partially sunny day and the sunshine. The air was humid, and she wondered if rain might be on the way later. Not worrying over it, she finished the work, put away the pitchfork and shovel, and walked outside. Paint, her two-year-old brown-and-white palomino, came racing to her side and nuzzled the pocket of her jacket.

"You just ate, remember?" she said, rubbing his neck affectionately. "No treats, and there'll be no carrots until I plant."

Paint kept up the nuzzling, which soon turned into playful bumping. Spring laughed as she tried to set her feet and not fall over. "Stop, silly!" Set on his fun, he kept it up. "Stop!" she scolded, laughing. "If you put me on my butt, you'll never get carrots again for as long as you live." The mares Lady and Sunrise watched silently. Stallion Cheyenne viewed the scene with kinglike disinterest from across the yard and she called to him, "Come and get your little brother."

The stallion of course ignored her and instead, lowered his head to drink from the water in the trough. Paint bumped her a few more times, almost succeeding in putting her on the ground, then raced away.

Shaking her head at his antics, she called out to Lady, who would help her with the next item on the day's list of chores. Cheyenne refused to be hitched to a wagon. It was as if he found such toil beneath his station as ruler. Lady on the other hand didn't seem to mind. She was a beautiful red-coated bay with a shiny black mane and tail, and strong black legs and matching hooves. Once Spring had her hitched, she called to Cheyenne. "I'll be back in a little while. Going to put Paint in the stable so he doesn't eat the cabin while I'm gone."

Cheyenne glanced over at Paint, who made a point of avoiding his gaze. Paint spent the first year of his life taking bites out of everything he came in contact with, from the wood on the cabin and the fences, to everything in Spring's garden. Returning from town one day, she found he'd jumped the garden's wire fencing and turned the newly emerging vegetables into his personal buffet. He'd eaten the tops of all the carrots, beets, and then all the beans and tomato plants. He paid for his greediness later that evening and was stomach sick for the next two days. Now a year older she hoped he was no longer bite happy, but she wasn't taking any chances. She walked him to the barn, put him in his stall, and locked his chest-high gate. "I'll let you out when I get back. You can't have my place for lunch, and if someone comes along and wants to steal you, Cheyenne will probably help them saddle you up. I don't want to lose you."

He stuck his painted face against her and whinnied.

"Be back soon." She gave him a hug and left the barn.

With Lady pulling the wagon, Spring took a slow drive around her property to check for damage left by the months of winter weather. McCray was also on her mind. She let herself admit to looking forward to having him back for dinner, and what might come after. Last night had not been enough. A couple of older trees had been downed by the storms, so she used an ax to chop the trunks into manageable rounds then struggled to place the heavy pieces into the bed of the wagon. The process took a while. Once she caught her breath and used a bandanna to mop up the sweat on her face and neck, she drove the wagon home. The unloading was just as arduous. After wiping her brow again, taking a few drags of water from her canteen, she let her arms rest for a few moments to free Paint and unhitch Lady. Once that was done, she picked up the ax again. The wood would be used for firewood later in the year. In the middle of the task, she spotted a buggy coming her way. Its occupants were Avery Jarvis, his business partner, and the young woman she'd seen the other day but had yet to be introduced to. Hoping they were just passing by, she resumed filling the air with the ring of the ax. When the buggy stopped and Jarvis and the others got out and approached, she snarled quietly.

"Afternoon, Miss Lee," Jarvis said. He was wearing a dark brown suit with matching vest over his white shirt, and a brown striped tie.

She brought the ax down on a log. It split and she pulled the ax free. "What can I do for you, Jarvis?"

"Thought I'd introduce you to my daughter, Hazel."

Spring eyed the woman. Dressed as finely as Glenda Cale in a pale gray walking ensemble and a fashionable little hat, Hazel gave Spring a quick nod.

"Hello," Spring said.

Jarvis continued, "And my secretary, Leland Swan."

"Miss Lee," Swan said, eyeing her distastefully.

"Mr. Swan." He was younger than Jarvis, also taller and leaner. She didn't know why he seemed so put out, but she didn't care. Wanting to get to the reason they'd stopped, she asked, "Lost again?" She saw her horses watching.

Jarvis smiled. "No. I came to inquire about the possibility of buying the land you own by the river. The parcel that used to belong to Matt Ketchum. I plan to open a mill. The one owned by Porter James is old and dated."

She resumed chopping. "It's not for sale."

"Suppose I make you a generous offer."

She brought the ax down again with such force, Hazel jumped. Spring worked the blade free. "Suppose you understand what I said. It isn't for sale."

"A woman alone can always use more money."

She almost asked him what he knew about a woman alone. His refusal to hear her was proof he was accustomed to getting his way, but so was she, and saw no need to argue or repeat herself. She addressed his companions. "Hazel, Mr. Leland. It was nice meeting you. Have a good afternoon, Mr. Jarvis." She turned to go up to the house. She'd finish chopping later.

Jarvis snapped, "Don't you dare walk away from me."

She stopped and asked quietly. "Or what? I'm carrying an ax and wearing a gun belt. What do you have to stop me besides your temper and a loud voice?"

She watched a smile curve Hazel's mouth before it quickly disappeared.

Her father's lips tightened. "I'm offering you good money for land Ketchum said you stole."

"Stole? When Matt Ketchum says it's raining, folks know to get up and go look for themselves. You should do the same."

He studied her as if assessing her mettle. "This is not the end," he finally promised.

"Yes, it is. Set foot on my land again and I'll shoot you for trespassing. If you believe I'm bluffing, Hazel will be taking your remains home in a box."

She set out towards her cabin and left them standing there. Hearing the buggy pull away a few moments later, she kept walking.

The work had left her sweaty and smelly, so she lit the outside boiler for hot water for a bath. Knowing the process would take close to an hour, she went into the kitchen, washed her hands, and made a sandwich. Placing it on a small plate, she took it out to the back porch along with a tumbler of water. Clouds were moving in and the sun was fading. Rain was definitely on the way. As she ate, she thought back on Jarvis, and wondered if Porter James knew the man wanted to put him out of business. With the help of Odell, Ben, and many others in Paradise, Mr. James built his mill before she and Colt were born. Yes, the stone structure was old and inefficient when compared to newer ones built in the larger cities, but it served their community well and Mr. James knew more about wood than anyone else around. Did Jarvis possess the same extensive knowledge? Did he own a mill wherever he was from? Would he try and build elsewhere along the river now that she'd turned him down? She had no answers, but she was certain that if Matt Ketchum was tied to the plans, Jarvis would have his hands full. In addition to being a foul-mouthed drunk, Matt was selfish, spoiled, and lazy. When she worked for his father, Mitch, there was no job the then-sixteen-year-old Matt didn't pass off to someone else. If he wanted to sleep in, he was allowed. If he showed up drunk, that was overlooked. Many of the hired hands grumbled about his irresponsible, self-centered ways, especially when they were forced to take on the work he didn't want to do, like mucking out stables or chopping wood needed to repair the fences, but no one dared approach his father to complain. Why his behavior was tolerated, she didn't know. Since it wasn't the hands' place to ask, they did his chores and cursed both father and son among themselves. After Mitch Ketchum's death, because Matt's whereabouts were unknown, the five thousand acres of Ketchum land went into foreclosure, contrary to his lies to Jarvis. At the bank auction, Odell and Spring purchased a few parcels that gave her and her horses access to the Paradise River. Her grandfather, the land's original owner, bought back a portion that held pine, creeks, and the foothills known for good hunting. Randolph Nelson purchased the remainder to access the grass-filled valley and rest of the river frontage for his cattle. Had Jarvis accused Nelson of stealing the land, too, or was the claim leveled at her alone? Either way, she didn't see Nelson relinquishing any of his vast acreage to accommodate a sawmill and the river access the enterprise would need. With any luck, Jarvis would accept defeat, leave Paradise, and go back to wherever he'd come from, but with Matt Ketchum involved and stirring the pot, that was probably just wishful thinking.

An hour later Spring stepped out of the bath and wrapped her wet body in a drying sheet. Fashioning a towel around her dripping hair, she padded to the kitchen in a pair of old moccasins to put on a pot of coffee so it would be ready when she dried off. Seeing McCray standing by the sofa stopped her cold.

Eyes wide, he stared at her in the thin, nearly transparent sheet and began coughing. Turning his back, he croaked, "Lord, Spring. Are you trying to kill me?"

Her smile peeped through. "How long have you been here?"

"A second or so." Peeking over his shoulder at her, his gaze slowly brushed her from the towel on her head to the moccasins on her feet, before he faced away again. He cleared his throat. "I knocked and got no answer, so I went to the barns. Didn't find you there, so I tried the back door. It was open. I've just walked in. I didn't know you were bathing."

He turned back to her and the intensity reflected in his eyes warmed her blood so thoroughly, she thought steam might rise from the sheet. He added, "I would've waited outside on the porch, but it's raining."

She saw the downpour through the window and his wet slicker hanging from a peg on the fireplace. "It's okay, put on some coffee. I'll be right back."

He gave her a nod, and she left him alone.

In the kitchen, Garrett hoped preparing the coffee would take his mind off what he'd just seen because he was hard as a length of oak. Granted, last night they'd made love and he'd seen her beautifully nude. However, having her appear with the thin sheet wrapped around her so sinuously in the middle of the afternoon was so unexpected, he was still trying to catch his breath. Tempted by the lure of her veiled nipples and the bare curves of her neck and shoulders he'd wanted to walk over and gently unwrap her as if she were his own personal boon. Even now, his hands longed to slowly circle the sheet over the swells of her hips and thighs before exploring the warm dampness hidden between. Realizing he was only making himself harder, he fought to focus on the coffee-making instead, but it was futile. He wanted her as much as he had last night.

Once the coffee was ready, he poured himself a cup and set the pot on the table. He'd just taken a seat and a sip of his coffee when she returned wearing her usual man's shirt and a pair of soft buckskin trousers. He was both relieved and disappointed. As if having read his mind, she said, "I can put the sheet on again, if you want."

He choked on the swallow. Picking up a napkin, he wiped his mouth and shot her an amused, quelling look. "You're really trying to put me in my grave, aren't you?"

Her sassy smile made him want to pull her onto his lap and kiss her until sunrise. "Be warned. The next time you're in that sheet, it won't be on you for long."

Having poured herself a cup, she sipped and replied, "I'm holding you to that."

He enjoyed this playful side of her and wished to be gifted with it more often.

She asked, "So how did you and my brother get along today?"

"We did well." He told her about meeting Lucky the dog, and Ed Prescott, but refused to bring up the visit to Boyer's hog farm. He'd taken a bath as soon as he reached the boardinghouse to rid his nose and skin of the putrid stench he swore still clung to him and his clothing.

Spring said, "Ed's grandparents were very kind to me and Colt after our mother passed on."

For a few moments she stared silently out at what he guessed was the past, and he was again reminded how much he didn't know about her. "What were you like as a child?" he asked softly.

"Quiet and well-mannered, like all little girls were supposed to be."

"Really?"

"Surprised?"

"A bit. I assumed you were rambunctious and rebellious."

"No. I learned to embroider and read. I knew how to set a proper table, play hymns on our old piano. I was the perfect, properly raised young woman—who loved horses." She quieted again, as if thinking back, then confessed almost wistfully, "That's the only part of that girl that remains."

"Your love of horses." He wondered if she missed being that girl, and if the cost of having to leave her behind still weighed heavily.

She nodded. "Once Ben and Odell taught me to ride, I fell in love. My mother tried to limit how often I rode because proper young girls shouldn't smell like horses, she often said. We argued about it a lot, but she finally just gave up, and I rode as often as I could."

"Why horses?"

"Because unlike some people, they're loyal, and if you treat them well and provide for them properly, they love you unconditionally and they don't judge. They also have distinct personalities. Some are serious like Cheyenne, some are jokesters. I've run into a few that were downright mean. I enjoy figuring out just who a horse is."

He'd thought back to Prescott's grieving mare. He'd received quite an equine education today. "You're a very fascinating woman, Spring Lee."

"Unlike Spring Rain, the quiet and shy little girl, Spring Rain, the woman, is rude, sometimes crude, obnoxious, and set in her ways."

"That's what's so fascinating."

"Is that the standard word you use for luring a woman into bed?"

"Is it working?"

She smiled, and he realized how much he enjoyed seeing it.

"It seems to be."

"Then how about you come over here and let's see if I can lure you with something more substantial."

She rose, walked over, and settled down on his lap. He ran a slow hand up her strong spine and down her soft but work-hardened forearm and savored her strength. As the silence between them grew thick with anticipation, he knew he wanted to be with this woman for the rest of his days. Rather than risk shattering the moment by confessing it, he leaned in and gently kissed her until it flared and deepened. Feeding on her rising desire and letting her feed on his, he eased her closer. Her body was warm, her soft-skinned neck scented from her bath. The thick black braid down her back, still damp. He moved his lips from her mouth to the shell of her ear and his hand to the small swell of her breast. Coaxing the nipple to come out and play, he savored the hushed sound of her arousal, and slowly began undoing her buttons. Drawn to her warmth, he nuzzled the exposed skin of her throat and asked, "Where's your shift?" She was deliciously bare inside the shirt.

"It was just going to be in the way," she replied breathlessly.

Amused by that, he moved the open halves aside and took a hardened nipple into his mouth. She crooned against the sound of the rain striking the windows. Turning attention to the other breast, he was rewarded with more vocalized delight.

"You're so good at this . . ."

He thanked her by giving another fervent kiss. "Thank you."

She reached down to his thigh and gave him a heated squeeze. "This feels pretty substantial."

He groaned with pleasure.

After a few more silent moments of kisses and potent strokes that set him on fire, she whispered, "Let's see how much more substantial I can make it." Standing, she took his hand and led him to her bedroom.

THE BEDROOM LAY in shadows from the darkness of the storm, but the desire in his eyes was as bright as her own. On their first night together she'd been unprepared for how powerful being with the right man could be. Now, as he eased her close and brushed his mouth over hers, she knew to expect the heat of his hard frame against her own, that his fiery, intense kisses would ignite a flame in her blood, and she'd savor the solid yet gentle weight of his encasing arm. When he languidly blazed a trail against the skin of her throat, cupped her breast bared by her already opened shirt, and slowly coaxed her nipple to life, the time he took no longer left her impatient. When he eased her shirt aside and bent to take her in his mouth, her core pulsed, and she crooned softly. He moved his mouth to lavish her other breast with lazy sucks and tiny bites. Never again would she be content with a quick, unsatisfying coupling. He'd proven there could be more, and as a result, she wanted to give him more: more kisses, more caresses of his strong arms and chest to seal her palms with the memory of his shape, form, and heated skin. She nibbled his bottom lip and slid her tongue temptingly against his own. He dragged her buckskins down and filled his large hands with her bare hips before fitting her to him.

"Substantial enough?" he asked playfully, moving heatedly against her.

She kissed him and reached down to boldly map his strong length. "I think so."

He eased a hand between her thighs. She hissed out her pleasure and widened her stance. He dallied, impaled her with a finger, then two, and her hips took up the sultry rhythm. Through the haze brought on by lust, she watched him watching her. The intensity in his eyes showed he was feeding on her responses and it increased the flame of her desire.

She raised a hand to undo the buttons on his shirt but focusing was difficult. Her body was greedily enjoying the art flowing from his wonderful hands. When the task was finally accomplished, she ran her fingers down the ten buttons anchoring his gray flannel union suit, then deftly undid the front of his trousers. Kissing him, she took his hardness in hand, enjoying the warmth of his body encased in the thin, smooth fabric, and heard him groan. He took a moment to rid himself of his pants while she freed the buttons that marched from his collar to his groin and brushed her lips softly against each patch of skin she bared—his collarbone, his strong hair-dappled chest. She flicked her tongue against each flat nipple and bit them gently. Noting he had his head back and his eyes closed as her hands circled his sculpted frame filled her with a power that sent her passion even higher. Lowering herself to her knees, she freed her prize and flicked her tongue over the round head. His hiss was like music to her ears. After a few well-placed licks that made the muscles of his legs clinch in response, she eased him into her mouth and showed him her own art. As she worked, he slowly shucked out of the top half of the suit and once he was bared to the waist, she flicked her tongue against his navel and pulled the garment down to his knees. She moved her hands over the strong, steely muscles of his buttocks and fed on him with such purposeful intent, he grabbed her head to guide her movements, rocking his hips with erotic response. Groaning, he pulled free and stepped back. His harsh breathing made her smile. When she met his blazing eyes, he crooked a finger at her and she rose. "Yes?" she asked innocently. She rid herself of the buckskins pooled at her ankles and closed the short distance between them. He pulled her to him and kissed her intensely.

Moving to the bed, they continued, while outside the thunder boomed and the lightning flashed. She again allowed him the honor of inserting her sponge and he rewarded her by spreading her legs wide to pay a tribute so filled with art, the wicked licks made her explode and scream out his name. Rising up, he teased a finger over the damp, swollen bud and smiled into her passion-lidded eyes. "You want more?"

Her hips rose to meet the rhythm set by his continuing teasing circles, and she said breathlessly, "You're so damn good at this, McCray."

He slid two fingers inside her and she crooned passionately.

Stroking his fingers languidly in and out, he leaned down to whisper against her ear, "And you're so damn alluring, I want to taste every inch of you . . ."

Spring wrapped her hand possessively around the part of him that she'd given her own lusty tribute to and he husked out, "Lord, woman." She smiled and sat up. Kissing him, she tasted herself on his lips and maneuvered herself in front of him. "Let me ride."

He lay back. She straddled him, and as she impaled herself, she watched pleasure close his eyes. Raising herself up until only the tip of his shaft remained sheathed, she teased him that way again and again, until he growled, clamped his hands on her waist, and set a pace that was both rough and delicious. "You are trying to kill me, aren't you?"

She met him measure for measure, enjoying the rawness, his growls, and the lust that pierced her like shards of lightning. When completion came amidst the answering springs of the bed, she again cried out his name while he emptied himself with a lusty roar. And when they were done, they melted into each other's passion-damp arms, hearts racing.

Later, after sharing the tub and having dinner, they sat nestled together on her fancy sofa, watching the crackling fire and listening to the patter of the rain against the windows.

"You should know that once I go home and take care of some things, I'm probably coming back."

She rose up and studied his face. "Why?"

"I'm thinking of making Paradise my home."

Spring wasn't sure how she felt about that. One part of herself embraced the idea. Other parts were concerned about the reasons.

He continued, "A bit has to do with you, but it's mostly because I like the freedom I find here. Porter James has offered me a job, so I'll be able to make a living. I'd eventually look into buying a small plot of land and building me a house."

She thought about the implications. "I'm not looking to marry, Garrett."

"Not expecting that. I'm content with whatever we're calling this for as long as it lasts. If it comes undone, I'll still want to set my life here."

Their eyes met and she said quietly, "I just wanted to make that clear."

"I understand. I'm not putting any expectations on you or the future."

"Good. I don't want you to be disappointed."

He placed a kiss on her brow. "I appreciate your honesty."

"How long do you think it will take to put your affairs in order back at home?"

"I don't know. There isn't much to do really. My parents are going to voice their concerns, so that will be the biggest thing to contend with."

"They'll probably worry about you being so far away."

"I know. We've lived fairly close to each since Freedom."

"They'll miss you, too."

"And I'll miss them, as well."

Where would they be in a year? she wondered. Still cuddling together like this or having gone their separate ways? Only the future would tell so she left it at that.

"Who should I speak with about buying land?"

"Arnold Cale at the bank, or Odell. He and Ben own most of the unoccupied land. I didn't get a chance to tell you, but Jarvis stopped by earlier and wanted to buy some of my land. Said he wants to open a sawmill."

"Are you selling?"

"No, but he also said Matt Ketchum is accusing me of having stolen the land from his father's estate."

"Do you have a deed?"

"Spoken like a lawyer. I do, and so do the others who purchased the bigger parts I couldn't afford."

"Like whom?"

"Nelson, Odell, and Ben. I'm wondering if Jarvis said anything to them about Matt's lies."

"Are you worried?"

"Not really. Randolph Nelson is one of the wealthiest ranchers in the Territory and the head of the Republican party. If Matt takes me on, he'll have to take on Randolph, too, and he'd be a fool to try and run roughshod over someone that influential."

"I agree but let me know if you need my help. I may not have liked being a lawyer but I'm good at it."

"I will."

"Sounds like the sooner I get home, the sooner I need to get back, if Ketchum's bent on trouble."

She agreed and it would be a lie to say she wouldn't miss him. Becoming attached to him was one of the most surprising things to happen to her in quite some time. That and learning from him that sex was a form of art. She smiled.

"Why the smile?"

"Just thinking about how good you are in bed."

"There's not a man alive who doesn't like hearing that."

"It's the truth, but don't let it swell your head. Sooner or later I'll find something you're terrible at." She turned to get a look at his face. "What are you terrible at?"

"Nothing that I know of."

She playfully punched him in the shoulder before resettling against the comfort of his chest. "Such modesty."

"You asked."

"Which I now regret."

Garrett wanted to spend the rest of his days holding her in just this way. Although he still had a few days to enjoy her company, he was missing her already. If the future was kind, he'd return, and over time have all his questions about her answered. Any she had about him would be answered, as well. Outside, he heard the rumble of thunder. "Does it storm this way often?"

"More in the spring and autumn than the rest of the year."

She asked, "Do you hunt and fish?"

"I do, but why'd you ask?"

"Just thinking about some things we might do together. Would you like to go fishing with me when you return?"

"I would."

He saw her nod. She was so unique. He'd never had a woman ask him that before. "Do you have a favorite place?"

"I do. It's a small cabin up in the foothills. I do most of my hunting from there."

He wondered how many men, if any, had been gifted such an invitation, but again he decided it didn't matter. She'd chosen him for now, so he contented himself with holding her close and listening to the rain.

# Chapter Ten

The following morning, after helping Spring with the breakfast dishes, Garrett prepared to leave for the day.

"What are your plans?" she asked.

"I want to stop by your brother's place and hopefully make arrangements to interview your sister-in-law before I depart for home, then ride into town. I need to send off this latest set of notes to my father and let them know the date of my return." His sadness tied to leaving her had not lessened.

"Dinner?" she asked.

"Here, if you aren't sick of me."

She rolled her eyes. "I suppose I can put up with you for another evening."

"You're so kind."

"Don't tell anyone. I've a reputation to maintain."

He laughed, then placing a light finger beneath her chin, raised her lips to his. The kiss, the first of the morning, added to the growing connection and pleasure he'd found in her. "I'll see you later," he murmured.

"I'll be here."

He left her, mounted the gelding, and rode off for his first stop.

The sound of a baby's angry cries hit his ears as soon as he stepped onto the porch. He debated whether to knock on not. By what he was hearing, Mrs. Lee had her hands full, so being the gentleman that he was, he decided to see her later on his way back to Spring.

Resuming his ride, he took in the beauty of the countryside and thought about his parents' reactions to his plans to leave the city. His father would be unhappy, mostly due to his desire to see his son married to a woman of class. His mother, always steady and practical, would miss him, as he would her, but she'd be more concerned with his happiness. His sister, Melody, would miss him, and he'd miss her sunny smile and sharp wit, as well. Hopefully, he'd return to visit when he could, and they'd find a way to visit him in turn. He was certain once they took in the Territory's beauty, they'd partially understand his decision.

Up ahead a mother duck and a line of ducklings were crossing the road. Smiling, he halted the horse to let the family pass. The sound of gunfire startled him. Hastily looking around for the source, a pain like a hundred hot pokers slammed into his back. Crying out, he gathered the reins. Before he could ride away, more bullets, this time shoulder high, toppled him from the saddle and onto the hard dirt road. More shots rang out. He knew he should scramble for cover, but his legs wouldn't obey. He couldn't breathe. In agony he touched his side and drew back blood-stained fingers. Again, he tried to get out of the road, but couldn't move. As consciousness faded, his last thought was of Spring.

SPRING SLID QUICKLY from Cheyenne's back and ran to her brother's office. A gaggle of people were out front. Pushing them aside, she yelled, "Get out of my way!" Ignoring their reactions, she reached the door, and, finding it locked, pounded on it like a woman possessed. Inside, Whit looked out the window.

"Open the door!" He quickly complied, and she entered. "Where is he?"

"Colt's working on him now. He's been in there awhile."

"I want to see him."

"Let your brother work. He doesn't need you distracting him. He'll come out when he's done."

Only then did she see her grandfather seated across the room. Ben was the one who'd found Garrett bleeding and unconscious in the road. After bringing him to town, he'd sent Odell to let her know about the shooting. Heart in her throat, she'd ridden off, leaving Odell to follow at his own pace. "Thank you for bringing him here."

Ben nodded.

"Did you see who shot him?"

"No. Whoever it was is either gone or hiding out of sight in the trees. From the amount of blood on him, I don't think he'd been in the road very long."

That gave her hope. She turned to Whit. "Ketchum did this. I know it as well as I know my name, and it's because of what happened at Glenda and Arnold's party."

"I wasn't there, so tell me what happened."

She did and when she finished he said, "Thanks, but I'll need evidence, Spring."

She had all the evidence she needed in her bones, and if Garrett died . . . She forced her mind away from that terrible possibility.

Whit told her, "I'll question Matt, but I can't charge him without a solid reason."

"He shot him in the back, Whit!"

"I understand. Nothing lower than that. Nothing. But you'll hang if you take the law into your own hands."

He knew her well. Fury made her want to hunt Matt down and treat him to a few well-placed bullets of her own. "Even if you do have solid evidence, Garrett's a Colored man. The courts aren't going to care."

"I'll do everything in my power to make sure they do. I promise you. If you hang it'll break Regan's heart," he said solemnly.

"Thanks for that," she countered coldly.

"It's all I have, Spring. I know you! Don't take this on yourself. Let me do my job."

He turned to Ben. "Where exactly did you find him?"

Ben explained, adding, "I tied a bandanna to one of the trees to mark the spot. I figured you'd want to take a look around."

"I do. Maybe I can find something that might narrow down who did the shooting. Spring, you're welcome to come along and help me look. Two pairs of eyes are better than one."

She agreed.

A pounding on the door heralded Odell's arrival. The curious crowd remained out front. Whit let him in.

Upon seeing Spring, his first words were, "Oh good. You're here."

"Where'd you think I'd be?"

"Already out gunning for Ketchum. The way you and Cheyenne took off, I was worried."

The concern in his eyes mirrored Ben's, so she said to him, "Whit says he'll handle things."

Odell replied, "And if he doesn't, I will. Shooting a man in the back justifies an eye for an eye."

Whit snarled, "Odell, you're not helping."

Ben warned, "Then you better find whoever did it and make sure he's brought to trial." His deadly tone made the hairs rise on the back of Spring's neck. Ben held her eyes for a long moment before declaring, "We live by mountain law. Justice will be served one way or another."

For the next hour it took Spring everything she had to sit and wait and not pace like a caged cat. The more she silently willed her brother to appear with news about Garrett's condition, the longer time passed with no word. Finally, Colt came out of the surgery. There was weariness in his face and blood staining the blue leather bib apron over his shirt and trousers. "I've done all I can for now, but he's strong. I'm confident he'll pull through."

Emotion clogged Spring's throat, and her shoulders slumped in relief.

"He had three bullets in the back and two in his right shoulder. I'll give them to you, Whit, soon as I clean them off."

"When do you think he'll be able to answer questions about what happened?"

"Maybe tomorrow or the day after. Not today though. He's full of laudanum."

"Okay. I need to send a bulletin on the shooting to the US Marshal in Cheyenne. Spring, stop by my office when you're ready to help me survey where McCray was ambushed."

"I will." The number of bullets caused Spring to wonder if Ketchum had enlisted help. Would Jarvis have assisted him? She didn't know enough about the man to speculate, but that Matt may have had accomplices was something to consider.

Whit asked Colt, "Can I let the folks outside know you think he's going to be okay?"

"Yes, if that will make them go home."

After the sheriff's exit, Spring asked, "May I see him?"

Her brother hesitated.

"Please." Spring rarely pleaded, and that must have made an impression.

"Come, but just for a minute."

Ben rose to his feet and joined Odell at the door. "I'll stop back later on my way home."

Spring took in the man responsible for setting her on the harsh road that led to the woman she'd become, and the decades of animosity cracked a little. "Thank you again."

He nodded and he and Odell departed.

She followed Colt to the back.

Garrett was lying so still it took her a moment to reassure herself that he was truly breathing. His chest was partially covered by a blanket, and the white bandages encasing his shoulder and torso stood out starkly against his brown skin. Her heart broke seeing him that way, especially knowing his injuries were tied to defending her. Eyes on him, she asked Colt quietly, "Are you sure he's going to be okay?"

"Pretty sure. It will take him a while to get back on his feet though."

Colt quieted for a moment, then asked, "You care about him, don't you?"

She nodded solemnly. "I do." There was no denying the truth.

"He cares about you, too. Very much."

Her awareness of how Garrett felt about her couldn't be denied, either. He'd made it plain in an unassuming way devoid of any expectations of commitment on her part. "Do you think we should let his family know what's happened?" she asked.

"Seeing as how it's going to be a while before he's able to travel, yes."

"Odell should know where his telegrams have been sent. I wouldn't know how to word it without scaring them to death. Would you take care of it?"

"I will. Let's let him rest."

"I'll be back this evening."

"That isn't necessary, Spring."

"It is. He was shot for standing up for me, Colt, and he'll need someone to watch over him while you sleep—at least for the first few days."

Colt sighed but didn't argue. "Okay. Let Regan know what's happened, and that I'll be sleeping here for a day or so."

"Will do." She ran concerned eyes over the sleeping Garrett—her partner. "Take good care of him."

He showed a soft smile. "I will. You remember to let Whit do his job."

She didn't make any promises. "I'll be back later." Glancing at Garrett one last time, she left him in her brother's care.

WHEN SPRING AND Whit spotted Ben's red bandanna tied to a low-hanging branch of a big oak near the edge of the road, they dismounted. In the dirt a few steps away was a patch of blood where they assumed Garrett had fallen. After viewing it, Whit scuffed it with the toe of his boot until it was gone. Swallowing her anger, a grim Spring followed him into the brush and trees lining the road. Because of the dense cover, they felt safe in assuming the shooter or shooters had hidden there as opposed to the more wide open landscape on the road's other side.

Figuring they could cover more ground if they split up, they went in different directions, and a short while later Spring came across boot prints in a small clearing between two pines. Noting that the spot offered a good view of the road, she called for Whit. He joined her and studied them.

"Looks like two different sets," she pointed out. "See the difference in the heel marks?"

"I do."

One had a well-worn uneven heel.

Like Spring, he glanced out at the road. "This could be where they were."

"Or where two people answered nature's call," she replied.

"That, too."

They investigated further but turned up nothing more.

To be thorough, they left the spot and searched the other side of the road. Whit asked, "Do you know if McCray made any stops on his way to town?"

"He said he was going to see Regan to set up a time to interview her, but I don't know if he did. I'm going to stop by there on my way home. I'll ask her."

"That would be helpful."

She glanced around the area again. They'd found nothing. "I wonder if whoever shot McCray had been keeping an eye on my place, hoping to catch him alone."

"That's a possibility."

"So had I been with him they might have shot me, too?"

"Maybe."

She wanted answers, but there were none, so they mounted up.

"I'll be back in town later," she said to him. "I'll let you know what Regan says."

"Okay, thanks." He paused for a moment, and said quietly, "Spring?"

She took in the serious set of his face.

He continued, "Sorry for yelling at you the way I did back there. I've known you most of your life and feel you're as much my little sister as Colt's."

"I know. Sometimes I need to be yelled at, so no apologies needed."

He nodded. "Be careful going home."

"I will."

They parted ways.

REGAN WAS APPALLED to hear about Garrett's shooting and agreed with Spring on Ketchum's probable involvement. "From what you've told me, McCray hasn't crossed anyone here but Ketchum," she said. "I hope Whit finds what's needed to place him before a judge."

"So do I. When Garrett left my place this morning, he planned to stop by here to set up an interview. Did he do that? He was shot not too far from here. Did you hear any shooting?"

Regan shook her head. "He didn't come by and I didn't hear any gunfire." She eyed Spring and asked, "And how are you feeling?"

"Angry enough to go after Ketchum myself, but Whit reminded me that it's his job. He said I'd hang if I take matters into my own hands."

"And that would break my heart."

"He said that, too. Now that I've cooled off I know he's right, but I still want to send Matt to hell."

"Has McCray's family been notified?"

"Colt's going to handle that. Not sure how he'll word it without scaring them to death."

"True, but this isn't the first time he's had to present bad news to a patient's family. I'm sure he knows what to say."

Spring agreed. She couldn't rid her mind of Garrett lying so still, but held on to Colt's assurance that he would recover.

"If it will help, I can put up a reward for information that leads to an arrest."

"That would be very helpful."

"And I think it should be a significant enough amount that anyone who may have been an accomplice will be seriously tempted to come forward. How about ten dollars gold?"

"I like the way you think."

"Let Whit know so he can have the posters put up as soon as he's able."

The sound of Colt Fontaine crying made Regan rise to her feet. "I guess my siesta is over. Thanks for letting me know about McCray, and that Colt won't be home this evening."

"Do you need me to get Anna from school?"

"No, Lucretia's bringing her home, but thanks for asking. Give me a hug."

They shared a tight embrace and Regan whispered, "I know you aren't showing how worried you are, but if Colt says Garrett will be okay, he will."

Spring was again grateful for having Regan in her life. "Thanks, and thanks for the reward offer. Now, go get my nephew before he screams the house down."

Regan smiled tiredly. "I'll see you later."

She left the parlor and Spring let herself out.

AT HOME, SPRING fed the horses and put Cheyenne in his stall. She grabbed her bedroll, placed a few toiletries and a couple of clean shirts into a bag, and saddled Lady for the ride back to town. Her growling stomach reminded her that she'd not eaten since breakfast, so a trip to Dovie's dining room was warranted at some point once she arrived.

In town, her first stop was her brother's office to check on Garrett. He was still sleeping.

"He's fine," Colt told her. "Did you speak with Regan?"

"I did." And she told him about the reward. "I'm so glad she married you."

He chuckled. "It was touch and go at the beginning, but I am, too. Where are you going now?"

"To let Whit know about the reward, then to Dovie's. I've not eaten since breakfast. Do you want me to bring you a plate?"

"No. She sent me food a little while ago."

"Good. I'll be back."

Leaving her gear in his office, she made the short walk down to the sheriff's office. After letting him know what she'd learned from Regan, and telling him about the reward, which he approved of, she left to go eat.

"How's Mr. McCray?" Dovie asked as Spring took a seat at one of the tables.

"Colt says he'll pull through, but it may take a while before he's fully healed up."

Dovie shook her head sympathetically. "Such a terrible thing to happen. Everyone I've talked to is pointing the finger at Matt Ketchum because of what happened at Glenda's party."

"So am I, but Whit needs evidence. If you hear anything let him know." She then told her about the reward Regan was offering.

"That's a lot of money."

"Yes, it is."

"You think I can talk her into offering a reward to anyone wanting to take Wallace Junior off my hands?"

Spring smiled for the first time since learning Garrett had been shot. Wallace Junior could be a terror, but she knew Dovie wasn't serious. She loved her son. "You can ask her next time you see her."

"Will do. What can I get you?"

Spring studied the chalkboard on the wall that listed the dishes of the day. "I'll have the beef stew and some biscuits." Dovie's biscuits were the best around.

"Okay. I'll be right back."

After she departed, Spring nodded a greeting to some of the others in the room. The elderly Emmett Davies, one of the local cattlemen, was seated with two other ranchers.

"I hear doc got McCray patched up," Emmett said to her from across the room.

"He did."

"Shame something like that happened. Worked with him on Porter's place. Nice fella. Hope Whit catches who did it."

Spring replied, "Mrs. Doc's offering up a big reward for information." Mrs. Doc was the nickname the locals lovingly bestowed upon Regan after she married Colt.

"Do tell."

Spring nodded. "Whit's going to put up posters to let everyone know about it."

The interest on the faces of the others in the room was plain. Once word got around about the size of the reward, she was confident someone would volunteer the evidence needed. It wasn't every day someone could earn ten dollars gold for simply turning on a skunk like Ketchum.

As if conjured up by her thoughts, Matt Ketchum entered the dining room with Jarvis, the male secretary Swan, and the daughter, Hazel. Silence descended as they took seats and all eyes watched. Spring took a perverse joy in seeing the lingering damage to Matt's face by Garrett's well-placed fist. It was bruised black-and-blue from his very swollen and crooked nose to his eyes. Upon noticing Spring, his mouth twisted nastily.

"I hear someone put that man of yours in his place," he said nasally. "Glad they did. I know you probably think I was involved, but you can't prove it."

Dovie returned with Spring's food. As she set the plate down, Spring replied to Ketchum, "You know, Matt, that might have had more sting if you didn't resemble and sound like a raccoon with cotton stuffed up its nose."

Snickers were heard.

Spring glanced up to see Dovie smiling. "Thanks, Dovie."

"You're welcome." Dovie then turned to Ketchum. "Any more of your ugliness and you'll be asked to leave."

"Says who?"

Dovie walked over to where he sat. Towering over him from her six-foot-plus frame, she replied calmly, "I whipped you when we were nine. I whipped you when we were fourteen. If you want to try me again, let me know." Matt turned beet-red beneath his bruises. Upon hearing the chuckling, and taking in the grins of those looking on, his face twisted with anger and he got up and walked out.

The amused Spring began eating her stew. For all his bragging and threats, he'd always had a thin skin. She expected Jarvis and his companions to follow his exit, but they stayed.

After placing their orders with Dovie, Jarvis got to his feet and walked over to Spring's table, much to her ire.

"Miss Lee?"

She looked up and waited for him to say more.

"I just wanted to let you know how sorry I am for what happened to McCray. I did warn him as you remember."

She wondered why he'd added that last part. If he'd come to express true concern, he could've done it and moved on. "Were you involved?"

"Of course not."

"Just wondering why you included the 'told you so.' Couldn't help crowing, I suppose."

His anger plainly showed he didn't like where she'd taken the conversation, but someone tried to put McCray in his grave. She didn't have to play nice. "You should probably go back to your seat."

He gritted out, "You might need to be taught a lesson, too."

"Someone already did. You're speaking to the result." She refused to be intimidated, especially by a man ignorant enough to believe being allied with Ketchum was a good idea. She again wondered what the two were really up to, but her food was getting cold. "Anything else?"

"I hope I'm around to witness you being brought down a peg or two. I'll enjoy it." He turned and went back to his seat.

She supposed she could've told him he wasn't the first person to wish her ill, and probably wouldn't be the last. Being a burr beneath some people's saddles seemed to be part of her charm, as McCray called it. Thinking about him put a damper on her mood, so sending good thoughts his way, she refocused on her meal.

When she finished eating, she paid Dovie and left.

Before going back to her brother's office, she wanted to talk with Odell, so she stopped at the telegraph office. To her surprise, there was no checkers game underway. In fact, Odell was alone.

"I sent the telegram to McCray's people," he told her. "Hoping we'll hear something back soon."

She wondered how they'd respond. Even if she and her brother were still estranged, getting word that he'd been injured, she'd've been on the next train heading his way. She wondered if his family would do the same. "Okay. Came to talk about the Ketchum land we purchased. Matt told Jarvis the acreage was sold illegally."

Odell rolled his eyes. "Matt's so full of manure, I'm surprised he doesn't leave a trail of pies every time he takes a step."

Tickled by that, she then relayed the details of Jarvis's visit, adding, "Says he wants to build a mill."

"According to what I've been hearing there's a bunch of back-East fellas wanting to buy land here so they can chop down all the trees."

Spring was confused.

He explained. "There's a big thirst for lumber to build houses and such, but not enough trees anymore. So companies are turning their eyes to places out West. Man like Jarvis could make a small fortune with a mill, especially a new fancy one."

"So has Jarvis approached you?"

"No. This is my first time hearing why he might be sniffing

around. He can't be very bright if he's hitched his wagon to Ketchum."

She agreed.

"And if Arnold Cale hears that Matt is telling folks his pa's land was sold illegally, Arnold's going to have his head. He takes a lot of pride in his reputation, and this would be a big smear if it were true, which it isn't. Cale put adverts in papers from San Francisco to Chicago looking for heirs after Mitch Ketchum died. Didn't hear a peep from Matt."

"Anybody know where he's been?"

"Hiding out, apparently. I heard rumors he was back East. That big politician in Cheyenne whose daughter Matt assaulted died recently, so I guess he figured it was safe to come back."

"And stir up trouble."

Odell nodded.

Spring admittedly didn't pay much attention to politics but wondered if the Territory politicians were promoting the land sales to the big back-East investors. There were certainly plenty of trees to be had.

Odell added, "If you're worried about your land being legal, don't be. It is. I'll be talking to Ben and some of the ranchers to let them know about the lies Matt and Jarvis are spreading and find out if Porter James knows about the mill Jarvis is talking about building."

"Thanks, Odell."

"You're welcome, and we will find out who shot McCray, one way or another."

"Regan's offering a reward for information." And she told him how much.

His blue eyes twinkled. "Mrs. Doc is such a gift to Paradise. That much money would tempt a saint."

"I agree."

He studied her for a few moments before asking, "The man means something to you, doesn't he?"

She gave him a nod.

"Not many men worthy enough to be with a woman as special as you. I hope you know that."

"I do." She valued herself even if others didn't.

"Walking through life alone has its advantages, but so does walking with someone you have feelings for. Keep that in mind."

"Thanks, Odell."

"You're welcome, Little Rain Girl."

His nickname for her made her smile. Over the years, whenever they discussed life or things close to the heart, he always affectionately addressed her that way. He also used it when he was upset with her about something she'd done, like not checking the hooves of her horse for stones or an ill-fitting shoe, or taking on a mustang he thought too dangerous for her to break. "Can I ask you a question?"

"Sure."

"Why am I named after my grandmother? The way Ben felt about her, you'd think my folks would've called me something else."

"Your mother wanted to honor your grandmother's memory. Ben pitched a fit of course, but Isabelle didn't care. She said your grandmother was due the tribute."

"So I've been a lightning rod of sorts since I was born."

He smiled. "I suppose you could say that, but like you, your grandmother had a deep well of strength. Ben stupidly used up every drop. It's why she left."

Her grandmother had rarely been discussed when Spring was young, but she knew a bit of the story about Ben and his Shoshone bride, and how he kept her from her people in a misguided attempt to turn her into what he called a civilized wife. She'd suffered loneliness, bore slurs from the townspeople, and one day Ben woke up to find his infant son Lewis tucked in bed beside him, and his wife gone. His search for her spanned years, but she was never found. "I'm going to check on McCray. You'll let me know when his folks reply?"

"Sure will."

# Chapter Eleven

For the next few days Spring divided her time between her place and helping with McCray's care so Colt could get some sleep. Odell and Whit took turns, as well. Colt showed them how many drops of laudanum to put in his tea to help him sleep, and how to change the dressings covering his back. The laudanum was alternated with bark tea. The bark tea wasn't as effective, but Colt didn't want Garrett to become dependent on the opium-based laudanum. On day four Dr. Crane, the Chinese doctor in Green River, sent word that Colt's help was needed with yet another measles outbreak, this time at a different mining camp.

As he prepared to leave, he told Spring, "I'd rather stay here and look after my patient, but babies are dying up there. Promise me you'll send someone for Lucretia if he gets a high fever or his healing stalls."

Lucretia Watson was the local midwife, and the grandmother of Anna's best friend, Livy. "I promise. Don't worry."

"Okay. I'm going by home to pack a bag, kiss my wife and children, and ride to the camp."

His weariness was plain, and she wondered when he'd get the rest he needed. "Be careful. Send word when you arrive so Regan won't worry."

"Will do. Take care of McCray. I'll be back as soon as I'm able." Picking up his medical bag and bedroll, he left the office. Watching through the window as he rode off, she sent up a silent prayer for his safety. During her wilder younger days, her outrageous behavior had caused a deep rift in their relationship. No matter how many times he tried to talk her into mending her ways, she'd refused to listen. Now, thanks to Regan, they were in a better place. It wasn't perfect and because of their personalities it might never be, but she was glad to have him back in her life, and she couldn't be prouder of his dedication to his profession.

That evening as she slept on her bedroll on the floor of the back room, she heard Garrett stirring. Still half-asleep, she got up, placing her hand on his forehead to assess his temperature.

He croaked, "Spring?"

Elated that he'd finally awakened, she replied, "I'm here."

"Where am I?"

"Colt's office."

He made a move to sit up, but she stalled him gently. "You have to lie still. You're hurt pretty bad."

He quieted for a moment as if assessing her words. "What happened?"

"You were shot. Hold on, let me light a lamp."

She did and when she glanced his way, found him asleep again. Sighing, she doused the lamp and returned to her bedroll.

GARRETT OPENED HIS eyes, glanced around the small windowless room, and didn't know where he was. Sleep tried to drag him under again, but he fought it to clear his mind enough to make sense of his surroundings. He tried to sit up, but pain dropped on him like an anvil, making him pant until the agony lessened somewhat.

The door opened. Odell appeared. "I see you're awake."

Garrett, still riding the wave of pain, thought he nodded but wasn't sure.

"How are you feeling?"

The call of nature was strong. He whispered, "Need to relieve myself."

"Got a chamber pot here."

"No. Outside."

"Letting you up is going to get both of us in trouble with Spring and Lucretia, but I understand."

Odell walked over to the cot. Garrett managed to get himself upright and sat head down on the edge of the cot. Shaking from lack of strength and doing his best to ignore the roaring pain in his back, he fought to catch his breath. He glanced at the loose nightshirt he was wearing and its origin was another mystery. "What happened to me?"

"You were backshot."

"When?"

"About five days ago. Ben found you and brought you here. Colt patched you up."

"Spring?"

"Been here with you the entire time. She went to eat. I'm watching you until she gets back." Odell assessed him. "You sure you want to go outside?"

"Yes."

"Okay. That door there leads out back. You'll have privacy. Let's do this quick before she returns and cusses us both."

Garrett agreed. Leaning on the old trapper for support, he shuffled his way on legs weak as wet string. His back protested angrily and sweat dampened his brow. Outside, the bright sunshine hurt his eyes. He couldn't tell what the temperature was. His focus was on answering his needs before he passed out.

Back inside and feeling better, he lay on the cot and waited for his ragged breath to return to a pace akin to normal. His back felt like a bonfire fueled by jagged pieces of glass.

"How's the pain?"

"Bad."

"Got some laudanum tea here."

Garrett struggled up, drank as much of the tea as he could, then lay back again. The many questions he wanted to put to Odell about the shooting were soon forgotten as sleep pulled him under once more.

Garrett awakened, and had no idea how much time had

passed since Odell helped him outside. Had it been hours, days? He was still in the windowless room, however. The pain in his back had subsided somewhat but was still viable enough to let him know he'd not be dancing a jig anytime soon. He was hungry and thirsty. "Anybody here?" he called out.

The door to the front of the office opened, letting in the light of day. Spring entered. Seeing her filled him with a soft glow.

"Hey there," she said, walking over to the cot.

"Hey."

She placed a light hand on his forehead. "No fever. That's good."

He agreed.

"Welcome back to the world."

"Thanks."

"Are you thirsty? Hungry?"

"Both."

"Colt said to give you soft things to eat first. Would you like some eggs?"

"Yes."

He wanted to tell her how grateful he was for her presence and her brother's care but his brain was scrambled as the eggs she'd offered.

Whit stuck his head in the door and Garrett was pleased to see him, as well. Spring said, "Odell told me about you going outside. I wasn't happy but I understand. Whit will help you if you need to again. I'll get those eggs from Dovie."

Feeling a bit closer to human as a man who'd been shot in the back could, Garrett silently offered up thanks for being alive.

AFTER PUTTING IN her request for Garrett's eggs, Spring sat in the dining room to wait for Dovie to bring the plate. Hazel Jarvis entered the otherwise empty space and walked over to Spring.

"Good morning, Miss Lee."

"Morning."

"If you have some spare time in the next few days, I'd like to speak to you."

"About?"

Overdressed as always, this time in olive green, she fidgeted for a moment. "I—I'd just like to get to know you better."

"Why?"

"I—you're not like any woman I've ever met before. How did you become so strong and fearless?"

Spring wondered what this was truly about. Hazel was a privileged woman of her race and class. Spring saw no reason for her to be interested in a Colored woman's life story. "I doubt your father would approve of you associating with me."

"Agreed. He doesn't care for you at all. Calls you unnatural and that you need to be shown your place."

Spring wasn't surprised.

"But I find you fascinating. And—"

"Hazel!" Her father's angry voice cut her off. He glared her way from across the dining room and the now tight-lipped Hazel scurried to his side. As he quietly berated her, her face was mutinous and remained so as they took seats at one of the tables.

Dovie brought out Garrett's eggs. The warm plate was wrapped in a towel to keep in the heat. "Thanks, Dovie."

"What does Mr. McCray plan to do about his room here?"

"Not sure, but I'll ask him and let you know what he says." Ignoring Hazel and her father, Spring went on her way.

Back at Colt's office, Garrett and Whit were talking when she entered.

"So what's the last thing you remember?" Whit asked.

Spring untied the towel around the plate and found scrambled eggs and two biscuits.

"The ducks."

Spring paused.

Whit chuckled, "Ducks?"

Garrett explained. "Just before I fell off the horse, I'd stopped to let a family of ducks cross the road."

Spring thought his gentleman's ways had almost cost him his life. Then again, she stopped for duck families many times, too.

With Garrett being unable to sit upright for any length of time and lacking the strength to feed himself, she and Whit ended up helping him into one of the office's chairs. It pained Spring to hear his labored breathing and to see the sheen of perspiration on his face brought on by such a simple maneuver.

"Did Matt Ketchum shoot me?" he asked them once he settled into the chair.

"More than likely," Whit replied. "But I need evidence to prove it."

Spring forked up some of the eggs and fed him a bit of it. "Regan has put up a reward for information but so far no one has come forward."

"Did you send word to my folks?"

"Yes. Odell said they sent back a number of questions, which he answered as best he could."

"I hope they're not too worried."

"We'll let them know that you're now awake and eating," she said reassuringly. "That might help ease their concerns."

By the time he finished the small helping of eggs and half a biscuit, he was exhausted and had to be helped back to the cot. Spring thought how much easier taking care of him might be were he at her place and able to rest in a real bed. Colt's back room wasn't equipped to house patients for lengthy stays, thus the reason he was having the hospital built, but she wasn't sure if Garrett had healed enough to make it to her place in the back of a wagon rolling on a rut-filled road. He must have read her mind because once he was supine again, he asked, "How much longer do I have to stay here? Sleeping on this cot is about as comfortable as a length of pine."

"I could move you to my place, but I'm worried about you

being tossed around in the wagon bed. Colt will have my hide if the ride undoes your healing."

"I'm willing to chance it."

"All right. Let's talk more tomorrow."

"I'd rather we do it today, Spring. Preferably now." There was a firmness in the eyes trained on her.

She looked to Whit. He replied with a shrug, adding, "I'm sure we could find something to pad the wagon. Dovie may have some old mattresses and pallets we can borrow. Odell may have something useful, too."

"I can't heal if I can't get some decent sleep," Garrett pointed out.

She knew he was right, but she still worried about making him worse. "Okay, let me ask around. My wagon is at home so I'll see if we can borrow Odell's."

"Thank you," Garrett said.

It took Spring an hour to get everything ready. Dovie donated two old mattresses. Odell offered to drive and threw in a couple of hides to cover the mattresses and offer more cushioning. Once they got Garrett aboard and comfortable, she placed in a bag clean bandages, a vial of laudanum, and a tin of the salve they'd been putting on his wounds. Word spread that McCray was leaving, so by the time the wagon was ready to go, a small crowd had formed. As she mounted Cheyenne, she saw Jarvis, his secretary, and his daughter watching from the edge, but Matt wasn't with them. In case of another attack, she was armed with her Colt and a rifle she'd borrowed from Whit. He was mounted on his stallion and would be riding along, too. She gave Odell the okay to pull off, and with her and Whit flanking the wagon, their small party headed out of town.

As THEY MADE their way down the road, Spring kept one eye on Garrett and the other on the surroundings. She doubted Ketchum or whomever had been responsible for the attack would be brave enough to repeat it with her, Whit, and Odell present, but she didn't let her guard down. Visually sweeping the road ahead, she focused on the trees and thick vegetation lining the way. Garrett had been given laudanum before they left town with the hope it would make him sleep for the duration of the journey, and so far, it was working. Each rut in the road tossed him, however, sometimes gently, other times roughly. A few deep holes shook the wagon so forcefully, winces crossed his sleeping face. She worried about him and would continue to until she had him home and in bed.

When they finally reached her cabin, getting him inside proved difficult. The laudanum had him so groggy and foggy-brained, Whit and Odell had to position him between them and wrangle him like a drunk. Once inside, they maneuvered him into the spare room and eased him down onto the big bed.

"Thank you," she said gratefully.

Odell asked, "You sure you're going to be able to handle this by yourself?"

"Pretty sure. How about you come check on me tomorrow, just in case."

"Will do."

Whit said, "Do you have everything from the wagon? The medical supplies and his clothes?"

She nodded. She'd packed up all his possession from his room at Dovie's. Spring hadn't the means to settle his bill but Dovie kindly told her not to worry. Garrett could pay what was owed when he was strong enough to come back to town.

After saying her goodbyes to Odell and Whit, Spring looked in on Garrett. He was beneath the blankets and quilts, and his breathing as he snored sounded less labored than before. The big feather mattress would cushion him in a way the cot hadn't. Moving him felt right. Having him with her felt right, as well.

She checked on him on and off during the day and each time she peeked in, a sense of peace rose inside. Who knew she'd become attached to a nosy newspaper carpenter. In some ways he was nothing like the men she'd grown up around. He didn't wear a gun belt and she'd never heard him curse. He'd cooked for her and didn't mind washing dishes. Kindness seemed to guide his steps, and he offered that same kindness to her freely and without judgment. He'd made her wonder more than once what it might be like to not walk through life as a woman alone.

As promised, Odell dropped by the next day and brought disturbing news. Porter James's mill caught fire last night.

Spring was shocked. "Was anyone hurt?"

"No, but the place is a total loss."

"How is that possible? Did he leave a lamp burning?"

"No. Seems deliberately set. Whit said there was a strong smell of kerosene when he rode out to look over what was left."

Spring thought about Jarvis and his talk of building a mill. "Could Jarvis have been involved?"

"No one knows. Dovie says he left for Cheyenne yesterday afternoon and is due back this evening, but it's pretty coincidental, don't you think?"

She agreed. "Poor Mr. James. Is he going to rebuild?"

"No. He says that's it for him. Once he tidies up his affairs, he plans to go live with his daughter and her family down in Denver. I'll miss that old codger very much."

As would everyone else around. He'd helped expand Regan and Colt's house last year, and did the work on fixing up the boardinghouse that Dovie managed. She thought about Colt's unfinished hospital. Progress on it had stopped because of winter, and now? Would his small crew of workers be able to continue without his supervision? If Garrett recovered would he be able to take over the construction when he healed up and returned from back East? She had no answers, but she was sorry Porter James would be leaving Paradise.

Odell said, "Speaking of Jarvis, he wants to meet with all the landowners on Wednesday to discuss what he's calling an investment opportunity we'll be interested in."

"Are you planning to attend?"

"I am. Know thy enemy is the first rule of survival."

"I'd like to hear what he has to say, too, but I can't leave Garrett here alone, at least not yet."

"Understood. I'll be sure to let you know how it turns out. How's your fella doing, by the way?"

She decided not to challenge Odell on calling Garrett her fella. Even if she did, he wouldn't stop, and honestly, thinking of Garrett in that way no longer made her grumble and gripe. "He slept well last night. Ate a little bit of breakfast earlier and is asleep again."

"Moving him was a good idea."

"I think so, too. Let's hope Colt agrees when he returns. Any word from Garrett's folks?"

"Got a wire late yesterday from a Melody. Says she's his sister?"

"Yes. He's mentioned her."

"She said to tell him he's in her prayers. She wanted to know how far Paradise was from Cheyenne."

"Maybe she's coming to visit?" Spring speculated. "If Colt were injured someplace far away, I'd certainly want to see him, no matter the distance."

"You might be right. We'll just have to wait and see. I'll let you know if she sends anything else."

Spring wasn't sure how she felt about meeting a member of Garrett's family but knew that didn't matter. If the sister did come, he'd be pleased, and Spring would do her best to be welcoming.

After promising to stop by again the next day, Odell left. Spring spent the rest of the morning taking care of her animals then peeked in at Garrett. He was still sleeping, so she left him to begin turning the soil for her garden. The growing season was short and now that the weather had warmed, she wanted to begin planting as soon as possible.

A short while later Lacy stopped by to drop off the kittens she'd asked Spring to take in. There were three. The fur of one reminded her of Odell's beard, so Spring named it Odell. A brown-and-white one that blinked up at her like an owl got named Hoot, and the third one, a gray with black stripes down its sides, hissed so angrily, Spring christened her Snake. She carried them to the barn where her mousers Queen Victoria and Cleopatra held court. When she entered, both black cats came slinking out of the shadows. Spring sat down on the hay-covered dirt floor to see if they'd venture over to investigate. The mewling kittens drew their immediate attention. When the queens began licking the little ones, Spring smiled. "You like your new babies?"

She ran a hand down the back of each of the big cats. "I'm going to get them something to sleep in. Be right back."

Leaving the kittens with their new mamas, she went to the house, grabbed two old pillows, a couple of ratty towels, and a big basket that she'd once used for laundry until Paint got a hold of it last year. His chomps reduced it from eight inches high to three. When she returned to the barn, she set the new bed near a wall and placed the kittens inside. As they immediately tumbled out, she added more feed to the queens' bowls and set some cream out for the babies. After stroking them all affectionately, she left them to get better acquainted while she went back to her garden.

Garrett opened his eyes and peered around the room. He didn't know how long he'd slept but he remembered eating breakfast. He just didn't know if that was the present day, the next day, or how much time had passed. The clock on the nightstand showed eleven. The windows were bright with the light of day, so it was morning. He needed to get to the washroom, but having no idea where Spring was, or the ability to maneuver down the short hallway to find her, he decided to attempt it without assistance. It was a slow go. He managed to get there and back without keeling over, but he was so winded from the journey, he instantly fell back into sleep.

When next he opened his eyes, the hands of the clock were on twelve and one. Sunlight continued to stream through the windows, so he assumed it to be the same day. His stomach growled with hunger, and again he wondered where Spring might be. And then, as if she'd heard his mental call, she was in the doorway. The sight of her filled him with something rivaling the day's sunshine. He didn't care that the front of her shirt and trousers were covered with dirt and that there was a matching streak across her forehead. To him, she was still lovely.

She said, "Glad to see you awake."

"Glad to be awake."

"Hungry?"

He nodded. "How long have I been asleep?"

"Just since breakfast."

"Today?"

"Yes."

Somewhat frustrated by his condition and being bedbound, he said wistfully, "Wish I could jump ahead a few weeks and be healed up."

"The future will come soon enough," she said softly. "There's potato soup. Do you want some?"

"Yes, please."

"Let me clean up and I'll be back."

When she returned he struggled to sit up.

"Hold on. Let me help." She set the tray down and gently added a slew of bracing pillows and a folded quilt against the headboard. Her nearness wafted over him, making him again wish to be fully healed so they could pick up where they'd been before he was shot. She must've seen something in his eyes because she paused and asked, "What?"

"Just missing you."

"I'm missing you, too," she said softly. "So let's get you healed up."

But just sitting up made him break out in a sweat.

"You okay?"

"Let me catch my breath a minute here." Having to admit he had about as much strength as a newborn sparrow played havoc with his manly pride, especially in front of the woman he cared so much for.

She placed a hand on his forehead. "No fever."

"Good. Hate being laid low this way."

"Understandable, but nothing to be done but bear it for now."

"A man doesn't like looking weak in front of his partner."

"It's not like you planned this, McCray. You didn't shoot yourself in the back."

"Still."

To his surprise, she leaned in and kissed him, leaving him dazzled and breathless in a different sort of way.

"Are you ready for this soup now?"

Wanting more than food, he returned the kiss, hoping it conveyed how much more nourishing he found her to be. When he'd gotten his fill, he reluctantly eased away. "Now I am."

She stroked the stubble that had grown out on his cheek. "Parts of you might be injured but your lips work just fine."

"Good to know."

Due to his bandaged shoulder and the wounds beneath, he remained unable to lift his right arm to feed himself. He'd been able to use his left hand for solid foods like eggs and bacon, but soup needed a preciseness his left hand couldn't manage.

Seated on the edge of the mattress, she spooned up a bit of the soup and raised it to him. "Here."

He couldn't decide whether he enjoyed being fed or not. On the one hand, he enjoyed her nearness and being fussed over, but on the other hand, he felt like a weak child.

She spooned up more. "Never fed a man before. Being around you is one new experience after another."

He'd missed her humor, too.

"What's going to be next?"

"Something much more substantial once I'm able to walk and talk at the same time," he quipped.

"I'm looking forward to your substantial attention."

His body was warming to the wordplay in a way that couldn't be satisfied in his present condition. "How about we talk about something else? I'm in no shape to be riled up."

She gave him a mock pout. "You're no fun, but okay. What would you rather we talked about?"

"Tell me what I've missed."

She began with the burning of Mr. James's mill. Hearing that the fire appeared to have been deliberately set left Garrett angry and concerned. "I'm glad he wasn't hurt. Was this Jarvis's doing?"

"Odell and I wondered the same thing." She then informed him of the meeting Jarvis was having.

Garrett asked, "Are you going to attend?"

"No. I don't want to leave you here alone."

"I can tend myself, Spring. It's not like you'll be gone overnight."

She studied him. "What if you need assistance getting out of bed?"

"I've managed twice on my own today."

She didn't appear impressed. "You're supposed to ask for help, mister."

"I didn't need any." He thought it best not to mention almost falling headfirst into the tub. "Go to the meeting. I know you'd rather be there in person than have Odell or someone else tell you what transpired." He knew her well enough to be certain he was correct.

"Okay, but if I come home and find you passed out on the floor, I'll be feeding you to a bear."

"Noted."

When he finished the soup, she set the bowl aside. "A wire came from your sister. She sends her love and prayers. Odell said she wanted to know the distance between here and Cheyenne. Do you think she's coming to visit?"

He was surprised by that. "I don't know. Did the wire contain anything else?" That Melody might indeed visit was exciting to think about.

"No, but Odell promised to let me know if she wires again."

He thought again how pleased he'd be to see her. "You'd like her, Spring. She and I have different fathers, but she's my sister through and through."

"I'm sure I would."

"What are you going to do for the rest of the day?" he asked.

"Hopefully make more headway plowing my garden so I can get the seeds put in. There's fences needing shoring up, wood to chop. Other than that, not much for a lady of leisure like myself."

"Yet another boring day."

"Exactly. Is there anything you need before I go back outside?"

"Yes, but I can't have it, at least not presently."

She gave him another soft, stirring kiss. "We'll make up for it soon. I promise. Get some rest. I'll be back later."

Buoyed by the soup, the kisses, and her promise, Garrett slept.

# Chapter Twelve

The Jarvis meeting was being held at the bank and when Spring arrived, most of the chairs in the room were filled with ranchers and other landowners. She nodded greetings to those she knew before finding a place in the back to stand. A few minutes later Odell entered and joined her. Jarvis made his entrance shortly after, along with Matt, Hazel, and Swan. Spring watched Swan set up an easel and a large map of the area on it. He then withdrew a stack of papers from a leather bag and set them on the table nearby. While he attended to that, Hazel sat silent and Spring again wondered what these people were really up to. Jarvis spent a few moments speaking with Arnold Cale, Matt, and Randolph Nelson before turning to assess the crowd.

Banker Cale started the meeting. "Evening. Thanks for coming. Many of you have seen Mr. Jarvis here around. He and his lovely daughter are visiting from back East where he's a very important man. He's called us all together because he has a few proposals he thinks we might be interested in."

Jarvis glanced around the room. He didn't say anything at first, making Spring wonder if he'd expected applause to greet his introduction.

He finally began. "As Banker Cale stated I'm Avery Jarvis from New York City."

Silence greeted that also.

He cleared his throat. "I met Matt Ketchum here a few months back and he told me what a fine community this was. He also told me about the acres and acres of lumber here, something those of us back East are in dire need of. I'm a lawyer and also a member of a group of investors who'd like to tap into those resources and offer you an opportunity to access what we're sure will be a promising enterprise."

The audience waited.

"First, I'd like to build a new mill to replace the one lost in the fire. It would be more cost effective to cut the trees into board length and ship the wood east than paying the freight for heavy uncut trees. A new mill would also give you access to a local business as opposed to having to patronize one that's not. My investor friends and I see this new enterprise as a partnership, and we'd match the funds that you raise."

Odell bluntly asked, "Who'd own it?"

"My people, and those who choose to invest. Now, the second opportunity I'd like to discuss is the planned railroad line that will run from Paradise to Cheyenne—" and he used a pointer to trace the proposed route on the big map resting on the easel, adding "—which is good news to the ranchers wanting to ship their beef, and to those who partner with our mill. In order to make this come about, the railroad needs to buy up the land along the route."

"How much are they paying?" someone asked.

Jarvis appeared thrown off by the interruption. "I'll get to that in a moment."

"Must be pennies if he's not telling."

A few people laughed.

Another voice responded sarcastically, "Okay, Jarvis, feed us more line. Let's see if we'll swallow the hook on this, too."

Spring wondered what Matt had shared with Jarvis that led him to believe this land buy would be an easy sell. Everyone acknowledged the benefits the railroads offered, but the companies were wholly hated. The trains killed livestock, the coal ash fouled streams, and more than a few landowners had been forced into foreclosure by the railroads' shady practices of selling bonds that weren't worth the paper they were printed on. She didn't see this going well for Jarvis if he couldn't prove this was an offer to be trusted.

Randolph Nelson asked, "So what are you selling, Mr. Jarvis?"

"Bonds in exchange for the land. The more profit the railroad makes, the higher the return on your bonds. You can cash them in once that profit is on the ledgers. I have brochures here that further explain the details."

Spring shook her head in response. Back when the railroad first began laying tracks, people were willing to offer up their farmland and everything else they owned for a shot at the promised profits. Now, after numerous scandals tied to fraud, government waste, and outright theft, people were now less gullible.

Nelson stood and said, "Thank you, Mr. Jarvis. Not interested." He started to the door. A few others followed. Spring watched Jarvis's eyes widen in shock and fright.

"Wait! Where are you going?"

"Home," Nelson replied.

"But I'm offering you the opportunity to reap a grand profit."

"Fleecing is for sheep and that's what this is going to be."

Jarvis said angrily, "What I'm offering is better than what you'll get if I sue you for the theft of Ketchum land. Once I'm done, you'll have nothing."

Nelson turned back. "What did you say?"

"Matt Ketchum is retaining my services to have the sale of his family acreage declared illegal and the land returned to him."

By then, every eye in the place was trained on Matt, who said defiantly, "My pa's land was stolen—"

"Wait one damn minute!" Arnold Cale interrupted angrily. "I conducted that sale. It was legal in every way. I did my best to get word to you when the land reverted to the bank, but you were nowhere to be found."

"You obviously didn't look hard enough."

"I didn't look under rocks if that's your meaning."

Nelson added, "I paid for that land fair and square, as did everyone else that day. If you're willing to believe Ketchum over the banker who conducted the sale, you truly are ignorant."

"And you'll be eating crow when he wins."

Randolph laughed. "Bring your suit and I'll tie you up in court so long my grandsons will be representing my estate before it's over."

Although the matter was a serious one, Spring thought this was better entertainment than the traveling stage shows that came through town every now and again. She glanced at Odell. He whispered, "They should've sold tickets."

She agreed.

As the squabbling continued, Nelson told Jarvis, "If I were you, I'd go back to New York. There's been nothing but trouble since you and this piece of offal—" and he glared directly at Matt "—came to town. First, McCray gets backshot, and then the mill burns down. Coincidence? Maybe. Either way, you need to leave."

Jarvis snapped, "Are you threatening me?"

"No. I'm telling you to go sell your snake oil somewhere else. We'll build our own mill without your help." And with that, he exited.

Cale said, "Your meeting's over, Jarvis. Get the hell out of my bank."

"I'll see you in court."

"I can't wait."

Jarvis glanced around at all the angry faces and apparently realized he had no support. Grim, he and Swan packed up the easel and map along with the stack of brochures, and he and his party left.

Arnold Cale was still fuming when Spring, Odell, and everyone who'd remained exited. Outside, Jarvis and his group could be seen walking swiftly back to Dovie's. Randolph Nelson, watching the retreat angrily, asked Odell and Spring, "Do you believe this?"

"I do," Odell said. "But only because Spring told me Jarvis approached her about selling her land."

"He did?" Randolph asked, sounding surprised. "When was this?"

Spring told him about the visit.

Randolph replied, "So he tried pressuring you first. Did he think you'd quake because you're a woman?"

"I got that impression."

"Then he doesn't know you, does he?"

"No." He wasn't the first man to think her gender was synonymous with weakness.

Nelson asked, "Matt doesn't actually believe that land was stolen from him, does he?"

Spring shrugged.

By then some of the others who'd been at the meeting drifted over and gave their opinions on what had transpired. Spring listened to a bit of it, but McCray, alone in her cabin, was on her mind and she wondered how he was faring. Needing to find out, she offered her goodbyes and rode for home.

In light of the attack on McCray, she kept an eye out as best she could for ambush. That Ketchum had turned what was once an uneventful ride into one that might cost her her life made her curse him inwardly. With any luck, the guilty would be found, tried, and jailed, and things would go back to being slow and peaceful again, but she didn't count on it being anytime soon.

McCray was in bed reading. His smile at her entrance touched her heart in a way that had become familiar as of late. Rather than question or ignore it, she chose to enjoy how it made her feel. He'd come into her life in the middle of a blizzard and proceeded to quietly challenge many things she thought she knew about herself. "Glad to find you in one piece."

"Welcome back. I told you I'd be fine." He set the book aside as she settled into the chair by the bed.

"What are you reading?" she asked. Other than Colt, she knew very few men who read sheerly for pleasure.

"The third installment of Fred Douglass's autobiography. How'd the meeting go?"

She gave him a quick rundown of the events, adding, "And Banker Cale was hopping mad having his integrity questioned."

"What do you think will happen next?"

"I have no idea. I do know that Randolph Nelson isn't going to be bullied by a big-city charlatan who thinks we're a bunch of ignorant small-town rubes. Nelson's wife, Audrey, has ties to people in the territorial government and they might be helpful getting this resolved. Jarvis should probably take Nelson's advice and leave town."

"He's probably not smart enough to do that."

"No. He seems hell-bent on getting his way."

"Are you worried about the lawsuit he's threatening?"

"I'd be naive to say no, but Odell and the others are certain his case won't hold water, so I'm choosing to believe them—at least for now." If she lost her land she wasn't sure what she'd do. More than likely, Odell and Ben would allow her to carve out a small piece from their extensive holdings, but she didn't want to start over someplace else. She'd worked hard to be able to afford the place she now called home, and after a decade of ownership, her roots ran deep.

"As a lawyer, I agree with Odell. If the bank owned the land, Cale had every right to sell it as he saw fit."

"Jarvis disagrees. I have to wonder how long he's known Matt to have put such faith in his side of the story."

"Sounds to me like there's some things we aren't being told."

"Wish we knew what it was so we could send the lot of them packing."

"The truth always rises."

"I'm hoping you're right. In the meantime, I'm hungry. Do you want a sandwich?"

"A few kisses would be better."

Amused by that, she said, "I thought you didn't want to get riled up?"

"I'm willing to risk a little commotion. It's helping me heal."

She laughed softly. "So kisses are medicinal?"

"Yours are."

Leaning close, she brushed her lips over his. "I wish I could give you more . . ."

The kiss was gentle at first, a short whispery reacquaintance that soon bloomed into the desire that had been left to simmer since his attack. They knew there'd be no full expression of their mutual passion, but she savored the tastes of him, the slide of her tongue against the parted corner of his mouth and the heat that slowly rose in her blood. He moved a bent finger teasingly over her nipple, reminding her how much she loved his touch and she murmured, "You really need to hurry up and get well, McCray."

"Open your shirt for me . . ."

Spurred by his tone and the intensity in his eyes, she moved closer to give him access. The slow licks and seductive tugs that followed made her melt and moan softly in pleasure-filled response. Reaching down, she found his hardness hidden beneath the blankets and once again sought his lips. Her hand played, he groaned. He raised his hips for more. Pain instantly tightened his face and his frame. "Too much," he panted.

She stopped. Feeling terrible, she laid her cheek against his brow and felt the slight sheen of perspiration on his skin. "I'm sorry."

"You've nothing to apologize for," he ground out, distress still evident. "Probably should've had the sandwich instead."

Concerned, she caressed his stubble-shrouded cheek. "No more kiss medicine for you."

He gave her a mock pout. "I suppose."

Once his breathing lost its harshness and slowed, she placed a kiss on his cheek. "I'll get your sandwich and make you some tea."

When she returned, Garrett used his left hand to take the small plate from her and set it on his lap.

"Better?" she asked, setting the steaming tea on the nightstand.

Seeing that she hadn't done up all the buttons on her shirt, giving him a partially veiled view of her small breasts, his smile was rueful. "I won't be better until I can show you how much I miss sharing a bed." He was pleased that she'd brought her food in, too, though. He missed her company as much as he did making love to her.

She moved her chair a short distance away from the bed. "I'm going to sit over here so I don't tempt you."

"Especially since your buttons are still undone."

"That's incentive for you to heal up."

With her wit and sass, Garrett thought men should be lined up outside her door for a chance at one of her smiles. Never mind that she'd probably shoot them all first.

Her voice brought him back. "Since we can't discuss or do anything substantial, what shall we talk about?"

Before he could think on that, she said, "I know. Tell me about being in the navy. You're the only sailor I've met."

"What do you want to know?"

"Where you went on the boat. What kind of work you did. That sort of thing."

"I was on a ship called the *Kearsarge*. Ever hear of it?"

She shook her head. "No."

"It was in one of the most famous sea battles of the war, the Battle of Cherbourg."

"Where's that?"

"Off the coast of France in the English Channel. The fight took place in July of sixty-four between our ship and the Confederate war sloop, *Alabama*."

"What were the ships doing in France?"

"The *Alabama* was there looking for a dock to make repairs. It had made a name for itself attacking Union merchant ships all over the world. We were docked in Holland."

"Why were the Rebs attacking merchant ships?"

"To stop the flow of food and supplies into the States mostly. Our navy sent twenty war ships out to capture it, but they weren't successful."

"Why not?"

"It was bigger, faster, and far better armed, but the *Kearsarge* was its equal in terms of size and guns. We were a war sloop, too."

"Was the *Kearsarge* named for someone famous? I've never heard that name before."

"No. It's a mountain in New Hampshire." The confusion and humor on her face made him smile. "I've no idea why the navy named it that."

"Okay, go on."

"When word spread the *Alabama* arrived in France, the French refused to let them dock."

"Why?"

"Because the French supported the Union in Lincoln's war. When our ship arrived three days later, the *Alabama* was anchored in the English Channel and the battle began."

"How long did the fight last?"

"Once we traded gunfire—less than an hour."

She startled. "Really?"

"Yes, the Rebs had been raiding Union merchant ships for almost two years, and after sailing around the Horn to reach France, their crew was tired, the ship needed overhauling, and their gunpowder was stale. A few good blasts from our cannons, and she started taking on water. Sank less than an hour later. Our captain wanted to bring the Reb officers back to the States for trial, but never got the chance because an English ship sitting in the Channel watching the fight rescued the Reb sailors."

"The English didn't turn them over?"

"No. The British supported the Confederacy. In fact, they'd built the *Alabama* for the South."

He then told her about the loss of his friend during the battle. "He was a Colored steward named Charles Foster. Knowing him changed me from an illiterate, shoeless country slave into a seasoned seaman." He quieted, thinking back. "Because of his duties as steward he was allowed to go into the cities where we docked to buy meat and vegetables for the crew, and he'd take me to help carry things back. Tagging along gave me the opportunity to see all kinds of new places and people not only in Europe but in places like the islands of the Caribbean and Cuba. He was also a member of the ship's band. When we were in Cadiz, Spain, he bought instruments: guitars, violins, cellos."

"There were navy bands?"

"Yes, and sometimes there'd be competitions with the bands on other ships. Foster was quite talented and had an excellent singing voice. Everyone thought very highly of him, even the White sailors and officers. When he died in the battle, the entire ship grieved."

"I'm sorry," she said quietly. "How many other Colored sailors were on the ship with you?"

"About fifteen. A couple were freeborn and the stories they shared about their families opened my eyes to the differences between their upbringing and mine. One man from Massachusetts had been a sailor for over thirty years. His family had been whalers since before America broke with Britain. Some of the freeborn had no slaves in their family whatsoever. That shocked me."

"My brother said he met a few men from Howard whose families had never been enslaved. One was a Colored student from Ireland whose mother was Irish and whose father was a Colored English sailor."

"I never knew there were Colored people all over Europe until I became a sailor. Being in the navy also turned me into a reader. A freeborn man named Harris helped me learn, and it was life changing. Once I began I never stopped. I have a book or a newspaper with me wherever I go."

"You said you and your uncle signed up together. Was he on the ship, too?"

"No. He, along with many others, were separated out and sent to fight with one of the USCT units. We were reunited after the surrender."

"Were you and the other sailors treated well?" she asked quietly.

He shrugged. "Sometimes yes, but most times not. Many of the officers were prejudiced. Sometimes the White sailors wouldn't allow us above deck. We kept to ourselves mostly. The only time no one cared about color was during battle."

She nodded understandingly.

"But the most valuable thing I learned in the navy?"

"Was?"

"How to walk in this world as a free man. Like reading, it changed me forever."

AFTER DINNER SPRING left Garrett to his resting and reading, and she took a seat on the front porch to enjoy the evening breeze. She thought back on their conversation about his service in the navy, and for the first time in her life found herself considering what it might be like to travel outside of the Territory. There'd been no interest before. She had her land, her horses, and didn't need more. But listening to Garrett speak about far-flung places like Spain, Holland, and the Caribbean, piqued her curiosity. She'd never seen the ocean, nor a ship large enough to sail on one. What type of food did the people of Cadiz, Spain, eat? What did they wear? Could you hunt elk in the Caribbean? Did herds of wild mustangs run free in Holland or France?

She had no answers. Being around Garrett McCray had altered her thinking about life and her place in it in ways that were new and challenging: from how she defined respect, to what she deserved from a man in bed. In his calm, quiet way he'd changed her, not necessarily into a better person but a different one. She didn't know how he'd magically accomplished this, nor put her finger on when it occurred, but she was not the same woman she'd been before finding him lost in the snow. And for the most part, she was fine with her transformation because it enabled her to open her feelings to him in ways she'd never done with a man before. She enjoyed his company and the ways he made her laugh. He accepted her as she was. Unlike some men in her past, he didn't waste time trying to best her at everything. She'd become accustomed to having him in her life, and she cared about his safety and well-being. It made her wonder if this was love.

Her musing was interrupted by an approaching rider. As he dismounted and made his way to the porch, she recognized him. Zach Hammond. Years ago they'd both worked for Mitch Ketchum, but in the time since, he'd moved away. Tall, gangly, and good-looking, with dark hair and eyes, she'd been sweet on him for a minute or two. He'd married the daughter of a Laramie preacher. Men like him used women like Spring for sport, not to take their name. Truthfully, she hadn't held it against him. She still didn't.

"Hey, Zach."

"Spring."

"What brings you to my door?"

"How've you been?" he asked.

"I'm okay."

She waited while he assessed her.

"You still look good," he said, showing the slow smile her younger self once loved having turned her way.

"How's the wife?" she asked pointedly.

He went red and laughed softly. "You're still hard as nails, Spring. My wife is well."

"Good to hear."

He drew in a deep breath and said, "I have a problem. Actually, Perry has one." Perry was his younger brother. "He wants to claim the reward Doc Lee's wife's offering."

Spring tensed. "Was he involved?"

"Not saying yes, not saying no. But if he was, he wants to tell what he knows secretly."

Spring remembered Perry. He'd been a friend of Matt's, but she hadn't seen him in quite some time. "Does he still live around here?"

"No. Cheyenne."

That confused her. "Why would he be involved?"

"Because he's stupid," he replied, looking and sounding exasperated. "Always has been where Matt's involved. They were good friends growing up. Still are, according to my brother. He said Matt showed up at the saloon in Long Pine, angry about the fight he'd had with your man. Matt was trying to get someone there to help him teach your man a lesson. Perry being Perry, and drunk at the time, was the only one to volunteer."

"And now?"

"His wife's been sick. Real sick. He wants the reward money so he can take her back East to one of the big hospitals. The doctors in Cheyenne say they don't have the skills to treat her."

"Why come to me?"

"The woman putting up the reward is your sister-in-law. You know the sheriff real well. Your man didn't die, so I was hoping you'd see if Perry could come in, point the finger at Matt, and get the reward."

"And he wants to do this anonymously, because he doesn't want to testify publicly?" she asked, making sure she understood.

"He's afraid of Matt."

"But not of his wife dying if she doesn't get treated." It was more statement than question. She also noted Zach hadn't mentioned Perry expressing any remorse for the shooting.

Behind her, she heard Garrett say, "Your brother will have to testify. Publicly. Before a judge."

She swung around to see Garrett standing behind the screen door. Her first instinct was to fuss at him for being out of bed. Making a note to do that later, she did introductions instead. "Zach Hammond. Garrett McCray."

Zach gave a short nod. "Sorry about the shooting."

"I appreciate that," Garrett replied. "Your brother needs a good lawyer."

He sighed. "Not sure how he can pay for one. I certainly can't."

Spring said, "I'll be letting Whit know you came to see me, and that Perry was involved."

"Understood." He stared off into the distance for a few moments before saying, "I've been rescuing him from dumb mistakes since our parents died when we were young, but this . . ." His voice trailed off. He looked to Garrett again. "He won't hang, will he?"

"They didn't kill me, so probably not."

Zach nodded as if finding that reassuring. "My brother said Matt had some back-East fella in a suit with him who was egging him on about getting revenge. A lot of talk about your man not having the right to put his hands on a white man, and that Matt owed it to his race to put McCray in his place. No offense," he said, looking up at Garrett.

"None taken."

Pretty sure the man in the suit was Jarvis, Spring wasn't happy.

Zach said, "Okay, I need to get going. Thanks, McCray. You, too, Spring. I'll talk to Perry and see if I can get him to do what's right. His wife will probably die if he doesn't."

He touched his hat in parting and walked back to his horse.

Spring rose to her feet and said to Garrett, "Finally, some solid evidence."

Garrett nodded as she stepped inside.

"I want to fuss at you for getting out of bed," she said.

"I know, but I heard you talking, and being a nosy reporter, I wanted to know who it was."

She rolled her eyes. "How are you feeling?"

"Like I should've stayed in bed."

A few minutes later he was lying beneath the quilts. "Do you think Hammond will convince his brother to come forward?" he asked.

"I hope so. I'd love to see Matt Ketchum go to jail." Matt's father had always stood between him and punishment. With Mitch dead that wouldn't happen this time.

Garrett quipped, "If times were different I'd be tempted to represent Zach's brother myself, if only to make Matt and Jarvis more furious."

"That would be a nice twist," she said, standing over him. "But now no more playing nosy reporter, or lawyer, Garrett McCray. Rest. Don't make me tie you to the bed."

"I might like that. You could have your way with me."

She snorted and gave him a mock stern look.

He replied, "Okay. Rest."

Still amused, she placed a soft kiss on his brow and left the room.

# Chapter Thirteen

Spring rode into town the next day to talk to Whit about Zach Hammond's visit and found the town abuzz. Dovie had been tied up and robbed by Avery Jarvis in the middle of the night. With him and Hazel and Swan being the only guests at the boardinghouse, she hadn't been found until morning. By then, Jarvis and the others were long gone.

"This happened last night?" a shocked Spring asked Whit as they talked about it in his office.

Lips thinned, he nodded tersely. "Yes. Heath found her on the floor in the kitchen when he came in for breakfast. He said she was furious."

"Was she hurt?"

"Just her pride. She said she woke up with Jarvis pointing a gun in her face. Made her open the strong box and took every dime. Then tied her up. They tied up her boy, too, but he's okay."

Spring was stunned and had so many questions, she didn't know which one to ask first.

Whit, seated at his desk, handed her a flier. "That came through in the mail Odell delivered this morning. Probably the reason they hightailed it out of here."

It was a Wanted poster featuring the drawn face of the man they'd known as Avery Jarvis. His real name was Walter Abner and he was wanted for embezzlement, robbery, and theft by authorities in New York, Cincinnati, Chicago, and St. Louis.

"Busy man," Spring noted as she continued to read.

"Agreed. I sent that on to the sheriff's office in Denver in case they're headed there."

Spring said, "Says here: known to be traveling with his daughter and an unknown man. Seem to be making their way west. So his talk of investing and mills and trees was just a flimflam?"

Whit shrugged. "I heard he managed to convince a few people to invest in the mill he supposedly wanted to build. Their money is probably long gone now."

"Do you think he was tipped off about this poster coming to you?"

"I don't know, but con men and grifters always say they can sense when it's time to pull up stakes and move on, usually one step ahead of the law. Maybe that's what happened here."

Spring had so many questions her head was starting to spin. "So him telling Matt Ketchum the land sale was illegal was just a ploy to get access to the people here so he could rob them? Matt isn't smart enough to have come up with something like this on his own."

"Who knows. There's also the unanswered question of who burned down Porter's mill and why?"

Spring had no answers.

"How's Garrett?" Whit asked.

"Healing." And she told him about Zach Hammond's visit.

"Good news. Not for Perry and Matt though. I'll ride over to the Long Pine Saloon and talk to the bartender. Maybe he can give me names of some of the men there that night who can verify Zach's story. It's a start. Perry's best bet is to turn himself in. He'll be charged and arrested but if he testifies against Matt, the court will probably go easy on him."

"Garrett told Zach the same thing. You'll let me know what you find out in Long Pine?"

"Yes, and I'll be talking to Zach, too."

Satisfied, Spring left.

* * *

OVER THE NEXT week Garrett gradually improved. The laudanum was discontinued. He slept less and ate more. Colt, having returned home, stopped by to evaluate his progress. Pleased with the wounds' healing, he replaced the mummylike wrappings with small cotton bandages attached by plasters.

Spring was pleased by his progress, too. His strength steadily increased, and by his tenth day at her place, he was better able to tend to his own needs like bathing and getting dressed, but still lacked the natural ease of movement he'd had before being shot.

After dinner that evening, they were sitting on her back porch enjoying the quiet of the evening. "I think I should be able to head home in another four or five days."

She turned his way. "Are you sure? You'll have a two-day ride back to Laramie on horseback. Maybe take the stagecoach or hitch a ride with Odell on his wagon when he goes to pick up the mail."

"That's a thought. Both might be less taxing. I'll think about it."

Spring was pleased by his response. The last thing he needed was to set himself back by doing more than he was physically capable of.

"Evening."

She looked over to see her brother walking toward them. She hadn't seen him or Regan in a few days. "Evening, brother. How are you?"

"Doing well. Came to check on my patient and to talk to you about something."

The serious set of his features gave her pause. "Concerning?"

"Ben."

"He isn't dead, is he?"

"No. Not yet."

She searched his face.

"Let me see to Garrett first and we'll talk after."

While the two men went inside, she sat wondering what her brother wanted her to know about Ben.

He returned a short while later and she asked, "How's the patient?"

He sat on the bench beside her. "Almost good as new. He says he's thinking of heading home in a few days."

"Can he handle a two-day trip on the gelding? I suggested he ride over with Odell or take the stagecoach."

"I think he may have less strength than he realizes so I suggested the same."

"So what's this about Ben?"

"He's dying. He has a growth in his upper chest and one on his spine."

Her heart stopped. "How long does he have?"

"Not sure. Could be six weeks, could be six months. You can never tell with these things."

Unsettling emotions filled her.

"Might be time for you two to make amends," he said.

That didn't sit well. "I doubt that his staring at the grave is going to make him apologize to me. When we bury him he'll still believe he was right."

"Then maybe consider forgiving him."

Her eyes narrowed. "Why?"

"For your own peace of mind."

"I'm already at peace," she lied. Probably never would be, but she'd be damned if she'd give him absolution.

"Let go of the past, Spring."

She knew he was trying to be helpful, but it irritated her nonetheless. Setting aside what she'd lived through wasn't something as easily done as dousing a lamp. "Do you know what I had to give Mitch Ketchum in order to work for him?"

He shook his head.

"My virginity."

His eyes widened.

"Imagine an eighteen-year-old child giving up her innocence

so she wouldn't starve to death, brother. Imagine her other choice was to marry an old man three times her age, who also wanted her innocence. Ben was my grandfather. He was supposed to protect me and watch over me when our mother died, but he saw me as a burden. You weren't here and he refused to let me live on my own. Not even wild animals sacrifice their young to the wolves, and you want me to forgive him?"

He whispered, "Oh, Spring."

She wasn't done. "And Mitch let Matt have me when he wanted to. He enjoyed using his fists."

He looked stunned.

"So don't ask me to forgive Ben because I can't."

"I'm sorry I wasn't here to protect you." The sorrow in his voice made her heart ache.

"I don't hold any of this against you, Colton. Please don't think I do. None of it was your fault."

"But—I didn't know, Spring. I'm so sorry."

She was, too. "Go home," she urged softly. "Give my love to Regan and the children."

He rose to his feet but appeared to be searching for a way to offer comfort, so she responded with as much sincerity as she could muster. "I'm fine. Been fine for fifteen years. Don't worry about me."

He didn't appear convinced.

"I'm fine," she echoed. "Go home."

He studied her for a long moment, then turned and left.

In the silence that followed, she heard Garrett quietly step out onto the porch behind her. Fighting her anger and pain, she stood and without turning his way, said, "I'm going for a ride. I'll be back later."

She didn't bother with a saddle. Fitting Cheyenne with a war bridle, she mounted and gave him his head as they galloped away. They finally stopped at a grassy ridge high above the Paradise River, where Spring watched a mama bear and two frolicking cubs take drinks from the water before moving on. An osprey swooped down and grabbed up a fish, and with outstretched wings flapping powerfully, headed back to its nest.

The evening was peaceful, and the quiet surroundings helped soothe her roiled emotions. She'd been coming to this spot since being old enough to ride alone. The first time, she'd been maybe ten summers. Although she had no memory of what sparked that visit, she did remember others: mourning her mother's death, nursing the sadness of Colt's leaving home to attend Howard Medical School. It was here that she'd wrestled with how to get around Ben's intractable decision to marry her off, and where the idea came to her to approach Mitch Ketchum about a job.

She glanced over at Cheyenne feeding on the thick grass and thought back on the different mounts she'd ridden here: a mare named Miss Lizzie, a gelding she'd called Fred, and a filly she'd named Cat's Paw for her white pawlike blaze. So many visits over so many years, and here she sat again.

She knew her revelations to Colt had left him reeling. She hadn't relished causing him so much distress, but he needed to know what she'd faced. For years she wanted to tell him the full story, but the time never seemed right, and coming up with the words had always been beyond her. Now that he was aware, she hoped he better understood why she'd been so wild and reckless when he'd returned to town after his studies back East. Making her body available to Mitch Ketchum killed the young girl their parents had raised, transforming her into a woman who'd felt dead inside, and as a result, every morning, whether rising from her own bunk or a Ketchum's bed, she'd cursed her grandfather.

Down at the river, a small group of elk strode majestically out of the trees. They stopped to scan for danger before lowering their heads to drink. She wondered if they knew how she was supposed to find it in herself to forgive Ben. News that he was facing death didn't bring joy. She'd always believed he'd live forever. And yet, as she'd noted before, long-buried parts of herself still loved him, and she'd mourn his loss. She just wished he'd loved her as much as she had him.

It was dark when she finally rode home. Garrett had left a lamp on in the front room. She extinguished it and headed down the dark hallway to her room. There was a sliver of light beneath his closed door and she supposed he was up reading while waiting for her return. Due to his healing she'd been sleeping in her own room, but tonight she put on her nightgown and went to his. Entering, she saw his surprise and concern as he viewed her in the doorway and set his book aside. Without a word, she crawled into bed beside him and nestled herself gently against his warm length. He draped an arm over her, placed a soft kiss on her brow that almost made her weep, and doused the lamp.

WHEN GARRETT AWAKENED the next morning, he was surprised to find Spring still asleep beside him. Usually after spending the night together she was up and gone before he opened his eyes. He'd been concerned about her when she'd taken off on her stallion yesterday, and wondered if her flight had been tied to the conversation she'd had with her brother. Once the sun set and she still hadn't returned, his concern grew. Reminding himself that she didn't need a keeper, he'd settled into bed with his book on Douglass, and forced himself to read. However, as darkness descended, her whereabouts remained foremost in his mind, along with his worries. Then she appeared in the doorway, dressed in her nightgown, eyes filled with an anguish she'd never displayed before, and he didn't know what to say or do. As she wordlessly slipped into bed with him, he instinctively knew not to pester her with questions. Sorting out the cause of her distress could be dealt with later. He simply held her close until she fell asleep.

And now her eyes were open and holding his. "Good morning," he said.

"Morning," she replied. She sat up and brushed the hair loosened from her braid by sleep away from her face.

"How are you?" he asked.

"Better." And added in a tone filled with sincerity, "Thank you."

He didn't pretend not knowing what she was referencing. "That's what partners are for."

A small smile curved her lips before she said gravely, "My grandfather is dying."

"I'm sorry to hear that."

"I am, too. My brother wants me to forgive him for all he did."

"How do you feel about that?"

"Even if I wanted to forgive him, I don't know how."

"Is that why you took off?"

She nodded. He sensed her sorting through her thoughts, so he remained silent and waited for her to speak again.

"I've shared bits and pieces with you of what happened back then. Can I tell you the whole story?"

"If it will help."

So he listened while she told him everything: what she'd sacrificed to work for Mitch Ketchum, how she'd felt inside, and when she finished her story, he understood. He now had the details he'd been missing; details the sheriff told him weeks ago that were only hers to give, and it left him angry. That she'd shared with him something so personal was also humbling.

She glanced over her shoulder at him. "Regan was the first person I told all this to. My brother didn't know any of it until we talked yesterday. It hurt him a lot, but he needed to know why the idea of forgiving Ben isn't so easy to do."

"Maybe now he has a better understanding."

"I'm sure he does, but it doesn't resolve anything. If anything, Ben should be apologizing to me. I feel as if forgiving him makes me weak, because he's still convinced he was right."

Garrett ran a comforting hand over her back. "No one will

ever accuse you of being weak, Spring. You're incredibly strong to have survived all that. Maybe it might help to look upon forgiving him as another way to show your strength."

"I suppose." But she didn't sound convinced.

Honestly, were he in her shoes, he didn't know if he'd be able to forgive Ben Lee, either.

"What would you do?" she asked.

"It would be hard for me to forgive him, too. Why does your brother think forgiveness is needed?"

"For my peace of mind."

"But you don't agree?"

She dragged her hands down her face. "I don't know. I don't see how it will. I've pretty much resolved myself to what happened and tried to move on with my life."

He watched as she stared off into the distance. After a few more moments of silence he prodded gently, "What are you thinking?"

"About Regan. When she was young, she and her sister were abandoned by their mother. Her sister has never gotten over it, but Regan refuses to wallow. In a way I've bits of both feelings inside. Regan's view is stronger though. Whether I forgive Ben or not won't change my life. I just wish he'd loved me enough to have considered what I wanted. That he refused is the part I'll probably never get over." She quieted again, then said softly, "I've never talked to anyone like this before. Thank you."

He stroked her back again. "I simply listened."

She gave him a ghost of a smile. "One more thing you do well."

He took in the emotion in her eyes and his heart swelled with his love for her, and knowing it wasn't reciprocated didn't change things.

She said, "I'd kiss you, but my mouth probably tastes like the road outside."

He chuckled and ran a finger down her cheek. "Mine is probably the same. You can give me one later."

"Deal," she whispered. After sharing a last long look with

him, she slowly scooted off the bed. "I'm going to wash up and start breakfast. Will flapjacks do you?"

"With bacon?"

"Always bacon."

"Then yes, flapjacks will do me."

She departed.

Alone, Garrett thought back on the small moment they'd just shared. Listening to her bare her soul endeared her to him all the more. He just wished he could somehow shoulder her pain or come up with a solution that helped her with the issue of her grandfather, but neither were possible, mostly because she was accustomed to bearing her burdens alone. He wondered if it was her way of protecting the brokenhearted young girl still inside. He thought about the young boy he carried within himself who'd been shoeless, illiterate, and unaware that the color of his skin was the only reason for his poor station in life; a boy who'd had no dreams. Even now, after seeing the world, having read for the bar, and having the ability to make his own decisions about life, that boy would always remind him of a past he couldn't change, and the quiet rage that still burned because of it.

The flapjacks were made special by the addition to the batter of the last of the blackberries she'd frozen for the winter.

"Where did you get the berries?" he asked as they ate at the table.

"I have a few bushes on the far side of the horse barn. The thorns are awful, but they keep Paint from eating them, so they serve a purpose."

"He's the Palomino?"

"Yes. I haven't introduced you yet, have I?"

"No."

"Then let's do that after we're done here. If the cats are around, you can meet them, too."

He felt very special being given the opportunity to meet the members of her four-legged family, but the introductions were mixed. The playful Paint kept trying to knock him over. The mares, Sunshine and Lady, showed him a small amount of interest and took dried apples from his hand, but the stallion ignored him.

"He ignores everybody," Spring told him. "So don't be offended." She looked over at him. "Is the walking tiring you out?"

"No. I'm not one hundred percent, but moving around feels okay."

"We'll walk slow."

He appreciated her concern.

The next stop was at the barn to meet the cats. The two older females chose not to make an appearance when called, but he did get to meet the kittens and learn their names.

On their way back to the cabin, Odell drove up in his wagon. Garrett now enjoyed the old trapper's visits due to the care he'd been shown after the attack. Odell got down and opened the gate on the wagon bed, calling, "Your ram's ready, Spring!"

Her face lit up and she ran to Odell's side, leaving a confused Garrett behind. Following her to the wagon, he stopped and stared with more confusion at what Odell handed her. It was a tan-colored head of what looked like a sheep with two large curling horns. "What is that?" he asked.

"A mountain goat!" she happily exclaimed, eyeing the thing as if it were made of gold. "Odell, you did a great job! Thank you!"

"Is it a real animal?" Garrett asked.

"Used to be before I stuffed him," Odell replied with a smile. "He's a youngster, though. The big males have horns twice this size. Maybe sometime soon we'll take you up where you can see a herd for yourself."

Garrett thought he might enjoy that. It was certainly unlike any goat he'd ever seen.

"I'm going to mount it above my fireplace," Spring declared proudly.

Garrett had noticed the stuffed animal heads on the wall of the telegraph office, but there hadn't been anything like this one.

Odell said to her, "Sorry it took me so long."

"Don't worry about that. I'm just pleased it's done."

Odell climbed back up to the wagon. "Got some more deliveries to make."

Garrett asked, "Any word from my folks?"

He shook his head. "Sorry, no. I'll let you know when something comes. Promise."

Garrett swallowed his disappointment. "Thanks."

With a wave, he was gone.

Spring said, "Going to hang this right now. Will you take it inside while I get some tools?"

"Sure."

She handed it over and hurried to the barn. He stared down into the glass marble eyes, chuckled at the wonder of the things he'd learned since arriving in Paradise, and carried the goat head into the cabin.

It only took her a short while to mount the thing, and once it was done, they stood back and admired Odell's handiwork.

She said, "It looks good there, don't you think?"

"I do." Admittedly, he'd never considered a stuffed goat's head as essential to a home's decor but it seemed perfect for her cabin. "Where'd Odell get it?"

"From me. I found the goat last autumn. Odell's been working on getting it ready all winter. He likes taxidermy. Even goes to conventions occasionally so he can learn better techniques and talk to folks who love doing these things as much as he does."

Garrett was finding Odell to be a much more layered person than he'd thought when they first met the morning after the snowstorm.

A knock on the door drew their attention. Spring went to answer it and returned with Ed Prescott. He and Garrett exchanged silent nods of greeting before Ed noticed the goat.

"Odell finished it, I see. It looks fine up there, Spring."

"I think so, too. What brings you by?"

"Hands brought in some new ponies and one of the mares is particularly ornery. Need your help calming her down."

"Is she broken yet?"

"No."

Garrett listened while they discussed the mare's size, breed, and how long she'd been in Ed's corral.

Once they were done, Spring said, "Let me get my gear and I'll be there shortly."

"Thanks." He turned to Garrett. "Good to see you're healing up, McCray."

"Thanks."

After Ed's departure, Spring said, "You're welcome to come along if you want."

The idea of watching her work piqued his interest. "I'd like that."

"We may be there a few days, so bring along anything you might need. Ed won't mind putting you up if we do need to stay. He has plenty of room."

"You're sure? I don't want to impose."

"You won't be."

He had many questions about what taming a horse entailed but didn't want to delay their leaving.

As if having peeked inside his mind, she asked, "How many questions am I going to be peppered with about this?"

He laughed. "You know me well."

"I've learned a thing or two about you."

"Like what?"

She moved closer and draped her arms around his waist. Looking up, she said, "You're a real good kisser."

"Am I?"

"Another item on that list of things you do well."

Fueled by how much he adored her, he moved his mouth invitingly against hers. "You did promise me a kiss earlier if I remember correctly."

"And I always pay my debts."

As their lips met and her fiery sweetness spread through his blood, he wanted to be indebted to her forever, so as to spend the next three lifetimes kissing her, making love to her, and being awed by her strength and courage. She was passionate, brave, and would hold his heart forever.

After a few more breath-robbing moments, she slowly drew back and looked up, eyes lidded with passion, and said, "We should stop. Otherwise, Ed won't see us until tomorrow."

He agreed. In spite of his still-healing condition, the urge to take her into the bedroom and satisfy their mutual desire was strong. Instead, he leaned down to enjoy one last kiss. "I'll get my things."

# Chapter Fourteen

Dressed in the leathers she always wore for horse breaking, Spring hitched Lady to the wagon and trailered her stallion and Paint to the bed. Sunrise didn't like crowds, so Spring left her in her stall with enough food and water to last until she returned home. Once all the gear was loaded and she and Garrett took their seats on the leather bench, they got underway. It was a glorious late-afternoon day. The blue sky was dotted with a few puffy clouds, the spring vegetation was in full bloom, and the mountains stood strong and bright in the sunlight. She glanced Garrett's way. He smiled and she replied in kind.

"So how do you tame wild horses?" he asked.

"Depends on the horse and who's taming it. I try and determine who the animal is inside. Being ridden is not their natural state. Ed and I respect that and hope the horse will allow us that privilege. Easier said than done most times though. After being separated from their herd and penned in, many are angry and scared. People would be, too, in that situation, don't you think?"

"When you put it that way, yes."

"We want them tamed, but not necessarily broken in spirit, so we use various ways to earn their trust—providing water, food, bedding down with them at night. Some of the feistier ones may have to be taken to the river and forced to swim until they accept a rider. Others we just let buck us off until they give up, which can sometimes take days. I used to enjoy going head to head with a strong-willed horse, but the older I get the less I like having sore limbs or broken bones."

His eyes shot through with concern.

"I've had a broken collarbone, broken ribs. Had my right arm broken twice. Left only once though."

His shock made her grin. "Pick up your jaw, McCray."

"But—"

Still amused, she cut him off. "I invited you along to watch, not to fuss at me about getting hurt. Odell and my brother think that's their job. More than likely they'll be at Ed's, too."

"Glad someone will be on duty."

She laughed. "I'll be fine, don't worry."

"Too late for that," he grumbled. "But I'll keep it to myself."

Turning her attention back to the road, she found his concern endearing. Only a handful of people cared about her well-being. Now she'd add her nosy newspaper fella to the list. That caring had been shown last night when she returned home and crawled into bed beside him. She'd never sought solace from anyone since going to work for the Ketchums, but in her heart, she knew she'd find it with Garrett. Having him silently pull her close, then place that tender kiss on her brow, put unshed tears in her eyes. And this morning, while she tried to explain the hurt she kept hidden inside, he'd listened without judging. He was a man who did many things well, but most of all he was kind, and again she wondered if this was love. She decided to believe it was.

When they reached Ed's property, Spring wasn't surprised by the wagons and buggies lining the road or the savory scent of roasting pork and beef.

Garrett was, however. "Why are all these people here?"

"It's a small town, and when the main source of entertainment is seeing what's new at Miller's store, horse breaking is exciting."

"Ah," he responded.

Heading towards the outbuildings, she skirted Ed's beautiful home, and past the people milling about, many of whom waved and called out greetings.

Eyeing the fairlike atmosphere, he asked, "How often do you bring horses in?"

"Two, sometimes three times over the course of the spring and summer. Depends on how many orders we receive. Some years it's a few, others more. The army contracts for the most, or at least they did. Now that the tribes are on reservations, they aren't replacing mounts as often."

Finally reaching their destination, she parked and they both climbed down. She undid the lead on Cheyenne and led him to the large fenced-in pasture holding Ed's main herd. Inside were horses of all ages and sizes. Cheyenne immediately let out a bellowing challenge, causing the ears of the others to perk up and people nearby to stop and take notice.

Spring sighed. "Everyone knows you're here, Cheyenne. Behave yourself. No picking fights with the other boys and no mounting the ladies. You hear me? They're Snow's mares, not yours."

Garrett laughed. Cheyenne ignored her and walked into the pen as if he owned each blade of grass.

She had other words for Paint. "Don't eat Ed's fence, and play nice."

He raced into the pen like a child let out of school.

Smiling, she took a moment to scan the area for Ed and spotted his tall, lean presence over by one of the three corrals reserved for the breakings. Upon seeing her, Ed walked over.

"You made it," he said and nodded to Garrett standing at her side.

"We did. How are things going?"

"Not too bad. None of the hands have been seriously hurt, and some of the ponies seem to be settling in."

"How many did you bring in?"

"Eight. Three have already been claimed. You can go over the orders and the books later this evening if you want."

"I do. Now, where's the mare you wanted my help with?"

"Far pen."

In addition to the large pasture where Cheyenne was lording over, there were three small corrals for unbroken newcomers.

"Anyone express an interest in her?"

"Yes, Randolph Nelson's daughter, Cass."

Spring showed her surprise. "Really?" Cassandra was sixteen.

"Yes, he came by earlier to look over the new stock and she was with him. Soon as she saw the mare, she asked him to buy her."

Spring had met her a few times in the past, but only to say hello. Cass was his only child, and Nelson set so much stock in her abilities he'd been training her since she was a little girl to take over the reins of the ranch one day. Spring found that admirable. Others did not. "Is she still here?"

He nodded. "Over by the fence. She hasn't moved since they arrived."

Spring and Garrett walked with Ed to the corral. Spring nodded at the small group of people watching the pacing, restless mustang inside. The mare was a beauty with a dark chestnut coat, a jet-black mane, and a white tail that matched the blaze between her eyes and the stockings on her legs. Spring was a tad jealous that Cass Nelson had already laid claim. Foals sired by Spring's stallion Cheyenne would fetch a pretty penny. Setting that aside, she focused on the mare now racing and rearing in the pen.

"When was the last time someone tried to ride her?"

"About three hours ago. She took a plug out of Elwood's leg and did her best to stomp him to death but he got the hell out of her way."

"That angry, huh?" Spring said, taking in the animal's deep chest and well-formed frame.

"Quite."

"Let me go get Lady and see if she can calm her down."

"Miss Spring?"

Spring turned at the sound of her name and met the shy brown eyes of Cass Nelson.

"I'm Cass Nelson. We met a couple of times when you did some work for my father."

"I remember. I'm hearing you want your pa to buy you that mare."

"I do." Viewing the mare with adoring eyes, she added, "I'm naming her Princess."

Something must have shown on Spring's face because the young woman asked, "You don't like the name?"

"I think she's more a queen than a princess, but you can name her what you want."

Cass studied the mare. "You're right, Queen is better. She's very regal, isn't she?"

"Yes, she is. Is your father here?"

"He left a few hours ago to fetch my mother. He should be on his way back by now."

"Okay. I want to talk to them when he returns. I'll need their permission for you to help me with her."

Her face brightened. "Me?"

"If you're to be her rider, I'd like you to assist with her training. Does that scare you?"

"No!" she said, excitedly. "I'd love to help."

Her eagerness made Spring smile inwardly. "Okay. I'll be back in a moment." Spring turned to Ed. "I'll go get Lady."

Garrett watched Spring hurry off and turned his attention to the surroundings. He was still caught off guard by the number of people in attendance. There were men throwing horseshoes, people lined up for the food being prepared. Children were playing tag and stickball, and the air was filled with the hoots and hollers of those near the corrals watching the ranch hands being tossed off the backs of angry horses. There was nothing like what he was seeing back home where people gathered for church socials, parades, and wedding celebrations. But as Spring explained, people took their entertainment where they found it.

Ed said, "These kinds of events probably don't happen in the District."

"No. We go to the breeder, pick out a mount, and take it home."

Ed smiled.

"Being here is giving me quite an education." Garrett met the man's amused eyes. "I'm a carpenter by trade, and if you wouldn't mind, I'd be real interested in talking to you about the design and construction of your home when you have time. It's one of the most unique places I've ever seen."

"Thanks. I put a lot of work into it. I'm an engineer by trade. Did the design and most of the construction myself."

"Amazing."

"I thought Odell told me you were a lawyer."

"I am, but not real interested in pursuing it as my life's work." Garrett smiled seeing Silas Taylor run past with his dog, Lucky.

"Where'd you train?" Ed asked.

"Howard Law School, and apprenticed with the Colored firm, Whipper, Elliot and Allen." Garrett asked, "Where'd you train for engineering?"

"A college in Minnesota."

Garrett found that surprising. "They allow your people to enroll?"

Ed shook his head. "I told them I was a Spaniard."

His knowing smile made Garrett laugh loudly. "The bamboozling we have to do to live in this country."

"Amen," Ed replied.

They shared a look and Ed stuck out his hand. "Glad to finally talk with you."

Garrett shook. "Same here."

"So what kind of carpentry do you do?"

"Furniture is my specialty."

Ed's surprise was plain. "Really?"

"I put as much heart into my builds as you did your home."

"There's a big demand here. Many of the wives of these rich ranchers would love to contract locally as opposed to dealing with places like Boston or San Francisco. You could make a lot of money if you're good."

"I am."

"After Spring and I get these ponies taken care of, you and I need to talk."

"I'll be all ears."

Spring returned riding Lady bareback. "Ed, can you open the gate, please?"

He complied and Garrett and the other spectators watched as she slowly entered the pen. As Ed closed the gate, the mare reared and let out a vocal challenge but didn't advance from her position on the far side of the enclosure. Spring let the mare get a good long look at her atop Lady before dismounting and climbing the fence to exit.

When she rejoined Garrett, he asked her, "Why'd you leave your horse inside?"

"Lady has a very calm nature. I'm hoping she'll help Cass's Queen not feel so alone, and eventually get her to relax."

Garrett knew nothing about breaking horses, but the strategy made sense.

Spring said to Cass, "Let's leave them together for a little while. Mr. McCray and I are going to see some of the other horses. Hopefully, your parents will have returned by the time we come back."

"Anything you want me to do?"

"Yes. Talk to her, sing to her, call her by her name. Gently though. It's pretty loud out here but horses hear real well, as you probably know. Let's try and get her accustomed to the sound of your voice for now."

"Okay. Thank you, Miss Lee."

"You're welcome."

Garrett and Spring spent the next hour taking in the other pens and the attempts by the ranch hands to tame the wild horses. Garrett winced each time a man was sent flying and hit the ground with a thud, and held his breath as they scrambled to escape the angry hooves. As Spring predicted, her brother was there treating injuries inside a small tent set up on the grounds. Even though Garrett had been advised not to worry about her, he wasn't looking forward to seeing her thrown, and hoped she'd be able to get through the rest of the day without paying Colt a visit.

On the way back to check on Lady and Queen they were stopped by the sheriff.

"Wanted to let you know that Perry Hammond turned himself in this morning and will testify against Matt in exchange for the reward."

Garrett was glad to hear it.

"So what about Matt?" Spring asked.

"He's pulled up stakes. No idea where he is. Landlady says she hasn't seen him in days. Could be he's with Jarvis and his people. Haven't heard anything on them so far either but the Cheyenne marshal has sent warrants as far west as San Francisco. Got my fingers crossed they'll be apprehended soon. In the meantime, I'll keep searching for Matt around here. I also alerted the railroad. The conductors are keeping an eye out in case he tries to buy a ticket."

More positive news, Garrett thought. "So do you think the judge will need my testimony?"

"I spoke with the marshal and he couldn't give me a yes or no. He said the statement you gave me on the shooting may suffice."

Garrett supposed he could live with that as long as Matt was convicted, which was in no way guaranteed considering the uneven justice the nation's courts tended to dispense in cases involving members of the race. The 1857 Supreme Court decision of Dred Scott vs Sanford continued to influence judiciary thinking, and he doubted its ramifications would be banished in his lifetime, if ever.

As the sheriff and Spring discussed where Matt might be, Garrett looked toward the road. Seeing Odell driving up on his wagon made his heart stop. Riding with the old trapper were his parents and sister!

Spring must have sensed the change in him. "What's the matter?"

"My folks!" he exclaimed and hurried to greet them as fast as his injured back allowed.

Spring smiled and stayed where she was, not wanting to butt in on their reunion. Pleased by the surprise and knowing how much seeing them meant to him, she watched for a moment as he embraced his family. Then she gave Whit her thanks for the news on Perry and headed back to the corral. She had a queen to tame.

Randolph and Audrey Nelson were standing by the fence, observing the pacing mare when Spring arrived. Randolph was tall and broad; his wife was short and thin-boned. Cass had inherited his stature and her mother's pretty face and brown eyes, eyes that were focused on the mare.

Nelson greeted Spring with a smile. "Cass said you wanted our permission for her to work with the mare."

"I do. I didn't want to involve her without speaking to you first." She looked to Audrey, one of the few women who'd never crossed the street when encountering Spring in town during her wild days.

"Makes sense to me," Audrey said. "Cass is pretty fearless when it comes to things. In many ways she reminds me of you, Spring."

Surprised by the compliment, Spring was rendered speechless. Cass, standing next to her mother, beamed shyly, as if pleased by the comparison.

"Thank you." Spring finally replied genuinely. Uneasy with the praise, she turned to Cass. "How's your queen doing?"

"Okay, I guess. Putting Lady in with her seems to be helping. She's been standing beside her and Queen hasn't been rearing or charging. Her ears are starting to perk up when I call her name and she looks over at me. I think she may be tired though. I asked Mr. Prescott if we could give her some water. He said to ask you when you returned."

Spring eyed the mare. She was moving slower and having spent the day charging and rearing, water was needed. "Let's get a bucket and see what happens."

After filling a bucket with water from the nearby pump, Spring climbed into the enclosure. Cass handed the bucket to her, and Spring set it on the ground by the fence. Lady immediately came over and Spring spent a few minutes quietly telling her what a good girl she'd been for watching over the mare and gave her a big hug. "Come, let's get you a drink."

Spring had been watching the mare the entire time, who in turn had been watching Spring and Lady.

"Cass, climb in and sit behind the bucket for me, please."

With everyone watching, Cass complied and took a seat.

"Put it as close to you as you can get it."

Once Lady drank her fill and moved off, Spring said to the observers, "I need everyone to be quiet now."

No one made a sound.

"Call your mare, Cass. Let her know you understand how thirsty she is, that you care about her, and whatever else you can think of to entice her. We need her to associate you with her well-being." Willing this to work, she waited.

Cass played her role well. Enticing the mare with words, she also placed her hand in the bucket and held it so the mare could smell the water. Spring was impressed. The mare remained skeptical, however, and kept her distance.

Thirty minutes passed, and as word spread, more people gathered to watch Cass and Queen, including Garrett and his family. Spring acknowledged him but stayed focused on her task. To tempt the mare even more, Ed brought Cass a bucket of feed. He'd purposefully withheld food for this moment, and Cass let the mare see the contents in her outstretched hand.

Lady walked to the feed and helped herself then whinnied to the mare as if to say, "Get over here and eat, little girl."

Everyone noticed the mare's rising interest by the way she kept eyeing what Cass had in her hand, so Spring warned the crowd, "When she does eat, anybody who cheers will have to deal with me. We don't want her spooked after all this." She punctuated the edict with a hard glance.

Finally, an hour after Cass took her seat, the mare walked over and drank from the bucket. Cass cried, and told her how proud she was. She reached out to touch her, but the horse shied and took off, but a moment later, returned for the feed. Spring saw Ed's grin. Audrey Nelson's tears matched her daughter's. Spring was pleased, and by the look on Cass's father's face and the shine of water in his eyes, he was, as well.

After her drink, Queen raced back to her spot on the far side of the pen, but Spring wasn't bothered by that. The mare was beginning to trust Cass. It was the big first step in the many to follow to help the horse and rider become one.

Most of the onlookers drifted away. Ed left to oversee other doings, and the Nelsons followed their daughter to where the mare stood, so she could continue familiarizing Queen to her presence and the sound of her voice. Spring watched for a moment then finally turned to Garrett and his family.

Garrett said, "Spring. I want you to meet my parents, Hiram and Fannie. My sister Melody and family friend Vernon Babcock. This is Spring Lee. Dr. Lee's sister."

"Pleased to meet you," Spring replied.

"What a lovely name," his short, wren-brown mother said, smiling.

"Thank you."

His father, as tall and lean-framed as his son, eyed her and her leather attire questioningly for a silent moment as if not sure what to make of her or what to say. "That was quite a show with the young lady and the mare. Is your family's business horses?"

"No. Just mine."

He cocked his head.

"Ed Prescott and I are business partners," she explained. "This is his spread. We sell wild mustangs."

Fannie said, "How interesting." She turned to Garrett with the same questioning look on her face as her husband's.

Garrett said, "She's a rancher, Mother."

"You own a ranch?" she asked, turning back to Spring.

"Yes, ma'am."

Garrett's father asked, "Along with your husband?"

She shook her head. "I'm not married."

He glanced from her to Garrett. "I see."

Melody, whose bright skin and chestnut hair made Spring wonder if she was mulatto said, "I've never met a lady rancher. Truthfully, I've never met any rancher. Odell said in one of the wires that you've been taking care of Garrett. Thank you for that."

"You're welcome, but the praise should go to my brother, Colton. Were it not for his skill as a doctor, the outcome might not have gone so well."

Vernon, with his well-trimmed beard, whiskers, and costly suit, added, "Then we're glad your brother's doctoring proved helpful. Burying Garrett would have put a damper on the wedding Melody and I have planned."

Melody rolled her eyes. "Nothing is set in stone, Vernon."

Spring found the interaction interesting. She was also aware of Hiram McCray's intense scrutiny. It was difficult to tell what he was thinking, so she decided not to worry over it. Whatever was going through his mind would reveal itself soon enough.

Hiram asked, "Is your brother here? I'm excited to finally meet him."

"He is. He's busy at the moment with the thrown riders, but I'm sure he'll make the time to come and say hello."

"I assume you leave that aspect to the men."

"If you mean the breaking and being thrown parts, no. I do that, as well."

He stiffened with shock. He again turned to the now-amused Garrett who shrugged and said, "Life's different out here, Hiram."

His father was now viewing her as if she'd grown two heads. Unconcerned by that, she asked, "How long do you plan to stay in Paradise?"

"Just long enough for my son to gather his things, so he can return with us."

Garrett didn't seem pleased by the response.

Fannie said, "But for the moment, I just wish to find a place to sit that isn't moving. Between the train, then the stagecoach, and the wagon ride here . . ."

"You can sit at one of the tables over there under the shade," Spring said sympathetically. Ed had a number of trestle tables set up. "There's also food available if you're hungry."

Melody said, "I'm starving."

"Then let's find a spot and get you all something to eat."

As they walked, Spring noticed Garrett gently stretching his shoulders and back. "Are you okay?"

"Just a little stiff."

His father asked with concern, "Are you certain you don't need more medical attention? We can probably find another doctor in one of the bigger cities."

Hearing that, Spring was offended on her brother's behalf.

Garrett replied plainly, "I'm fine. Dr. Lee is a superior physician. I owe him my life."

His mother rubbed his forearm comfortingly and asked, "Have the villains been found?"

He told her the news Whit shared earlier.

Melody said, "That's good."

Garrett added, "The sheriff is hoping to find Matt Ketchum soon."

"I hope so, too," his father said. "Seems like a pretty lawless place."

Spring took offense again but remained silent.

Garrett didn't. "I'm fairly sure more people are attacked in the District than here."

Hiram grumbled, "If you say so."

On the way to the table they stopped by the food station run by Chauncey Miller's wife, Lacy, and Lucretia Watson and filled their plates with pieces of roasted chicken, slices of beef, vegetables, and biscuits. They then took seats at a table with enough free space to accommodate them, and the visitors sighed with relief.

"I'm exhausted," Melody admitted. "Garrett, you're never allowed to travel this far from home ever again."

"Understood," he replied, smiling.

Fannie noted that Spring hadn't gotten a plate. "Are you not hungry, Spring?"

"I'll eat later. If I have to help with one of the mustangs, it's better if my stomach is empty."

"Oh."

Vernon glanced up from his plate. "You're just pulling our leg about riding those bucking horses, right?"

"As Garrett said earlier, life here is different."

Hiram asked, "Do other women do what you do?"

"I'm sure there are some in other places, but around here, I'm the only one."

Spring turned to Garrett. "I see where you get all your question asking."

He chuckled. "They're just as impressed by you as I was when we met."

Hiram said, "My son said in one of his letters that you met in a snowstorm?"

"Yes. Came across him in the middle of a blizzard."

Garrett said, "The Lee family has kept me alive three times now. Her grandfather Ben found me in the road after I'd been shot, and took me to Dr. Lee's office. I'm forever in their debt."

Spring met the sincerity in his gaze and saw his mother watching them for a moment before she returned to her plate of food.

A few moments later Spring noticed Colt coming their way

across the grass. He was wearing the black suit he always favored and she realized it had been quite some time since she'd seen him in anything else. His legendary devotion to caring for people was honorable but she worried that he never seemed to rest. "Here comes my brother now."

Hiram hastily wiped his mouth with his napkin. He'd removed his brown suitcoat earlier due to the warm day, but now put it back on. Watching him brushing himself off and straightening his vest as if he were about to meet royalty was amusing, but she was pleased by the show of respect.

Colt nodded Garrett's way when he reached the table. "Odell said your folks were here. I wanted to come say hello."

Garrett did the introductions.

"Pleased to meet you all," Colt responded. "And Mr. McCray, it was an honor to be interviewed by Garrett for your newspaper."

"People back East need to know about you, and I can't thank you enough for saving his life."

"You're welcome. Things like that rarely happen here, but I'm glad to have helped."

"Is he fit to travel? I'd like to return home as soon as possible. He's enjoyed himself here, but his true place is back East."

Garrett's jaw tightened. Colt's eyes glanced at Spring's. She kept her face blank.

"He and I have discussed his options," Colt replied. "He's free to share them with you at his convenience."

Spring noted how gracefully her brother avoided Hiram's trap. Garrett was a grown man, yet his father acted as though his son had no say in his own future. Did the man always ride roughshod over the lives of his children? Did they object? Her thoughts were interrupted by her brother saying, "Spring. Odell had to leave. He's asked if you could take Garrett's visitors back to town when they're ready. They're staying at the boardinghouse."

The request caught her off guard because she'd planned

to help Ed with the mustangs all day, but she answered, "Of course."

"Good. Thanks. You folks enjoy your stay. Nice meeting you." With that, he departed.

Watching him walk away, Melody asked, "How many doctors are there here?"

"He's the only one in Paradise," Spring replied.

"The whites don't mind him treating them?"

"Some do, but most don't. He's held in pretty high regard."

Hiram said, "That's good to hear."

They'd just finished their meal when an unhappy-looking Ed rode up on his white stallion, Snow. Behind him were Cheyenne and Paint on a lead.

Spring stood. "What's wrong?"

"Take your children home."

"Jesus and three fishes," she snarled with frustration. "What did they do?"

"Cheyenne keeps challenging the young stallions and Paint is running amok. As always. Between them they have the whole herd riled up."

She dropped her head. "I'm so sorry."

"We probably won't need you for the rest of the day anyway. Helping Cass and her mare was my biggest concern. Thanks for working with them."

"You're welcome."

Spring saw the visitors eyeing him. "Have you met Garrett's family?"

"No. But I heard they were here. I'm Ed Prescott."

Garrett introduced them, and Ed nodded in response. "I hope you'll enjoy your stay."

They nodded and stared, but Ed didn't seem bothered by it. "Spring, if I need your help tomorrow I'll send one of the hands over to let you know. Here are the ledgers." He handed her the leather pouch he'd placed them in.

"I'll check the numbers tonight."

"Thanks. Nice meeting you folks." He touched his hat and rode away.

Hiram said, "Not to be disrespectful, but is he a foreigner?"

"No. He's a member of the Bannock tribe."

Melody asked, sounding confused, "Tribe?"

"He's what people back East call an Indian," Garrett replied.

Vernon smirked. "What's he call himself?"

"Ed," Spring said coolly.

He seemed startled by the tone of her reply and the harshness in her glare.

Garrett added, "This is his land. That beautiful house on the hill? He built it. He's an engineer."

Vernon scoffed. "You don't actually believe that, do you? Everyone knows they're savages."

Garrett snapped, "Some people view our race the same way. Are they correct?"

"Of course not."

Spring wanted to rip out his heart. "My grandmother was Shoshone. How about you walk back to town? I'm sure you don't want to ride in the wagon of a savage."

Seeing all the angry eyes trained his way, he swallowed visibly. "My apologies for speaking out of turn."

"Keep your bigotry to yourself." She turned to the others. "I'll be back with the wagon."

She stalked off and her horses followed.

# Chapter Fifteen

Spring's temper was still simmering when she ushered her visitors inside her cabin. She'd stopped there first to change clothes before driving into town. They glanced around the cabin's small interior and silently took seats. Hiram stared at the stuffed head above the fireplace and asked. "What is that?"

"A mountain goat," she said. "There are herds of them here. This one had been caught in a rockslide and was buried from the shoulders down when I came across it. I dug it out hoping it could get back on its feet but the back legs were broken. The bleating was terrible."

"Poor thing," Fannie whispered.

"It was in a lot of pain, and wasn't going to survive, so I showed it the mercy it deserved and took the carcass back to town—"

"You killed it?" Hiram asked, interrupting.

"Yes. Otherwise, it would've taken days for it to starve to death, and no animal or person should endure that."

He studied her for a long moment before saying, "I suppose you're right."

Spring knew she was right, and because he was Garrett's father she didn't allow her irritation to rise and take hold. She was already mad enough at Vernon. "We respect life here in the mountains, Mr. McCray. Anyone coming across an injured animal beyond help will do just as I did. You don't do them a favor by allowing them to die in pain or from starvation."

He nodded tersely. "I understand. It's just women back East wouldn't consider doing such a thing."

Spring said, "You aren't back East, sir."

Fannie smiled. "Touché!"

Her husband grumbled a bit but had nothing further to say, which suited Spring just fine. She glanced Garrett's way and saw his chilly eyes focused on his father.

Melody was at the window looking out. "I can't get over the beauty of these mountains."

"I know. I enjoy waking up to them each morning. If you'll excuse me for a few minutes, I need to change clothes before I take you to town. This leather is pretty warm."

Fannie said, "Take your time."

"Thanks."

Spring noticed Vernon watching her. There was a veiled anger in his eyes but she ignored it and him as she left the room.

After her departure, Hiram said, "Garrett, I see your books and journal on the table there. Are you living here?"

Garrett expected the blunt question. The unexpected part was that his father had waited until after Spring's exit. "She and Odell moved me here so I could sleep and heal in a bed. After the surgery I was sleeping on a cot in Dr. Lee's office that was as uncomfortable as a floor."

"The woman at the boardinghouse said you'd rented a room. Why weren't you taken back there?"

"Because Dr. Lee was called away on an emergency, and the boardinghouse proprietress, Dovie, has enough to do without having to deal with a bedridden man. Spring volunteered to take me in." He knew this wouldn't be the only thing his father would want to know, and at some point Garrett would have to remind him that he was fully grown and no longer subject to his authority.

His mother said, "Miss Lee seems very unconventional."

"Is that a compliment?" Garrett asked.

"Truthfully? I'd have to know her better to be certain, but I believe it is."

He could always count on his mother to be fair-minded. "She's quite a force, Mama. I've never met anyone like her."

The next question came from Melody. "Do many of the women here dress the way she does? In trousers? I saw a few at Mr. Prescott's place."

"A few, yes. Spring's a rancher. She can't do the work that needs to be done in a gown."

Vernon asked, "So she really isn't married?"

"No."

"A widow?"

"No. She's never been married."

Hiram huffed. "The way she carries herself, I see why not."

The statement raised Garrett's ire. "Meaning?"

"What man would want a woman who wears trousers, and boasts of killing sheep, or goats—whatever that thing is?" he said, pointing to the stuffed head over the fireplace. "Men of our class prefer someone with the elegance and grace of say an Emily Stanton."

Garrett offered a bitter chuckle. "I'm not marrying Emily, Hiram."

"You certainly aren't marrying Miss Lee."

"She wouldn't have me if I asked."

Sounding puzzled, his mother asked, "Why not?"

"She doesn't plan to marry anyone. She's content with her land and her horses."

Fannie eyed him as if attempting to gauge his feelings on Spring's stance before replying, "That's her choice, I suppose."

Vernon said importantly, "Every woman wants a husband."

Melody chimed in, "Emily doesn't."

"Emily will do what her parents decide is best," her father countered. "As will you."

Resentment flashed over Melody's features before she turned back to the view through the window.

Garrett knew that at some point he'd have to talk to his father about forcing his sister to marry. Vernon was a lawyer, a member of the city's elite, and fit the mold of what Hiram viewed as her ideal mate. But in talking with her, Garrett knew she had no tender feelings for the man. She'd always tried to please their parents, especially Hiram. Garrett thought it stemmed from the fealty she believed she owed him for claiming her as his daughter, in spite of being sired by the brother of Fannie's master. Melody had been a year old when their family reunited after Freedom.

His father said, "Back to the question of returning home. When will you be ready?"

"Whenever you are, but I'll only be returning to put my affairs in order. I'm coming back. I'm planning to purchase some land and live here permanently."

His mother looked stricken. Melody turned from the window in surprise. His father, features tight, asked, "Is it the woman?"

Garrett replied honestly, "Partially yes, but mainly, I've enjoyed being here. The pace, the people, this way of life suits me."

"You almost lost your life," his father pointed out.

"True, but this is where I prefer to be."

"A future with Emily would be far more advantageous to you in the long run."

Garrett had no plans to argue. He knew how much it upset his mother when they did, so he said simply, "My mind's made up."

Melody asked, "How will you make your living?"

"Ed Prescott thinks my furniture-making skills will be in demand." Ignoring his father's sullen face, he added, "There's always a call for carpentry. I'll be fine."

Spring returned a few moments later. She'd traded her leather pants and vest for a pair of denims and one of the numerous men's shirts she tended to favor. "Are we ready to leave for town?"

They were, and followed her out to the wagon. Fannie and Melody joined her on the bench while the three males climbed into the bed.

As they got underway, Hiram asked Garrett, "She always wear that gun belt?"

"Always."

Vernon asked, "Do you plan to do the same once you move here?"

"I do. I'm probably the only person around who doesn't carry a Colt or a rifle. Spring carries both."

"I don't like her," Vernon noted. "Too unnatural."

"She doesn't care for you, either," Garrett tossed back. "Too bigoted."

A small smile curved his father's lips. Pleased by that, Garrett settled in for the drive.

As they entered town, his father said, "I can't get over how small and quiet this place is. No crowds or streetcars. No vendors on the streets."

Garrett understood. "Took me some time to get accustomed to it, too, but the silence grows on you. At least it has on me."

His father added, "Moving here will mean turning your back on Quincy and all he's done for you by taking you under his wing and teaching you carpentry."

Garrett wanted to roll his eyes. "Your brother has always encouraged me to be my own man. I know I'll miss him, but I also know he'll support my decision. And who knows, once I tell him about the wealth of trees here, he may want to pull up stakes and join me. Maybe establish his own carpentry business here."

The wagon pulled to a stop in front of the boardinghouse. Once everyone climbed down Garrett said to them, "I'll join you inside shortly."

Fannie and Melody called out their goodbyes to Spring. Hiram offered her his thanks for driving them, but Vernon climbed to the porch and entered without a word.

Once Garrett and Spring were alone, she told him, "If your folks ever visit again, make sure they leave Vernon at home."

"I promise." Thoughts of Vernon were immediately eclipsed

by the knowledge that he'd be leaving town soon and it came with a sadness that he felt in his bones. That the separation would be temporary only helped a little bit. "We'll probably be leaving the day after tomorrow."

She nodded tightly and there was sadness in her eyes, too.

He added, "I'll spend most of tomorrow with them, but I'd like to spend my last night here with you."

"I'd like that."

"We probably won't get much sleep though."

She chuckled. "Probably not. Let's hope you don't hurt yourself."

"If I do, I'll have a cross-country train ride to heal up." His love for her was also bone deep.

For a moment neither spoke; they simply drank in each other with their eyes. She finally said, "I should probably get going. I'll look forward to seeing you tomorrow."

"Same here."

"Your father's head will probably explode if he sees us, but I need a goodbye kiss, McCray."

"I thought you'd never ask."

She leaned down and the kiss they shared was as sweet with longing as it was tender. It exuded the sadness of the looming separation, but their mutual passion fed the bond they'd built. When it ended, he ran a caressing finger over the soft skin of her cheek. "Be careful going home. I'll see you tomorrow evening."

"I will. I think I'm in love with you."

His mouth dropped. Before he could respond verbally, she shot him a wink and drove off.

Outdone, he yelled, "Spring! Get back here!"

He heard her laughter as the wagon rolled away.

Watching the wagon disappear from sight, surprise and elation filled him. They had a lot to discuss tomorrow, including the way her parting words stunned him like being kicked in the chest by a mule. Ignoring the few people standing in front of Miller's General Store eyeing him oddly, he ascended the steps of the boardinghouse as if floating on air. Smiling, he opened the door and went inside.

His father sat alone in the dining room and upon seeing Garrett's face asked, "What's happened?"

"Nothing," Garrett replied, tamping down the glee brought on by Spring's startling declaration. "I thought you'd be upstairs resting after all you've done today."

"I'll do that in a moment. Wanted to speak with you first. Is there somewhere more private we can sit?"

Garrett sighed. He'd had enough of his father for the day but wanted Hiram to get whatever it was he had off his chest now rather than later. "There are chairs out back. We can talk there."

Outside, they took seats in the old armchairs set in a cleared portion of the grassy field. It was early evening and the sun was making its way across the snowcapped mountains. Hiram said, "I have to admit the scenery is outstanding."

"Glad we can agree on something."

His father smiled before asking with serious curiosity, "Why her, Garrett?"

He shrugged in response. "From the moment we met, something about her settled into me that I can't dislodge." He again told the story of his rescue. "I'd've probably died had she not come along during that storm."

"So your life's been in danger twice since you arrived, and you still want to live here?"

"I do."

"Makes no sense."

"It doesn't have to, does it?"

"I suppose not. but you'd be better off back home where you aren't in danger of being killed by blizzards or guns. Tell me about the ambush."

So for the next little while they talked about his fight with Matt Ketchum on the night of the Cale party.

The telling left his father both angry and afraid for him. "I appreciate you coming to Miss Lee's aid, but men of the race have been killed for less, Garrett."

"True, but the color of his skin doesn't allow Ketchum to spit in my face."

"I've endured more."

"I understand, but when do we reach the point of saying: No more?"

His father didn't respond.

Had the country wanted him to remain subservient, it should never have let him enlist in the navy. Being able to see the world and the possibilities it held as a free man had removed the scales from his eyes. "Although the law may never reflect it, we are not less in any way, and I refuse to believe that I am simply because others do."

"You're right, and that fire you have inside would be good in a courtroom."

"And more than likely get me killed. I don't have the desire nor the patience to argue laws that only one race has to abide by. There are men back East far more skilled at that than I."

"So you want to move here."

"I do, and no disrespect but this is my life, not yours."

There was sadness on Hiram's face as he looked out into the field. "Forgive an old man for wanting his son by his side so that he knows he'll be safe." He met Garrett's eyes. "The thought of you being here and out of my sight is something I'm having trouble with."

"Why?" Garrett asked softly. "We were apart when I went into the navy."

"But I knew Quincy would keep you safe. I suppose this need to hold on to you is tied to our being slaves. I was sold as a babe, and to this day have no idea who my parents are. When you were small and it looked like you'd grow up to be big and strong like me, I did everything in my power to keep you from being sold. Men of our stature were worth small fortunes on the block. When it became certain that Master McCray was going broke, he wanted to sell you, but I begged him not to sell us separately. I took on work in his fields hoping to help increase his profits. Fannie volunteered to be auctioned off if it meant you and I could stay together."

Garrett never knew that. His heart ached.

"Neither of us wanted our only child to grow up and not be raised by at least one of us, so you'd know how much you were loved. I've watched over you, guided you, comforted you from the nightmares you had after Fannie was sold. I know you're a grown man, Garrett, but turning you loose is difficult."

"You raised me well, Hiram, and I will never not appreciate your love and care. I'm going to move here, but I will visit, write—send you wires. You aren't losing me. Please don't think that you are."

"My head knows that but my heart . . ."

"And please don't force Melody to marry someone she has no feelings for just because you want status."

Hiram sighed. "All my life I've wanted to be more. To be recognized as something other than how I'm defined. Is it so wrong to want that for my daughter?"

"You and Mama love each other. Melody should have a chance at that, as well, not be with a man she has no feelings for simply because he's wealthy. Why did you even bring him along?"

"He loaned me the money for the train tickets. The hotel where I work is being renovated and will be closed for the next few months. They're paying me a small portion of my salary until it reopens but it isn't enough for extras like train tickets. I'll repay him when I go back to work."

"Loan or no loan, Vernon proved today he's not worthy to be her husband, and she doesn't deserve to be unhappy for the rest of her life." He wanted to tell him about Spring and her grandfather but had no right to share her painful story without her consent.

"The bigotry was surprising."

"As was Spring's restraint."

His father searched his face. "You love her, don't you?"

"I do. Probably from the moment she shook me awake and threatened to feed me to a bear if I ruined her new sofa."

His father stared.

"Long story. I'll share it with you some other time. How's the paper? Were the subscribers pleased with the installments about Dr. Lee?"

"They were, but it's no more."

Garrett was taken aback. "Why?"

"It was another of the extras I can no longer afford. Do I buy ink or do your mother and I have food on the table?"

He understood. "I'm sorry to hear that. Will you start up again when the hotel opens?"

"I don't know. We'll see."

He knew how much the newspaper meant to him and hoped he'd be able to print it again. "You should go get some rest."

He nodded and asked, "Is there any chance you'll change your mind about moving here?"

"No."

He sighed with surrender. "Okay. I suppose I'll have to live with that. And so you'll know, your mother isn't keen on me deciding who Melody will marry, either."

"Good for her."

His father smiled. "I'm surprised she still loves an old fool like me."

"Me, too."

"Watch it. You're not that grown."

They laughed and stood.

Hiram viewed him affectionately. "Are you too grown to hug your old father?"

"Never."

The embrace was as strong as their bond. He was glad they'd had the opportunity to talk and were now moving forward. As they parted, Hiram said, "Convince Miss Lee to marry you, so I can hold a freeborn McCray babe in my arms."

Garrett wanted that, as well. Freeborn children meant the

world to families that had only known enslavement. "I'll see what I can do."

"Good."

They left the chairs and returned to the boardinghouse.

SPRING ARRIVED HOME still smiling at Garrett's reaction to her revelation. Having come to the conclusion that she did indeed care for him in a way that had to be love, and spring it on him as a surprise, made the moment memorable. Her humor deflated seeing her grandfather seated atop his old wagon.

Sighing, she parked and walked over to him. "What can I do for you, Ben?"

Clad in the worn, shaggy buffalo coat he wore no matter the weather, he asked, "Did your brother tell you I'm dying?"

"He did. I was sorry to get the news."

"I'm leaving you everything I own."

She stared. "Why?"

"Who else is there? Your brother's already married to Queen Midas and doesn't need my money. Odell will be joining me in the grave soon. So, you're it. All my land, mining interests, water rights, gold, back-East investments, and the rest. Had a lawyer do up the papers. They're in a deposit box at the bank."

"I don't want it."

"I don't care, and if you're dumb enough not to take it so you can have a better life, shame on you."

"Do you hear me? I don't want it."

"Did you hear me? I don't care."

He slapped the reins down on the backs of his mules and the rickety old wagon rambled off.

Snarling, she watched him go.

She walked into her cabin wanting to punch something. Instead, she made coffee. When it was done, she carried her cup of the brew outside and sat on the back porch. That he would leave her everything was not something she'd expected. Granted, she could use the financial boon because for the past few years poverty had been pinching her like a pair of too-small boots. With profits down from the horse business, she'd have no hogs to slaughter and sell this autumn. There was no extra money to purchase piglets, let alone the feed necessary to raise them and fatten them up.

But considering her anger at Ben, would accepting make her a hypocrite? She hadn't asked him to leave her anything, so did that make a difference? She didn't know. She'd had no idea his holdings were so vast. Saying yes would potentially make her a pretty wealthy woman. A part of her hoped he'd come to his senses and change his mind so the matter would be out of her hands, but there was little chance of that occurring. Once Ben set a course there was no going back. His decision that placed her eighteen-year-old self on the path that would become her life stood as testament to his stubborn resolve. She wondered if this was his way of apologizing. He certainly owed her something for putting her through hell, and as he'd plainly stated, she'd be dumb to turn down a gift that would make life easier. Outside of nuns, priests, and Jesuits, no one in their right mind chose to be poor, not even hypocrites.

After going back inside, she washed her cup and set it on the counter. The cabin interior echoed with silence. In the past, it had been companionable. Now something seemed missing and that something was Garrett. His presence drifted in the air like an unseen spirit, as if the cabin had become his, as well. It was an odd sensation, but not an unpleasant one. She felt that if she went to his room and knocked on the door, he'd set aside his book and respond. He'd been a constant companion lately, her partner, and she'd grown accustomed to having him near. In a few days he'd be returning to the place he called home, yet, during the past few weeks, she'd come to consider this cabin his home. They'd shared meals, conversation, passion, and she admitted that in the back of her mind, she worried he'd go back East and decide not to return. If so, she'd mourn what might have been then retrain herself in how to be a woman alone. For the moment, however, she looked forward to tomorrow evening and the night they planned to share.

Later, as she prepared for bed, she opened the door to his room and looked inside. Most of his belongings were still there. In a corner by the wardrobe were the new boots he'd been unable to remove on his own the day she rescued him from the storm, and the memory of that encounter evoked a soft smile. Who knew he'd work his way into her life and heart so effortlessly, and that she'd be changed as a result? Her eyes lingered on the bed. Some women might be comforted by sleeping in their love's bed while he was away, but Spring thought that pretty sappy—she hadn't been changed that much. After closing the door, she walked through the silence to her own room.

# Chapter Sixteen

The following morning Spring knew she'd spend the day pacing and making herself loco while waiting for Garrett to arrive, so she ate breakfast and rode over to see Regan to pass some of the time.

"I'm in love," Spring confessed.

Holding the baby, Regan got up from her sofa, walked to the closest window, and looked out.

"What are you doing?"

"Trying to see the pigs flying around."

Spring shot her a look and laughed. "I will hurt you, you know."

Regan grinned and retook her seat. "No, you won't. Congratulations on finding someone who fills you heart."

"It wasn't my intention."

"Love has a way of finding us anyway. Especially when we're not looking. Have you told him?"

"I have." Spring described the moment.

"That was so wrong but so perfect."

"I know." She could still hear Garrett yell, "Spring! Get back here!"

She spent the next few minutes telling Regan about meeting Garrett's family, and Vernon's reaction to Ed Prescott.

Displeased, Regan said, "Let Melody know we don't marry bigots in this family."

"My feelings exactly. I understand that newspapers back East don't paint a true picture of the tribes, but we were on Ed's land. Vernon had seen that beautiful house, the horses, and still called him a savage."

"You wanted to do him bodily harm, I take it."

"Very much so." And she still did.

Regan looked down at Colton Fontaine and said quietly, "He's asleep. Let me put him in the crib."

When she returned, she said, "Colt said you told him the full story about working for Mitch Ketchum."

"I did. He wants me to forgive Ben, so he needed to know the truth." She'd shared the details with Regan right after she became Colt's wife.

Regan said softly, "I've never seen your brother cry, Spring, but he did when we spoke about it. He thinks he failed you."

Emotion clogged Spring's throat. "I told him it wasn't his fault."

"I did, too, but he was heartbroken and angry at himself for suggesting you hold out the olive branch to Ben."

Spring supposed she and her brother would need to discuss it further. The last thing she wanted was for him to berate himself for something he played no part in. "Ben told me he's leaving me everything after his death."

Regan looked surprised.

"I don't want anything from him, and I think accepting this inheritance will make me feel like a hypocrite."

Regan scoffed. "Please, don't be ridiculous. Take whatever he gives you, so you can stop robbing Peter to pay Paul. If Ben's trying to buy his way into heaven, fine. But accepting doesn't make you a hypocrite. I've been dirt poor and wealthy. Wealthy is better."

Spring loved her so much.

"Besides, you need that money to buy hogs so I can have my bacon."

Amused, Spring hung her head.

Regan added, "And, I'm still upset with you for not letting me help you financially."

"I know."

"Sisters help each other, Spring. You can't eat pride."

Regan was right, but accepting help in any form was difficult, even when necessary as it had been earlier in the year when she offered the means to buy the piglets and feed Spring needed.

Regan said sincerely, "I don't like knowing you're going without, Spring. Neither does Colt."

Spring's tight nod conveyed she understood. As she'd noted before, only a small handful of people cared whether she lived or died, and Regan Carmichael Lee was at the top of the list. She had to learn to do better and accept that care in the spirit it was given because it was so rare in her life.

They talked for a while longer about Ben's gift and the things she might do with the money, the reward claimed by Perry, and speculated on where Matt Ketchum might be.

Regan said, "Colt was part of a posse that went out with Whit last evening. Somebody thought they spotted Matt up by Eagle Point. Whit said some of the summer cabins near there had been broken into. He thinks Matt may be the culprit."

"The posse find anything?"

"No, but Whit was going back up there this morning."

Eagle Point was not far from Spring's battered old cabin. The land around it was owned by her grandfather and named for the many eagles nesting there due to its proximity to the Paradise River. The area was densely wooded, but many spots offered great hunting and spectacular views of the mountains. The rich from back East were beginning to build summer cabins there.

The loud cries of the now-awake Colton Fontaine signaled an end to the sisters-in-law's visit, so they both stood. They'd discussed Garrett's departure, and as they shared a parting hug, Regan said, "Give Garrett my goodbyes, and prayers that he and the family have a safe journey."

"I will."

"And, Spring, try not to hurt the man tonight, you hear?"

Chuckling, she replied, "I'll do my best is all I can promise."

SPRING SPENT THE rest of the day seeing to her horses and the newly emerging shoots in her garden, then made bread for dinner. With no idea what time Garrett would be arriving she wasn't sure if she should cook dinner for just herself or for him, too. In the end, she pulled two steaks from the last of the ice in her outbuilding and took a bath while they thawed. After the bath she went through her wardrobe in search of something special to wear. The only fancy items inside were the gown she'd worn to the Cale dinner, and the burgundy off-shoulder beauty she'd worn to Regan and Colt's wedding. She wanted the evening to be special. The burgundy was jaw-dropping gorgeous, so she chose it.

The clock in the kitchen showed the time to be just past six when a knock sounded on the door. Letting her excitement have its head, she went to answer, and there stood Garrett. As if the evening was special to him, as well, he'd worn his brown suit. He ran his eyes over her in the gown and said, "Trying to kill me before I even step inside, are you?"

"I can take it off, if you want."

Eyes locked on hers, he replied, "That'll be my job."

She stepped back to let him enter, and as he did, he eased her close and greeted her with a kiss that turned her legs to sand. The kiss was a masterful combination of heat and rising desire. Leaving her lips, he kissed his way down her throat to the bared scented skin above the low-cut top of the gown. Hands filled with the rustling burgundy silk covering her hips, he fit her possessively against his hardness. "Feel what you do to me."

She ran an equally possessive hand over his length, savoring the power her body had over his and the growl he uttered in response to her caresses. "Dinner's ready. Do you want to eat first?"

"Yes." He pushed the top of the gown aside and took a bare nipple in his mouth. Her grin slid into a high-pitched croon that ruffled the silence. He feasted and lust sparked in her blood like tiny lightning bolts. Exposing the other breast, he helped himself. Her head dropped back and the world went hazy.

Moving his lips to her ear, he whispered, "Go over to your fancy couch, raise this fancy dress, and spread your gorgeous legs—wide. You owe me for saying you love me and then driving away."

Heat, hot as the desert sun, rushed through her. Undaunted, she ran her hand over his hardness and boldly undid the buttons on the placard of his trousers. Freeing him from his inner clothing, she wrapped her fingers around his strong, warm girth, asking teasingly, "Am I being punished?"

Eyes closed, and rising to her wicked ministrations, he replied, "In the best way, but only if I don't die first."

Smiling, she walked to the sofa, turned to face him, and slowly raised the yards of burgundy silk to her waist. Gaze locked with his, she paused to let him see she was wearing nothing beneath but her stockings and rhinestone-studded garters. He stroked himself in reaction, whispering, "Scandalous woman."

She made herself comfortable and spread her legs. "Wide enough?"

"Wider."

The lust in the room and in his voice was thick. She complied, then slid a finger between her damp folds. "You've made me very wet, Garrett McCray. Come look and see."

"I prefer to come lick and see."

Spring shivered with the promise he exuded. "You're way too good at this."

"Part of the art."

"One day you'll have to tell me where you learned this."

He knelt in front of her, gently fit her hips in his hands, and eased her closer to the sofa's edge. "A gentleman never tells."

After gifting her with a long kiss, he ran his hands languidly up and down her firm thighs before placing his lips gently against each sparkling garter. "You ready to take your punishment?" He slipped a finger into her core and then a second. She tightened and moaned. "Yes."

And he began with touches and licks and a magic display of art that soon had her hips rising. He feasted; she gasped passionately. He told her all the wicked things he had in store for later, and she was certain she'd die from the pleasuring. It didn't take long for her orgasm to build and rise inside like a sensual mountain. He made her mindless, whimper, grab his head, twist and turn, and when he gave her a tiny but fiery little bite on the nub at the apex of her thighs, the mountain shattered and she screamed his name loud enough to be heard by the stars in the night sky.

Driven by their rising passion, they made love all over the cabin; on her dining table, in the tub where they'd gone to clean up, and then in his bed. And for each encounter Spring used her sponges. As they lay together by the light of the turned-down lamp in the aftermath of yet another round, he said softly, "If I was a wealthy man, I'd give you rubies to thread in your hair. Put diamonds on each fingertip and garnets on your toes." Swirling his finger lightly over her navel, he murmured, "And here, I'd put a sapphire."

Spring's heart soared in response to his tender words.

"I'd drape you in jewels, because you are my jewel, Spring Rain."

She whispered, "You don't have to say those kinds of things to me, Garrett."

"They're not to you. They're for me. It's how I feel. It's a declaration, a statement, a truth."

His eyes met hers in the glow of the lamp. "You are diamond-hard in mind and spirit. You glow inside with the fire of rubies. And you're as vibrant as a sapphire when we make love."

He eased her closer so that her back was against his chest,

then draped an arm over her waist as he placed a kiss against the edge of her shoulder. "I want you with me always, Spring. I want to wake up each morning and see your smile. I want to hunt with you and fish with you. I want to have babies with you that are freeborn instead of slavery-born like I was. Little Springs who ride horses—"

Spring eased away from his arms and sat up. She glanced over her shoulder at him then away.

"What's wrong?" he asked.

Her heart aching, she knew they had to discuss this, so she said, "I don't want children, Garrett."

He sat up. She looked back and saw the confusion filling his features.

"What do you mean?" he asked. "Are you saying you can't?"

She shook her head. "I don't want children. I never have."

"But—"

"I love you very much, but I'm not going to give you those freeborn babies, and I won't apologize for being who I am, or change my mind."

He searched her face for a long moment then fell back onto the mattress like a sail losing its wind.

In the thick silence that followed, she sat there for a few moments, waiting to see if he had anything else to say, but he didn't speak. Resigned, she stood, left the room, and closed the door behind her.

GARRETT AWAKENED IN the dark early hours before dawn to the sound of heavy rain pelting the roof and windows. Not happy at the prospect of having to ride to town in a downpour, he nevertheless got up. He had a train to catch.

He wanted to speak with Spring first though. He'd lain awake most of the night thinking about her revelation. He'd felt gutted, still did, but didn't want to leave with them at odds. Tired and bleary from too little sleep, he took care of his morning needs, got dressed, and went to her room. The door was closed so he knocked softly. When no response came he knocked again, this time more firmly. Nothing. Concerned, he eased the door open just wide enough to peek inside and was met by the perfectly made up bed but no Spring. He listened for her moving around in the front room. Getting a bad feeling he went to the kitchen and found it just as empty and silent. Frantic, he called her name, then grabbed his slicker from the peg and ran through the cold rain to the barn. Paint, Lady, and Sunrise were in their stalls but the stallion wasn't. She was gone. Where to, he didn't know, but sensed it had to do with last night. Disheartened, he returned to the cabin. Only then did he see the folded piece of paper on the dining table. His name was printed on the front side. Picking it up, he read:

*I didn't want say goodbye. Thank you for loving me and showing me that I can love in return. Have a safe trip home. Spring.*

Filled with emotion, he debated whether or not to stay and wait for her to return but he didn't know how long that might be or if she'd be happy to find him there when she did come home. He kicked himself for not talking to her last night before she slipped out of the room, but he didn't know what to say. Still didn't. So he packed up his belongings. Before leaving, he tore a sheet of paper from his journal and wrote her a note in reply. He placed it solemnly in the spot on the table where his had been. With that done, he took one last look around the place that had come to be home, filled himself up with the memories he'd made, and stepped out into the rain for the cold, wet ride back to town.

Up on the ridge, protected from the weather by her slicker and flat-crowned hat, Spring watched the watery dawn try and pinken the slate-gray sky. She supposed Garrett was gone by now and she could return home. She'd had too many conflicting emotions to pretend things were okay while wishing him a cheery goodbye, so she'd left. She hoped he found her note though. It said all she needed to say. They'd had a good time as partners, and she'd remember him fondly, but she didn't think he'd be coming back to Paradise.

When she returned home, she checked the table where she'd left the note and was surprised to see a different one in its place. Taking a deep breath, she picked it up, unfolded it, and read: *Until the mountains are no more I will love you. G.*

Spring prided herself on being someone who never cried but his words made her drop into the nearest chair and weep.

On the train ride East, Garrett did his best to hide his misery. It didn't help that they were forced to ride Jim Crow out of Cheyenne. Vernon, who apparently had never traveled far from the District, was outraged when the conductor directed them to the gambling car.

"I want to speak to whomever is in charge!" he'd demanded.

"I'm in charge," the man responded. "So, take yourself to the gambling car with the rest of your kind. Or get off the train."

That left the light-skinned lawyer red faced and sputtering. Melody finally hooked her arm in his and led him away. "Come on. We'll be fine."

Now, a day and a half out of Cheyenne, Garrett sat in one of the booths by the window watching the train take him farther and farther away from Spring, while cigar-smoking gamblers suckered rubes out of their meager funds, and rouged up good-time girls promised quick delights on the small platform outside the car—for a price.

His mother had asked after him when he'd met them at the boardinghouse on the morning they'd left Paradise, but he told her he was fine. He knew she hadn't believed him, but she hadn't pressed for the truth.

Now, as she came to sit opposite him, she eyed him with concern. "What's going on with you, Garrett?"

"I'm fine."

"Don't lie to your mother," she said with gentle humor. "The Good Lord doesn't like it."

He smiled and sighed. "Just need to figure some things out."

"Such as?"

He didn't respond.

She did, saying, "A mother's job is to be nosy, so tell me what's wrong or I'll have your father be nosy on my behalf."

"Lord, help me."

She folded her hands. "I'm waiting."

"I love Spring very much, but she doesn't want children."

"And?"

He was confused. "But I do."

"Then let Spring go, and find a woman who wants what you want. Simple solution."

"But—"

"Is she willing to change her mind?"

"She said no." And he searched for the words to convey his thoughts. "I've never met a woman who didn't want children."

"There are plenty, believe me. Some of whom have given birth only because of the expectations of society and husbands."

"But think of how wonderful it will be to hold the family's first freeborn child."

"That will be a joyful occasion, but that child will apparently not come from you and Spring, Garrett."

He gazed unseeing out at the passing landscape.

His mother asked, "Suppose she was unable to have children. Would you be so at sixes and sevens over that?"

He thought about it and admitted, "Probably not." And had a small clarifying moment. "I never thought about it in those terms."

"You may want to. Ask yourself, do you want Spring because you love her or because of her potential to breed?"

"Because I love her."

"Then you have your answer."

And he did.

The next day when the train pulled into the station in Omaha, Nebraska, Garrett gathered his belongings and prepared to tell his family goodbye. He'd return East before the trees turned in autumn but now he had to return to Spring and set things straight with her. His father wanted to contest the decision but his mother gave him her blessings. Garrett hugged Melody and while doing so whispered that she find someone she actually loved and invited her to come to Wyoming when she had the chance. As for Vernon, Garrett thanked him for footing the bill for the train tickets and vowed to help Hiram reimburse him as soon as possible.

And with that, Garrett left the train. Luckily for him, a train heading west was leaving within the hour. According to the conductor, they'd pull into Cheyenne in three maybe four days, depending on variables like weather and track conditions. He sent a hasty wire to Odell to meet him in Cheyenne but to not let Spring know. He feared she'd take off again and it would be winter before they had a chance to speak.

As the train with his parents continued its journey east, Garrett's westbound train left the station at the same time—and he didn't have to ride Jim Crow. On the empty seat beside him was a day-old Chicago newspaper someone had left behind. Leafing through it, some familiar faces caught his attention and he smiled reading the caption beneath: *Dastardly embezzlement gang jailed for attempted robbery.* "I hope they lock you up and lose the key, Mr. Avery Jarvis, or whatever your real name turns out to be." He placed the newspaper in his bag to show to Paradise sheriff Whit Lambert in case he hadn't been informed.

# Chapter Seventeen

Spring spent the first two days after Garrett's departure feeling sad and miserable. The nonstop rain only added more gloom to her mood. Being able to leave the house might have helped her not think about him so much, but because she was stuck inside, his presence came to mind relentlessly. She thought about him at breakfast, when she had her coffee, changing the bedding in his room, and of course every time her eyes settled on her sofa.

On day three, she woke up to sunshine and shouted for joy. Deciding she'd go up to the ridge and maybe do some fishing, she hitched Lady to the wagon and swung by Colt's place first to speak with Regan. She was hoping her sister-in-law had advice on how to stop thinking about Garrett McCray.

Regan greeted her arrival with a smile.

Not seeing her nephew, Spring asked, "Is Colt Fontaine asleep?"

"No. He's in the baby jail."

Spring stared then laughed. "The what?"

"Baby jail. Come see."

In the parlor on the floor was a fairly large polished wooden box with slats on the sides. It looked like a fancy crate. Strung across the open top was a length of ribbon. Dangling from it were colorful tops, little wooden horses, and other small toys. Inside, lying on his back atop a thick pallet was the smiling giggling baby. "My sister, Portia, sent it. It's really called a playpen but she calls it a baby jail. Keeps them in one spot while you get things done. Best gift she ever sent." She turned from the jail to ask, "So how did your night with Garrett go? Did you hurt him so bad that he's still in bed?"

"It went well until he mentioned wanting freeborn babies."

Regan's humor faded. "Oh dear."

"I told him the truth. I don't want children. He didn't have much to say after that. The next morning I went up to the ridge before he got up, so I didn't have to say goodbye. I couldn't, Regan."

"I'm so sorry, Spring."

Spring shrugged. "Not happy with this falling-in-love thing. It hurts. Any idea how to make it stop or to stop thinking about him?"

Regan shook her head. "No. Did he say he wasn't coming back?"

"No." Spring didn't mention the note. The wording was too personal to share, even with Regan. "I didn't think there'd be a magic solution but I wanted to check with you just to make sure."

"Only time passing will heal things."

"While I wait for that, I'm going fishing. Do you want some if I catch any?"

"Yes, please. That would be wonderful."

"Okay." Spring walked over to the baby jail and reached down to give her nephew an affectionate auntie cheek pinch. "No breaking out, you hear?"

He giggled and waved his chubby little arms and legs. Spring smiled in response before turning to Regan. "I'll be back later."

"Okay."

SPRING CAUGHT A mess of fish. After stringing them to a line, she thought she'd make a quick climb up the ridge to take a look at her place. As old and broken down as it was it held nothing of value—there wasn't even a sleeping bag inside, but she hadn't been up there in a while, and wanted to make sure no vermin or varmints had taken up residence. She took the fish with her because if she left the string on the wagon, the local eagles would treat it as a free meal and fly off with them. She had a barrel to put them in but if any nosy bears came around, they'd see it as a free meal, too. With the fish in tow, she took the narrow trail up the mountain. It was heavily wooded on both sides with a variety of old-growth trees, chest-high shrubs, and tree roots the size of her grandfather's arms. Maybe when she inherited Ben's gifts, she'd get someone to build her a real hunting cabin to take the place of her old ramshackle one.

When she reached the listing place with its partially missing roof, she opened the door and met the smug eyes of Matt Ketchum and the business end of a Colt pointed her way. "Well, well, well. I wondered how long I'd have to wait for you to show up."

She immediately threw the string of fish at him, and as he fumbled, she ran outside and slammed the door. Bullets rang out, shattering the old wood. Bent low, she kept moving. If she could make it back down the hill to her wagon, she might stand a chance.

"Get back here, you bitch!"

Another bullet cracked loud. Squawking birds took flight while she did her best not to trip over tree roots or lose an eye to the low-hanging branches whipping against her face as she ran. A quick touch to her face showed blood on her fingers. She kept running. He was crashing through the vegetation behind her. All the noise and commotion would draw curious predators; bears, cats, wolves, but the two-legged one was her main concern. Heart pumping, she slid on her butt down the rest of the hill and upon hitting flat ground, increased her speed to get to the wagon. It was a risky move, because he'd have a clear shot now, but if she could reach the wagon and use it for cover she could return fire. She drew her gun out of her holster but before she could turn, her leg exploded. She cried out in pain, clutched the leg just long enough to confirm she'd been shot.

"Drop the gun or I'll put a bullet in your other leg."

She glanced up to see him closing the distance between them. He was only a few feet away, still coming and grinning.

"Drop the gun! Now!"

Tossing her gun aside, she faced him. Her leg was on fire. Putting weight on it only increased the pain.

He came close and said, "Women like you is only good on her knees, so kneel, bitch."

"And men like you are only good for shooting people in the back, fucking coward!"

Red with fury, he backhanded her. The force knocked her to the ground. Standing over her, he sneered. "I've hated you for a long time, and do you know why?"

She didn't and didn't care. She dragged the back of her hand across her bleeding lip.

"I hated you because my father called you a better man than me. Said your rode better, roped better. Wished his son had half your balls."

Smiling, she asked, "Do you know who else is a better man than you? Him." And she pointed at her grandfather approaching Matt like a stalking grizzly.

Eyes wide, Matt emptied his Colt's last few bullets into Ben's buffalo coat-covered chest, but the old mountain man didn't slow. Matt turned to run. Ben's hunting knife flew from his hand and the gleaming blade hit the back of Matt's thigh like a lightning bolt from the heavens. Matt screamed and fell. Ben reached down, raised him to his feet, and said, "See you in hell."

He snapped Matt's neck and tossed him aside. It happened so quickly, it took her a moment to process what she'd seen. She looked up into Ben's feral eyes only to watch him slowly drop to his knees. Alarmed and recalling the bullets he'd taken, she crawled to his side. "Are you hurt?"

He was by then stretched out on the ground. She opened his coat and all the blood covering his chest scared her. "We have to get you to Colt."

He pushed her hands away. "I'm going to die, so let me do it here. I'd rather go out this way than by a disease that'll leave me good for nothing but shitting on myself."

"You are not going to die."

"Sure I am. Tell Odell to burn me. You take my ashes up to Eagle Point and put me in the wind. That way I can sleep with the mountains."

Frantic, she looked around for a way to save him. "Don't you dare die on me, old man! We have things to settle."

"Too late, Little Rain. I did you wrong but look how strong and brave it made you. Tell Colt I said goodbye."

And he slipped away.

"No!" she screamed, and the pain in it echoed across the stillness. Holding and rocking his body against hers, she wept.

IT'S SAID THAT in times of great stress the human body is capable of amazing feats. Spring was unable to recall how she got her grandfather's body into the bed of the wagon, but somehow she did.

Driving slowly into town, dirty, bleeding, and shot, she pulled back on the reins in front of Colt's office and a crowd of people ran to her aid.

Later in Colt's office, as he removed the bullet from her leg, she distracted herself from the painful process by telling the story of what happened.

"Where's Matt's body?" Whit asked when she was done. Odell was there, too.

"On the ground where Ben tossed him."

He sighed. "I'll get Lyman Beck and bring his remains back to town."

Spring hoped scavenging predators had dragged him into the brush to feast, but she kept that to herself. "I should've been able to do something to keep Ben alive until I got him here."

Colt shook his head. "There was no way he could've survived those wounds. You did your best, Spring. Don't beat yourself up, please. I'm just glad Matt didn't hurt you any more than he did."

She was, too. Had Ben not shown up . . . She forced her mind away from what might have been. She glanced down at the bandage around her leg. Colt had cut off one side of her denims from the knee down in order to get at the bullet. "Can I go home?"

"Only if you promise to rest and stay off that leg for the next few days."

She looked at him as if that was the dumbest thing she'd ever heard him say, but she said, "Okay."

Odell said, "I'll bring you food from Dovie so you'll eat and not have to worry about cooking for yourself."

"Thanks."

"I'll also drive you home. You ready?"

She nodded and said to Colt, "Tell Regan I lost all the fish."

He smiled. "I will."

She leaned over and kissed his cheek. "Thanks for patching me up."

"Anytime."

He loaned her a pair of crutches and she managed to leave the office and climb onto the bed of Odell's wagon. The bed of hers needed a good scrubbing to rid it of Ben's blood. Odell volunteered to take care of that for her, as well.

When she got home, she and her crutches hobbled slowly into the house. She was exhausted. She sat on the bed and fell back onto the mattress.

He asked, "You sure you'll be okay here by yourself?"

"I will. Just come check on me in the morning."

"Will do."

She sat up again. "I wanted to resolve our problems and now, we never will."

"I know, but he gave his life for you. That has to mean something."

"True." And it did. She owed him her life for the rest of her life.

"I'm going to miss him a lot. We've been blood brothers almost sixty years." There were tears in his eyes. "Going to get drunk, but I'll be back to see you in the morning. Give me a hug, then you go to sleep."

They shared a strong hug and she kissed his whiskered cheek. "I'm sorry for the loss of your friend," she whispered.

"So am I." He wiped his eyes. "I'll make you some bark tea and head back to town. Do you need anything else?"

She shook her head. "I'll probably be asleep by the time the water boils so go on and leave. I can heat water when I wake up."

"You sure?"

"Positive."

He kissed her cheek. "Get some rest."

She nodded and was asleep before he drove away.

WHEN SHE AWAKENED later it was night. She thought it odd that the lamp on her nightstand was lit because she didn't remember it being that way when she went to sleep. She then decided she must be dreaming because Garrett was seated in the chair by the fireplace. He set his book aside and asked, "How are you feeling?"

Confused beyond measure, she countered, "What are you doing here? Why aren't you with your family?"

"Left the train in Omaha and came back."

"Why?"

"To tell you I love you, and that if you don't want children I won't love you less. To hope you'll overlook me being a ham-handed rube for my backward thinking and forgive me and let me love you until the mountains are no more."

Her heart soared. "That's certainly a long list."

"I know. I can probably add more if you need me to."

"Maybe later." She studied him. "You aren't saying all that hoping I'll change my mind sometime in the future?"

"No. I meant every word." And he added, softly, "I don't care if we marry or not, but I want to grow old with you, Spring. You and I. Partners."

Moved by that, she whispered, "You're a very special man, Garrett McCray."

"And I love a very special woman."

"Can you add one more thing to that long list?"

"Sure."

"Will you heat some water and make me some bark tea? My leg hurts like hell."

He smiled. "Be right back."

He walked to the door.

"Garrett."

He turned.

"I'm glad you're back. I've missed you terribly."

He gave her a wink and left the room.

Alone, Spring wiped at her wet eyes. She'd cried more in the past week than she had in years, but she felt no shame. She now had her land, her horses, and a man who loved her for herself. He even made tea. She was content.

# Author's Note

A few years ago, as I traveled around the country in support of Regan's book, *Tempest,* many readers pleaded for Spring to have her own book. You were intrigued by Dr. Colton Lee's sister, Spring Rain, and I must agree, I was, too. I loved writing her story and having her fill in the parts about herself I didn't know. She's bold and fierce, and my tribute to those women who prefer to be child free. Garrett McCray was fun to write, too. He doesn't have a lot of swagger nor the overwhelming personality displayed by some of the men in my previous books. Instead, he's sweet, kind, and yes, bookish, but loves Spring deeply. In romance, we call a man like Garrett a cinnamon roll. He's probably the first cinnamon roll hero I've written. I hope you enjoyed him as much as Spring did.

Back when Garrett attended Howard, the U.S. had no real standards for becoming a lawyer. Men and women did what was called read for the law. It was usually a years long study of English law books under the supervision of experienced lawyers. A small number of U.S. jurisdictions still permit this practice today. A budding Black law student like Garrett may have been taken under the wing of Macon Bolling Allen. His firm of Whipper, Elliot and Allen was one of the first Black law firms in the nation.

When studies are done on the contribution of African Americans to the Civil War, most of the scholarship focuses on the role played by the 179,000 United States Colored Troops (USCT). Less attention has been given to the 19,000 Black sailors of the Union Navy.

For an in-depth look at these brave men, please check out this outstanding article from the National Archives: www.archives.gov/publications/prologue/2001/fall/black-sailors-1.html.

Another great resource that delves into the history of Black seamen is *Black Jacks: African American Seamen in the Age of Sail* by W. Jeffrey Bolster. Also see: *The Negro in the Civil War* by Benjamin Quarles.

The history of Black newspapers is not well known outside of academia, but during the years between the 1827 birth of the first Black edited paper, *Freedom's Journal,* and the end of the 19th century there were over 500 nationwide. Most were sundown papers like the one owned by Garrett's father, and others only published for a short while. But they were all dedicated to being true voices for the race, especially during the rise of Jim Crow. For more info on these newspapers and their editors, please see: *The Black Press 1827-1890,* edited by Martin E. Dann. See also: *A History of the Black Press* by Armistead S. Pride and Clint C Wilson.

In closing, let me thank my publisher, Avon Books, my editor, and my agent. My biggest thanks go out to you, dear readers, for your love and support. There will be one more book in the Women Who Dare series. At this point, I have no idea who she will be, but I'm looking forward to meeting her. In the meantime, happy reading. See you next time.

Sincerely,
B

Did you miss the origin of
Regan and Colt's romance? Then turn
the page for a taste of

# TEMPEST

Available now!

# Chapter One

*Wyoming Territory*
*Spring 1885*

Regan Carmichael was tired of riding in the stagecoach. The beauty of the Wyoming countryside with its trees and snow-topped mountains had been thrilling to view at first, but after traveling for three long days in a cramped coach that seemingly had no springs, she longed for the journey to Paradise, Wyoming, to end. Even her excitement at meeting the man she'd come to marry had been dulled by the lengthy trek, and she was certain her bottom would bear bruises for the rest of her days. Her mood was further challenged by having ridden the past day and a half alone. She did enjoy no longer being squashed between the other passengers who'd since departed, but missed the conversations they'd shared. Up top, sat the driver, Mr. Denby, and the guard, Mr. Casey, who due to their duties had no time to lighten her boredom with conversation. The wheels hit another rut on the uneven road causing her to bounce, land hard on the thin leather seat, and her poor sore bottom wailed again.

That it might be months before she saw her family again temporarily took her mind off the uncomfortable ride. She began missing them the moment she boarded the train in Tucson. Her

Aunt Eddy and Uncle Rhine. Her dear sister, Portia. The last time she'd been away from home for more than an extended period had been during her studies at Oberlin College, but unlike then Regan wouldn't be returning home. This would be the start of a new life in a place she knew little about other than it was mostly wild and untamed, the two largest cities were Laramie and Cheyenne, cattle raising reigned supreme, and women were given the right to vote in 1869; a national first.

Suddenly, the coach picked up speed. Mr. Denby could be heard hoarsely urging the horses to run faster. Concerned, she quickly pushed aside the leather window shade and looked out. Three men wearing bandanas over their faces were riding hard in their wake. Mr. Casey began firing his shotgun, and the riders, swiftly closing in on the coach, returned fire. Regan snatched up her own Winchester, tore down the shade, and added her weapon to the fray. Seconds later, she no longer heard the shotgun from above.

"Mr. Denby! Are you two okay?" she shouted.

"No! Keep shooting, miss!"

He didn't have to tell her twice.

The outlaws were nearly on them. Even though the careening pitch of the coach played havoc with her aim, she managed to hit the nearest rider, which made him drop the reins, grab his arm, and slump forward in pain. His partner rode past him and positioned himself adjacent to the coach. He took aim at the uncovered window but Regan was already squeezing the trigger on the rapid-fire rifle. The cartridges exploded in his chest and he tumbled backwards off his mount.

The coach thundered on.

The third hombre must have realized the odds weren't in his favor. A grim Regan watched him grab the reins of the riderless horse. He and the slumped man she'd shot in the arm rode back the way they'd come. Whether the one they left behind was dead, she didn't know.

Breathing harshly and shaking, she fell back against the

seat. Only then did she acknowledge how terrified she'd been. Her roiling stomach made her think she might be sick, but she thanked her recently deceased neighbor, Mr. Blanchard, for his rifle lessons. Shoot first, puke later! he'd told the then eleven-year-old Regan and her older sister, Portia. The memory made her smile and she drew in a deep breath that calmed her frayed nerves.

The coach slowed, then stopped. When the door opened, an alarmed Regan grabbed the Winchester. It was the driver, Mr. Denby. For a moment, he stared at her in awe.

"That was some mighty good shooting, miss. Wasn't expecting that—not with you all fancy dressed the way you are."

Regan silently acknowledged the compliment. "Are you and Mr. Casey all right?"

"No. Casey's heart gave out. He's dead."

"Oh no! I'm so sorry."

"I'd be dead, too, if it hadn't been for you. Do you mind riding up top with me so I can put his body in the coach?"

"Of course not."

With her help, Casey's body was placed on the seat. After handing Denby her rifle, she hiked up the skirt of her fancy blue traveling ensemble and climbed the large front wheel to the seat.

"You do that like you've been climbing wagons all your life."

"I have. I drove the mail back home in Arizona Territory."

He chuckled. "Really?"

She nodded.

"You here to visit family?"

"No. I'm a mail-order bride. The man's name is Dr. Colton Lee."

Denby began coughing.

"What's wrong?"

"Nothing. Just a tickle in my throat. Let's get going. We should make it to Paradise before sunset."

He got the horses moving but Regan swore the coughing fit

must've meant something else because when she glanced his way, Denby was smiling.

Before they'd gone another mile, she spied another group of men riding hard in their direction. This time there were no bandanas and their open dusters were flapping like birds of prey. She grabbed her rifle and took aim. "I think the man that got away has returned with friends. You keep driving, I'll try and hold them off."

He let out a curse and slapped the reins down on the horses' backs. The coach picked up speed, but she could tell by the rate they were moving that the poor beasts were tired. "How many men?" Denby yelled. He was unable to see the riders from his seat.

"Eight!" Regan knew there was no way she'd be able to hold her own against so many armed men. She was terrified, but as they got within range she steadied her aim and fired repeatedly. There were three men riding point. She hit one in the shoulder, but apparently, the bullet only grazed him because he slapped a hand over the injury and kept riding. They began returning fire but she realized they were firing in the air. They'd also halted their mounts. Curious, but not drawing down, she waited over her pounding heart.

"What's the matter?" Denby asked.

"They've stopped."

He pulled back on the reins to halt the coach and stood up cautiously. After assessing the riders, he waved his arms as if signaling them and asked her, "Did that rifle of yours hit anybody?"

"I caught the one in the black duster in the shoulder. Why? Do you know them?"

"Yep. It's the sheriff, Whit Lambert."

Her eyes widened. "I shot the sheriff?"

"No, ma'am. The man in the black duster is Doc Lee. You just plugged your soon-to-be husband." And by his chuckles, he apparently found that humorous.

Regan was mortified.

The sheriff and his men approached on mounts held to a walk. Regan couldn't take her eyes off the grim ebony face of the man she'd come to marry. He was tall and lean and sat his big bay stallion proudly. A mustache accented his tersely set mouth. A close-cropped beard dusted his jaw. She was pleased to finally put a face to the man she'd been corresponding with for the past few months, but her main concern was how he'd react upon learning who'd shot him. Regan also noted belatedly that the men who'd attacked the coach were also with the sheriff's posse. Their hands were cuffed and neither looked happy about being apprehended. She assumed the body lying across the back of a black horse was the one she'd shot in the chest.

"Sorry about the shooting, Sheriff," Denby called out. "We thought you were part of the gang that rode down on us earlier. She really didn't mean to shoot the doc."

The tall auburn-haired sheriff appeared as confused by Regan's presence as the men of the posse seemed to be. "You were the one shooting at us, ma'am?"

"Yes."

"I'm Sheriff Whitman Lambert. And you are?"

Drawing in a nervous breath, she gave the doctor a hasty glance. "Regan Carmichael."

The doctor's dark gaze flew to hers. "I'm truly sorry," she replied guiltily.

The sheriff turned to the doctor and although his barely veiled amusement mirrored the reactions of the other posse members, the doctor's jaw was tight with displeasure.

She felt terrible.

"Where's Casey?" the sheriff asked Denby.

"Inside on the seat. He's dead. I think his heart gave out during the gun fight earlier."

The doctor dismounted, wincing a bit as he moved and entered the coach.

"Was it those two?" Lambert asked, pointing to the sullen, dirty-faced outlaws.

"Their faces were covered," Regan replied, "but I believe so. I hit one in the arm and another in the chest."

"That's him back there," he said, indicating the lifeless body. He viewed her with the same wonderment Mr. Denby had earlier.

Denby came to her defense. "You aren't going to charge her, are you? Had it not been for her, I'd probably be dead as Casey. The stage line will probably give her a reward for helping keep the gold I'm carrying safe."

Regan knew stage lines sometimes did such things, but she didn't need rewarding for protecting herself. She was a woman. Had the outlaws taken the coach, she might have been prey to an unspeakable assault and they may have discovered the large amount of gold coins sewn into the hems of her gowns. She took no joy in having caused the man's death and if she was charged, she knew her Uncle Rhine would provide her the best lawyer his money could buy.

The doctor exited the coach. Ignoring her, he gave the sheriff a terse nod, as if verifying Mr. Casey's demise, before haltingly climbing back into the saddle. His stilted movements made her believe his injury was more serious than the simple graze she'd assumed earlier. Again, she felt awful.

The sheriff said, "You won't be charged, Miss Carmichael, but they will. They've been ambushing coaches up and down this trail for weeks. In fact, they took down a coach earlier today. The driver and guard were wounded and we were out looking for them when we came across them after you and Denby sent them skedaddling. Thank you for your help."

"You're welcome." She was relieved, but so far, Colton Lee had yet to speak to her directly. And as the sheriff and his men escorted the coach the remaining few miles to town, that didn't change.

"STOP LAUGHING AND take the damn bullet out," Colt snarled, removing his shirt. The last thing he needed was more of Whit's needling.

"Got yourself quite the delicate bride-to-be there, Dr. Lee. Hold still." Whit used the tip of his big bladed knife to expertly dig into Colt's shoulder, causing him to hiss out a curse in response to the sharp pain.

"Got it." The bloody bullet went into a chipped porcelain basin on the desk. Whit sloshed whiskey over the oozing injury. Colton hissed again and immediately reached for the clean square of white cotton sheeting he'd taken from his medical bag and pressed it against the wound to ease the bleeding.

"Want me to ask her in to sew you up?"

Colton glared.

"Just asking. No need to get surly."

Colt knew Whit was having a good time. Were the shoe on the other foot, he'd be the one poking fun, but it was on his foot and it pinched like hell. What kind of woman shot her intended? Yes, it was an accident but his pride was as wounded as his shoulder.

Whit added, "If you're going to send her back let me know. The way she shoots, I might like to swear her in as a deputy." The two surviving outlaws were locked up in the small jail behind his office.

Colton ignored him, or as much as one could a six-foot-five-inch former cavalry soldier who on better days was called friend. Instead, his thoughts were on Regan Carmichael. What kind of woman had he asked to take the place of his late wife, Adele? What other nonladylike skills did she possess? Had she lied to him about being educated and cultured? A part of him was half-ready to scrap the marriage agreement and send her packing. Colt's grandfather Ben would undoubtedly agree. Whit's humor notwithstanding, Colt found nothing funny about it, and neither did his gunshot shoulder.

REGAN, WHO'D BEEN told by the sheriff to wait outside while he patched up the doctor, paced the wooden walk in front of his office. How was she supposed to know the riders were a sheriff's posse? She'd been too busy protecting herself and Mr. Denby to stop firing and politely ask their identities. Colton Lee seemed furious, and on the ride to town hadn't once looked her way. She supposed he was allowed. After all, how many men met their prospective brides via a bullet from her Winchester? She couldn't blame him if he decided to send her packing, thus preventing her from trying to make things right—not that she knew how that might be accomplished.

Word must have gotten around about the shooting because a small group of men were on the other side of the street watching her from in front of the general store. One, sporting whiskers, long white hair, and wearing trousers and a shirt made from deerskin called out, "Did you really shoot the doc?"

Her cheeks burned. "It was an accident."

Another man shouted, "This called a shotgun wedding where you're from?"

They all laughed. She didn't respond.

The door opened and the sheriff stepped out.

"May I see him?" she asked anxiously.

"I think I should probably take you over to Minnie's. She takes in boarders. You'll stay there until the wedding. You can see him later."

That wasn't the answer Regan wanted, so she sailed past him and went inside. Her steps halted at the sight of Lee attempting to drag his union shirt up and over his bandaged left shoulder. Seeing her enter, he stopped and her first thought was that the tall slender Colton Lee was as handsome as an African god. The second thought: the riveting eyes were as foreboding as a gathering thunderstorm. All they lacked were lightning bolts. "I . . . want to apologize. I didn't know you and the others were a posse."

His gaze didn't waver, and again she expected lightning. Instead, he resumed his one-handed attempt to cover his bared left shoulder. She took a step forward to assist him but his silent rebuke froze her in place. Regan swallowed in a dry throat. She noticed him wince again as he finally got the shirt positioned. He used his right hand to do up the buttons, then picked up a blue denim shirt and slowly worked it on.

"Where'd you learn to shoot?" he finally asked quietly.

"A neighbor."

"What else he teach you?"

She took offense at both the question and his tone. Surely he wasn't intimating that Old Man Blanchard had taught her anything unseemly. "To hunt, shoe a horse. Shingle a roof. Again, I'm sorry for wounding you."

His continued displeasure made her temper rise. In her mind, he was being terribly unfair. Even if he was still angry, he could at least acknowledge her apology.

"I'm not sure we'll mesh," he finally said.

"Neither am I. A grown man should be able to acknowledge a sincerely offered apology and converse in sentences consisting of more than five words. Good day, Dr. Lee."

She turned on her heel and stormed out.

Outside, she found Sheriff Lambert talking with Mr. Denby. All her trunks and valises were off the coach and waiting. "I'm ready to go to Minnie's," she declared hotly. "Wherever that may be."

"Got a temper, too, do you?" the sheriff asked, taking in her tight face.

She glared.

His thick mustache framed his smile. "You may be just the tonic Colt needs."

"The doctor needs a colonic. Not a wife."

Denby hooted.

The sheriff laughed, too, and after Mr. Denby left them, turned his attention to her trunks. "All these yours?"

"Yes."

"You going on safari?"

She gave him another glare, even though she did have a small mountain of belongings.

"Just pulling your leg. Give me a few minutes to get a wagon from the livery and we'll be on our way."

"Thank you."

While waiting for his return, she noticed a man on a bay stallion riding towards the outskirts of town. It was Lee and she wanted to yell after him, "Coward!" Instead she settled for fuming. This was not how she'd envisioned her journey as a mail-order bride would begin.